BLACK DEATH

M.J. Trow

CRÈME de la CRIME

This first world edition published 2019
in Great Britain and the USA by
Crème de la Crime an imprint of
SEVERN HOUSE PUBLISHERS LTD of
Eardley House, 4 Uxbridge Street, London W8 7SY.
Trade paperback edition first published
in Great Britain and the USA 2019 by
SEVERN HOUSE PUBLISHERS LTD.

British Library Cataloguing in Publication Data
A CIP catalogue record for this title is available from the British Library.

ISBN-13: 978-1-78029-116-1 (cased)
ISBN-13: 978-1-78029-601-2 (trade paper)
ISBN-13: 978-1-4483-0218-5 (e-book)

Typeset by Palimpsest Book Production Ltd.,
Falkirk, Stirlingshire, Scotland.

ONE

The Pestilence came to Dowgate that summer. The Spaniards sent it, the rumour ran, in plague ships that drifted with the tide up the river in the dead of night. The Lord sent it because the City's Livery Companies had displeased him, worshipping Mammon as they did. Above all, it was the Devil, the old serpent, keen as always to add souls to his legions. What if they shivered when he sent for them, if their bodies bulged with black sores and oozed blood? It was all one to him, the great searcher, hobbling on his cloven hoofs down the cobbled smock alleys and prancing through the steelyards, ringing to his tune.

Meg Honeytree had seen him creeping along Elbow Lane; Jane Griggs had caught a blast of his foul breath as he brushed past her on his way to the Vintry. She hadn't believed a word from the plague doctor in his leather beak, spouting some rubbish about the miasma that rose from the old Walbrook, the stream that lay buried under London's streets. It was the Fiend, simple as that.

Robert Greene didn't know. Robert Greene didn't care. He sat in his house along Kyroun Lane, watching the Baltic ships riding the river's tide. The huge cranes in the Vintry swung above the Thames mist, groaning as their ropes took the weight of the dark timber, the silver furs. Silent in the shadows, cats prowled, fat on the rats that streamed from the ships in their hundreds. Even at dusk the docks were alive, the sailors' calls rising above the hum of a never-sleeping city, the lanterns darting like fireflies on the water.

Robert Greene was in his thirty-fifth year, but today he felt as old as Methuselah. Around him, in his garret room, the spiders ruled, weaving whole kingdoms in the casement, pattering over his parchment, leaving trails of God-alone-knew-what all over his *Friar Bacon and Friar Bungay*. He dipped the quill into the ink. There would be no plays tonight, no poetry; not his own, nor anyone else's. Tonight, he had to write a letter – just one – to a man he hated more than anyone in the world. He shivered suddenly as a draught caught him. He thought he heard a creak on the stair, a muttered word, a whisper just on the cusp of sound. It couldn't be Mrs Isam; she never came this high into the eaves, not when Dominus Greene was there. And besides, she never spoke below a dull roar, being hard of hearing and of most other senses beyond cooking and laundering. And Dominus Greene had not stirred from his room for three days and three nights. Only one man had come to see him: not Doll, not the snivelling Fortunatus; no one, except that one man.

Greene felt cold and old as he dipped the quill again. How could he start this letter, after all this time? Yet, how could he not, when his life depended on it? He took a breath as deep as his rattling lungs would allow and pulled the linen shroud up over his head. The candle guttered as his hand moved past it and the quill tip scratched the vellum.

'To Christopher Marlowe,' he saw the words appear and nearly shrank from them. They seemed almost to glow in the gloom of his chamber. 'Dominus of Corpus Christi College, poet, playwright, friend to the afflicted.' It was in Greene's nature to grovel, to compliment, to laud, even the most undeserving. But would the recipient of this letter appreciate it, that was the question? Marlowe, who could see deep into men's souls with those dark eyes of his. Greene paused, a glutinous drop of ink frozen on the tip of the feather. He toyed with screwing up the letter and starting again. But time was of the essence and the sand in his glass had long ago run out. He dipped the quill again and forced his aching fingers to move to the next line – 'Kit,' he wrote.

'There is Pestilence north of the river,' Tom Sledd said it again, like a mantra, hissed on every outward breath he made. Beyond him, in the wooden O of the Rose, carpenters hammered and sawed, hauling on ropes and splashing paint. Sledd took in their work. Then he shook his head; it didn't look much like Paris to him. It looked like bits of wood and canvas that yesterday had been Tamburlaine's fortress. Before that, if memory served, it had been a castle in some godforsaken drivel by Shaxsper. To say it had failed at the box office would be being kind to it, but the Warwickshire man worked for nothing and there was something to be said for having a grateful, if second-rate, playwright up your sleeve for when the Muse's darling was elsewhere. And say what you liked about Shaxsper, he didn't ask for the moon when it came to scenery. Blasted heaths, beaches, graveyards, he'd tried them all and although the plays had been rubbish, Tom Sledd was always home betimes when the scenery was being made for a Shaxsper epic, so his long-suffering wife always said the Warwickshire man was her favourite writer. Tom smiled to himself. Will would love to hear that; the hysterical laughter immediately afterwards, perhaps not so much.

But Kit now, ah, Kit . . . he could weave magic out of thin air with his words, but the wood and canvas still had to be in place. He didn't want much, he would always say. 'Just the inner sanctum of a magus, Tom. Just the fires of Damnation.' And now, the towers and turrets of the second greatest city in the world. Charles IX, King of France, was strutting around the stage, trying on his crown and getting in everybody's way. The Lord High Admiral was fussing about his chain of office – it was *way* too heavy for an actor of his calibre; it weighed on his chest and interfered with his enunciation. Little Benny was doing his best with the hooped petticoat of Catherine de Medici, the Queen Mother; and he'd got to be better than best or Tom Sledd himself, stage manager to the great Philip Henslowe, owner of the Rose, would have to put on the frock and the lipstick once again. And then, the entire company would know all about it.

'Kit!' Sledd saw a flash of quicksilver out of the corner of his eye. 'Holy Mass, Kit.'

'What about it?' Marlowe looked up at the rafters. This wasn't his idea of Paris, either. 'Act One, Scene One, if memory serves.'

'Yes, and elsewhere. It's just that . . . well, it's a bit tricky, all things considered.'

'Is it?' Marlowe stood stock still and frowned at him. When Tom Sledd said things were tricky, it was as well to listen; the man could virtually weave gold out of straw.

Sledd looked at the man. He would go through fire for Kit Marlowe, had *gone* through fire for him. But Kit Marlowe was a dangerous man to know. Working with him, drinking with him, even talking to him; it was all at your own risk. 'Er . . . you *do* know there's been a sort of Reformation in this country?' Sledd checked.

'Before my time, I'm afraid,' Marlowe smiled, the dark eyes twinkling.

'Yes, and mine, but even so – where am I going to get a crucifix?'

Marlowe sighed and placed his hands on Sledd's shoulders. 'Tom, Tom,' he said, softly. 'This is a play called *The Massacre at Paris*. Paris is the capital of France and France – or at least most of it – is Catholic. The bit that isn't is centred on La Rochelle. Now, I could have written a play called *The Massacre at La Rochelle*, except that there wasn't one and that wouldn't be fair to the fee-paying audience, would it? We have to have all the Papist claptrap or the whole play's meaningless. Besides,' Marlowe felt the lad's shoulders sag, 'you're stage manager at the Rose, for God's sake. Right-hand man to the great Philip Henslowe himself.' He lowered his head and let his eyes burn into Sledd's. 'And I happen to know you can work miracles.' He slapped his friend's shoulder and spun away, making for the light.

'Oh, Kit, I nearly forgot.' Sledd was fumbling in his doublet pocket. 'This came for you.'

'What is it?'

'A letter from Dowgate, the lad who brought it said.'

'Dowgate?' Marlowe took the folded vellum. 'I don't know anybody in Dowgate.'

Sledd shrugged. 'You do now,' he said.

The candles guttered that night in the Palace of Whitehall. The wind from the river blew the early Fall leaves around and rattled the shutters in the stables.

Lord Burghley trembled a little these days. There had been a time when he had run from his great house along the Strand to Whitehall; now he was brought in a litter by men wearing the Queen's livery. He preferred milk to a glass of Rhenish.

His rheumatism plagued him and it was difficult to read by candlelight. But all that was between him and his Maker. The outside world must never know. Little Robert wasn't ready, not yet. Burghley had made his dwarf son a Spymaster, but he was no Secretary of State.

'How often have I told you, my boy?' The old man looked across the vast table at his son, 'Be neither Essex nor Ralegh.'

'Not a good time to be either of them, father,' the younger Cecil said. He had all his teeth and found the Burgundy refreshing as August faded to September and the Fall was in the wind.

'What have you heard?' Burghley leaned forward. He had spent too long in the summer at Hatfield. The younger Cecil was nearer to the pulse of things here in London, the heartbeat of the nation.

'No more than you, father,' the Spymaster assured him. 'Ralegh is rotting in the Tower, thanks to his dalliance with Bess Throckmorton.'

'You've got to keep up, Robyn. The Queen intends to release Ralegh on a damned fool expedition with his Devon sea-dogs.'

'Really?' Robert Cecil could play the innocent when he needed to, even with his father. He knew perfectly well what the Queen's plans were.

'It'll all end in tears, of course,' the old man sighed. 'What of Essex?'

'Kept his head down since the Queen recalled him from France.' Cecil looked up sharply at the old man. 'You were there, father. Just how angry *was* the Queen?'

Burghley chuckled. 'Let's just say I've never seen the royal signet put to better use.'

'Oh?' Cecil was grinning along with his old man.

'Split the bumptious little shit's lip. It was a joy to behold. In the meantime,' Burghley's face fell, 'I have more pressing problems.'

'Purveyance,' the Spymaster nodded grimly. 'This Burgundy, for instance. The counties cutting up rough, eh?'

'We don't ask much of them,' the old man spread his arms. 'It's their feudal obligation to cough up. The provisions for Her Majesty, that's all.'

'And Her Majesty's government,' Cecil spread the problem – and the cost – wider in four words.

'It's the damned Puritans,' Burghley muttered, 'and I speak as one of them.'

Cecil raised an eyebrow. What he knew about his father's religious beliefs would see the old man writhing in the fire, but now wasn't the time to say so. There never would be a time.

Burghley went on. 'Know what they call Her Majesty's government now? The Regnum Cecilianum, the rule of the Cecils! What nonsense!'

'Nonsense, indeed,' the younger man smiled. He changed the subject. 'I hear there's Pestilence in Dowgate ward.'

Burghley nodded, 'The blackest of deaths, Robyn. Can you leave London at the moment?'

Cecil shook his head.

'Nor me,' the old man said. 'We'll just have to think pure thoughts and hope for the best.'

'And put our trust in the Lord,' Cecil added.

'Oh, that too, of course.'

TWO

T he mist wreathed from the river the next morning. In a day, it seemed, the summer that had brought the Pestilence had gone and a chill Fall had taken its place, creeping up the ramps where the wharf rats scurried, and coiling around the green, slime-coated props of the jetties.

Marlowe walked along the road that skirted the steelyard. The clang of metal was all around him, even this early in the morning and the smiths' fires belched flame and smoke as the hammers rang. Beyond that, the playwright might have been at home in his native Canterbury, the stench of the dyers' and skinners' crafts, cloth stretched on the tenter grounds and leather hanging to cure its putrefaction. The bright painted arms of the Worshipful Companies creaked in chains above the Walbrook, floating with only God-knew-what; the crowns and ermine of the Skinners' Company, the tuns of the Innkeepers'.

Marlowe turned the corner where the spire of St Michael Paternoster disappeared into the mist. The gravestones of the great and good lay crusted in lichen, leaning towards each other, the dead still whispering together after all these years, swapping secrets that were secret no longer. He saw them before they saw him, the constables of the Watch. They had not been relieved from the night before yet and they were cold and dripping with the morning dew dropping from their helmet rims and sparkling on the rimy stubble on their chins. They straightened at his arrival. A gentleman, they knew, by his doublet and Colleyweston cloak. Now, what was he doing in this God-forsaken part of London and at this hour of the day?

'Morning, sir,' one of them hailed him. 'You know we have the Pestilence here?'

Marlowe nodded. He knew. He knew as every man knew. The sweating. The cough. Black swellings and rotting flesh. And over it all, the solemn tolling of the bell.

'Better run far, run fast, then,' the second constable muttered. Six hours pounding the unforgiving cobbles had done nothing for his bonhomie.

'You're still here,' Marlowe pointed out. He had stopped walking now.

'We're Dowgate, born and bred,' the first man said, shifting his weight as he leaned on his pike. 'Besides, it's our job.'

'And mine,' Marlowe smiled. 'I have come to pay my respects to an old enemy.'

The constables looked at each other.

'It's complicated,' Marlowe laughed, sensing their confusion. 'The cobbler's house in Kyroun Lane – is this the way?'

'Mrs Isam,' the younger man nodded. 'Yes. First left beyond the churchyard.'

'You sure you won't change your mind, sir?' the first constable asked. 'I wouldn't have thought paying your respects to an enemy is worth dying for.'

'Perhaps not.' Marlowe turned as he went on his way. 'As I said, it's complicated.'

The cobbler's house was like any other. Kyroun Lane was like any other. Old buildings, mildewed with damp that had seeped into the oak timbers in the days of Geoffrey Chaucer, jostled each other, fighting for space, trying to breathe. Now and then was a gap, weed-strewn lumps of lathe and plaster the only remnants of a building which had lost the unequal struggle and collapsed with scarcely a sigh to the ground. It was a dull, grey day but Marlowe knew the sun never shone here. He rapped on the door, a rusty iron knocker echoing through the passages of the house. And he waited.

A bonneted matron slid back the bolts and peered out at him.

'I got a letter.' Marlowe held it up. 'From Robert Greene; late, I understand, of this house.'

'You'll be that Kit Marlowe,' the woman said, looking him up and down.

'I am,' Marlowe half bowed, 'though whether I am *that* Kit Marlowe depends on who you've been talking to.'

'I've been talking to Dominus Greene,' the woman said. 'He was a University scholar, you know.'

'So he kept telling me,' Marlowe said. 'You are?'

'Not a university scholar,' she scowled. It was an unnecessary statement, but it gave Marlowe a sense of where this woman's loyalties lay. 'You'd better come in.'

Marlowe did. The ceiling was low and he had to duck as she led him along a passageway and down stone steps into a kitchen. If there was refreshment here, Marlowe was not offered any. The fire was burning sullenly under the soot-caked kettle, which was not so much singing as humming a miserable dirge.

'I am Eliza Isam,' she said, offering her visitor a chair at least. 'Dominus Greene's landlady.'

'Charmed,' Marlowe smiled.

'We've got the Pestilence here in Dowgate,' Mrs Isam said. That was the second time that Marlowe had heard that this morning.

'I saw no cross on your door,' he said; and he wouldn't have crossed the threshold if he had. There was not much that rattled Kit Marlowe, but a slow, agonizing death from a cause no one knew; *that* rattled him.

'Nor will you. Dr Forman says the humours are in the right balance in this house. The Pestilence holds no fears for me.'

'Dr Forman?' Marlowe had heard that name somewhere.

'The plague doctor. Actually, he's more than that.' A smirk had spread over the hard features of Dominus Greene's land-lady, a smirk that developed into a smile. 'He's a magus. Understands the stars – or, as he calls them, celestial bodies. He's ever so clever. And handsome! Ooh, he's lovely!' In a few sentences, the morose Mrs Isam had changed into a giggly girl, all dewy-eyed at the memory of the gorgeous Dr Forman.

Marlowe knew all about men like him. They didn't have to be magi to have a way with ladies of a certain age. The trage-dian Ned Alleyn had cut his teeth, if that was the right phrase, on more rich widows than Marlowe could – or would – shake a stick at. Even Richard Burbage, not so handsome, not so elegant in the calf, not as slick of tongue, was rumoured to have a nice little thing going with one Mistress Quick down at Bow. She was a leaving of Shaxsper's, or so rumour had it, but when a man was being kept in hose and a manner of other fripperies, who was counting? Marlowe toyed with bursting Mistress Isam's bubble, but she was still glowing at his elbow and he relented.

'Did the good doctor officiate at Master Greene's passing?' he asked.

'Well, he was in the area. I knew it wasn't the Pestilence, anyway. Dominus Greene had been ill for days but he didn't show the signs. No black buboes. No pus. No shivering. Nothing like that.'

'What signs *did* he show?' Marlowe asked.

A quizzical expression spread over the landlady's face. 'Was you at University with Dominus Greene?' she asked.

'Same University,' Marlowe nodded. 'Different college. He was at St John's, I at Corpus Christi.'

'He never spoke of you,' the landlady said, 'until the end, when he decided to write that letter.'

'What did he say?' Marlowe was almost afraid to ask.

'Not a lot. He said you would understand his problem. You, of all people, he said. I told him he could confide in Dr Forman if he needed to clear his mind, him being in tune with the celestial bodies and all, but no, he must needs write to you and no one else, he said.'

It was getting hard to keep this conversation under control. Mistress Isam was like some demented mayfly, darting here and there, always coming back to her magus. 'His problem?'

The woman shrugged. 'He was a deep one, was Dominus Greene; you probably know that.'

'We'd rather lost touch,' Marlowe said. 'Did he have any family?'

'His wife, Doll.' Mistress Isam's face had resumed its scowl. Clearly, the memories of the luscious Forman had vanished, chased away by the thoughts of Greene's erstwhile spouse. 'She's no better than she should be, you mark my words.'

'Consider them marked,' Marlowe said. 'Children?'

'Fortunatus. Stupid name for a snot-nosed bastard, I always thought, but it wasn't my place to say so.'

'Where are they?'

'God knows,' Mrs Isam shrugged. 'Dominus Greene was

estranged from Doll and Fortunatus lives with her. I don't know where.'

'No one else?' Marlowe asked.

The landlady shook her head and her lugubrious cheeks trembled, taking a few seconds longer to stop than could be considered attractive.

'What about friends?'

Mrs Isam knew that Robert Greene didn't have a friend in the world, but it wasn't her place to say that either. 'There was only one cove kept hanging around. Hoity-toity he was. Giving orders like he owned the place. And me, the owner of this house since Mr Isam, God rest his soul, departed this vale of tears.'

'Who was that?'

'Another doctor,' she said and her eyes briefly lit up again. 'Oh, not like Dr Forman, of course. What was his name, now? Harbottle? Shrewsbury? Name from the Bible, that I know. Job, was it? Ezekiel? Not Nebuchadnezzar, surely? An angel . . .' She pursed her lips and tapped her chin with a wrinkled finger. 'Could it have been . . .'

'Harvey?' Marlowe asked. 'Gabriel Harvey?'

She looked at him and seemed about to shake her head again, then thought twice. 'I believe that might be the name, yes. That, or close to it in any case. Gabriel Harvey, or close to it, yes, certainly. It might have been Azrael . . .'

But Kit Marlowe had gone.

Tom Sledd was catching a very well-deserved few minutes' rest under a sloping piece of scenery when he was suddenly rudely awakened by some thoughtless bastard who clearly didn't have a teething child at home kicking his ankles. He drew up his legs, turned over resolutely and squeezed his eyes shut. He had hidden from better men than whoever it was. Hell and damnation, he had hidden from Philip Henslowe, and Philip Henslowe could ferret out anything, from the smallest coin down the side of an overstuffed chair upwards.

'Tom! Tom!' Again, the kicking.

'To Hell with it,' Sledd muttered to himself and curled up even smaller.

'Thomas,' the voice sang out, sweet as a lark.

Sledd groaned. Kit. Kit never gave up once he had started something, everyone knew that, so he would happily stand there kicking the stage manager's ankles till Kingdom come. 'Stop, stop, I'm coming out.' He struggled out of his tight cocoon and emerged, blinking and covered in dusty paint smudges and cobweb. 'What do you want?'

'There was no need to get up,' Marlowe said. 'I just wanted to know if you had a shovel. And I don't need that until dark, in any case.'

Sledd's eyes narrowed. 'A shovel? What do you want with a shovel? You've never done a day's hard labour in your life.' Tiredness had made him testy.

The playwright looked stricken. His eyes grew big and melancholy and Sledd felt the old guilt wash over him. If he had a groat for every time Marlowe had made him feel like shit on his shoe, he wouldn't be skivvying for Philip Henslowe, that was certain.

'Sorry, yes, I know writing is hard work.'

Marlowe had raised a calloused right forefinger, still stained with ink, but now lowered it again, a sly smile on his lips. It was almost too easy, but still a lot of fun, to make Tom Sledd do his bidding.

'What do you want a shovel for, Master Marlowe?' Sledd sounded like a child repeating a long-learned lesson by rote.

'I might need two shovels,' he said, not really answering the question. 'There's a need for speed, you see.'

Sledd leaned forward. He knew sleep had eluded him for today. If he didn't get his forty winks before the cleaners, the scene-painters, the walking gentlemen and the rest arrived for the afternoon, he never would. 'So . . . who would be wielding this shovel?'

'These shovels.' Marlowe could be a stickler for detail.

'These shovels?'

'Well, I would be one, of course.' Marlowe struck something of a labouring man's pose, arms akimbo and ready for anything.

'And the other?' Sledd leaned on the scenery, which shifted slightly under his weight and rather spoiled the insouciant pose. He had a rough idea what the answer might be.

'Do you know,' Marlowe said, looking up into the sky above the Rose, softly glowing with the warmth of a late September day. 'Do you know when we last spent an evening together? A few ales in a friendly inn? Banter with the serving wench? Rolling home in the wee small hours?' He smiled at Sledd again, using all his wiles.

Sledd tapped his chin and looked thoughtful. 'Never?' he ventured.

Marlowe was crestfallen. 'Now, come, Tom. You know that's not true. We have been out together, on many an adventure.'

Sledd stepped forward, a finger jabbing at Marlowe's chest. 'An adventure, yes. An *adventure*. But I'm a married man, now, Kit. I have responsibilities. And anyhow, there is Pestilence in Dowgate.'

Marlowe's eyes flew open. He was quite genuinely amazed. 'How did you know I wanted you to dig in Dowgate?'

'I'm not *stupid*, Kit!' Sledd was on his high horse now. 'You get a letter from Dowgate. You come in here, stinking of half-cured hides and talking of shovels. *Ergo* . . .' Sledd spat his Latin out proudly '. . . ergo, you've been to Dowgate and you want to dig something up there.' He chuckled. 'Probably the fellow who sent you the letter.' He laughed again, nervously.

Marlowe's face was unreadable.

Sledd suddenly felt the hairs on the back of his neck crawl. 'No, Kit, no, I won't do it. And neither should you. Your life is charmed, I will admit, but not to that extent. No.' Sledd stamped his foot, a trick that always seemed to work when little Neddy did it at home. 'No. I will *not* dig anyone up, not in Dowgate or anywhere else.'

A face appeared around the flats leaning on the opposite wall.

'Dig someone up? For money?'

Marlowe and Sledd spun around. The weaselly face of Ingram Frizer wore the beam it always did when coinage was on offer. The man was a walking gentleman, in the language of the theatre. He was also, in the language of more than one magistrate, 'a liar, a scoundrel and a rogue'. He could play all three together, if the money was right.

'Just planning our next theatrical epic,' Sledd said, unconvincingly.

'Sounds a pretty simple scene,' Frizer said. 'Gravedigger – not a very convincing character, I wouldn't imagine. Who could empathize with a gravedigger?'

Another head came round the scenery, large as a moon on a midsummer night and just as round and bald.

'I think I could write that scene, Tom. I can just picture it now—'

'For the love of God!' Sledd was at the end of his tether. 'Frizer, Shaxsper, we are *trying* to have a private conversation here. Is there nowhere a man can go to have a quiet colloquy with a friend?' Will Shaxsper may have been Johanna Sledd's favourite playwright, but he wasn't her husband's. The man was a hanger-on of the worst water, a picker-up of other people's trifles.

Marlowe touched his sleeve. 'We *are* on a stage, Tom,' he pointed out. 'Most people don't go there for privacy.'

'Even so . . .' Sledd's wind had been taken out of his sails. Frizer and Shaxsper stood there still, almost panting in their enthusiasm to be included. 'If you want men to dig, Kit, there they stand. I refuse to help you and that's an end to it.' And, with as much grace as he could muster, he exited, stage left.

The soft Fall day had given way to a night which held a tinge of frost in it. The moon was full and made the sky cold with its white, ethereal light. The skittering of night creatures sounded preternaturally loud inside the high walls of the New Churchyard and the cries of the Watchmen and late carousers along Bishopsgate Street could have been from another world. The sleepers in the graveyard made no sound. Not for them the soft susurration of blood whispering through their veins, nor the murmur of air in throat and lung. They lay, wrapped in wool or linen, their eyes far away and sunken into their heads, thinking what thoughts the dead might think, endlessly, until the final trump might sound.

The men who walked above their sleeping heads made little sound either. Their shadows on the grass were silent, deformed by the beaks of the masks they wore. The scent of rosemary and vinegar wreathed around them, efficacious against the plague, or so men said. They swung them from side to side as they looked through the eyeholes, trying to find the man they sought, tucked up tight below the hastily removed and replaced earth and sod.

Without a word, the man at the back of the little row of four tapped his neighbour on the shoulder and pointed to a corner of the graveyard. In the pitiless light of the moon, a newly turned mound stood out in sharp relief. He nodded his head in its direction and the men turned their steps towards it. One of them leaned over and picked a sliver of wood from the head of the grave. 'Dominus Greene,' he muttered. '*Resquiat im pace.*'

'Close enough,' muttered one of the others. 'This is the one.' He gestured and they bent their heads together, to be reminded of their task. 'Dig quietly. Dig fast. The Pestilence is in Dowgate, don't forget.'

'Not likely to,' muttered the man to his left and got an elbow in the ribs for his pains.

'The night Watch have just passed. It will be another half an hour before they come back round again. That's the time we have. Now – dig.'

All four bent to their task, breathing stertorously through the herb-packed beaks. Not three feet down, a shovel hit wood and one of the diggers tutted.

'Three feet,' he said, dismissively. 'Skimpy.'

'I suspect the sexton was busy,' Marlowe said, straightening up and pushing his mask back to wipe his sweating face. He gestured around them to all the new mounds, black in the moonlight amongst the grassy beds of the longer dead. 'But he did us a favour, that's for sure.' He pulled his mask back on and his voice became muffled again. 'Now, lads, shovels to each corner, like we planned. And . . . heave.'

The coffin sprang out of the ground as though it were on springs. With a deft twist of the shovels, it was rested across the corners of the grave. It had been a hasty job, that was obvious. The nails were proud of the deal planks of the lid in several places and, halfway along one side, a wisp of linen shroud had been trapped in the undertaker's haste to get the

man nailed in and underground. Marlowe put the edge of his
shovel under one corner of the lid and turned it sharply. With
a crack and a scream of tearing timber, the planks sprang free
and the men leaned in, pushing their masks up onto their
foreheads to better see what was revealed. Their motives varied.
Frizer was a ghoul, always had been, since a lad, when he
had plucked the wings from flies just to see what they might
do. Dead men's faces had a fascination for him. Shaxsper
never turned down an opportunity to gather experiences for
the plays he knew he could write one day. Tom Sledd didn't
want to, but just couldn't help himself. When Marlowe said
'Dig', Tom just asked, 'How deep?'

Marlowe knew what he was looking for. He had spent the
afternoon with John Dee, who had wanted to come with them,
but had been dissuaded – he would say, prevented – by his
wife, the redoubtable Jane. Marlowe, Dee said, was to look
for swelling, discolouration, twisting of the body, bared teeth
and a host of other symptoms which would invade his sleep
for weeks to come. He was to cut away portions of the shroud
carefully. Dee had been his usual matter-of-fact self. When a
man raised the dead for a living, doing it with a shovel held
no terrors for him.

'Near the anus, the mouth and the organs of generation, my
boy,' he had said, rubbing his hands together. 'Where things
seep, you know.'

Marlowe knew.

The men stood back to let the moon shine down and illu-
minate the scene. The shroud was spattered with stains.
Marlowe cut them away and stowed them in a pouch he had
brought for the purpose. He cut the cord gathering the shroud
over the scholar's head and let the linen fall away. The face
he revealed was peaceful. No one could ever have accused
Robert Greene in life of being handsome, but there was now
a certain nobility in his features, a sense that he had come
willingly to the end of a road which had given him no pleasure
in its travelling.

'No buboes, then,' Frizer said, pragmatic to the last, poking
a finger into Greene's armpits.

'He didn't die of the plague,' Marlowe reminded him.

'Everybody says that, though, don't they?' the walking gentleman said. 'Nobody wants the neighbours to know what their folks died of. How're you going to sell their clothes for a good price then?'

Shaxsper and Sledd shrugged. The man had a point. Marlowe looked at the moon. It had moved a fair way across the sky already, silver frosting the rooftops beyond the churchyard walls. The Watch would soon be back. 'Will,' he said. 'Use this cloth to sop up some of the . . .' wordsmith though he was, he was stuck for the proper term '. . . stuff at the bottom of the coffin. Put it in this waxed bag.'

Shaxsper looked as though he might vomit, but controlled himself enough to manage a nod.

'Frizer,' he passed across another waxed paper. 'Trim his beard, his hair, his nails and put them in here.'

Frizer was unfazed. He would have happily sopped up anything without demur, but trimming a dead man's beard was no trouble to him either.

'Tom . . .' Marlowe looked up to where Sledd stood at the head of the grave, his eyes big and frightened in his dead white face and his conscience, for once, gave him pause. 'Tom, go and check for the Watch, there's a good man. I can do the rest of what is needed here.'

Tom Sledd was no coward, but sometimes a man should take any small favours that come his way. He edged round the grave and walked as quickly as he could without running to the gate. He knew that if once he broke into even a trot, he would just run and run until he was home and under the covers with his lovely Johanna.

He crept on silent feet along Bishopsgate Street, in the direction from which he knew the Watch would come, south from the Vintry, across the Moor Field. Every few steps he stopped and listened for the tramp of booted feet and the hum of quiet conversation. He kept his eyes peeled for the dim light of the hooded lantern that he knew the Watch always carried at the slope. But so far, so good – nothing.

At the next corner, he glanced back over his shoulder. He could see the spire of All Hallows on the Wall, tall and black against the moon. He didn't want to be too far away when the others got to the gate; he wouldn't want them to think he had bolted for home. He strained his eyes and ears but could hear nothing, unless it was a very distant sound of earth on pine, but perhaps that was just his imagination. He turned back to look around the corner and almost swallowed his tongue. About three inches from his nose, a man's face was peering at him in the gloom. When he could speak and his heart was back in his chest, he managed to croak out, 'Who are you? And where in Hell did you come from?'

The man took a step back and flung out an arm, simultaneously pointing an elegant toe. 'I,' he cried in ringing tones, 'I, you oaf, am the greatest actor of the age. I, fellow, am Edward Alleyn.'

Tom had wondered whether this frowsty fellow wandering the streets at dead of night might not be quite the full groat but now he knew for sure. Only a total lunatic would pretend to be Ned Alleyn. 'I . . . see,' Tom said, keeping his tone gentle and even, so as not to provoke the man. Only now did he remember that the dark wall bulked above his head was all that stood between him and the inmates of Bedlam, where the mad were chained to walls, and worse. How this one had got out he had no idea. Or, he thought to himself, perhaps he was trying to get *in*. In any event, he had to keep him quiet but, more importantly, he had to get away.

'I am surprised you did not recognize me,' the madman intoned. 'I am loved and feted throughout this realm.' He had a rather irritating way of rolling his 'r's almost to exhaustion, but it did remind the stage manager of the original and it was all he could do to suppress a smile.

'Now I come to look again,' he said, 'I do recognize you. I don't get to the theatre much, you see.' Ingram Frizer wasn't the only liar in London.

'Poor wretch!' The lunatic was heartbroken to think of Sledd's misfortune. 'And here we are, within a stone's throw of the Curtain. Let me give you my Faustus! It is my most resonant role!'

Sledd thought fast. 'I don't go to the theatre,' he said, 'because of my ears. I must have silence, you see.'

The madman stepped back again. Much more of that and he would be far enough away for Sledd to make his escape. 'I will be silent,' he shouted. 'I shall roar you as gently as any sucking dove.'

'Er . . . thank you, Master Alleyn,' Sledd said, 'but even that would be too loud for my poor ears.'

'Really?' The man leaned forward, his rags hanging loose from his shoulders. 'They are as bad as that, are they? *You* would be no good as an actor. You need to project!' He shouted the last word so loudly that the echoes all but exploded. 'The groundlings must hear every golden word from your lips, don't forget.' He peered at Sledd. 'And yet, you know, I have seen you before. Are you sure you are not an actor?'

Of all things, Sledd knew that that was true. Although he had at one time earned what his adoptive father, Ned Sledd, the actor manager, had told him was his living by acting, he knew he was hopeless at it. And, as long as the law and tradition had stood on their dignity and not allowed women on the stage, Tom had squawked his way from Mistress Gotobed to Dido, Queen of Carthage. Then, his voice had broken. 'I am certain,' he said, but the word was cut off as a hand went over his mouth.

'That's enough, my lad. You just come along o' me.'

'No, no, Jack,' another voice said. 'That's not our boy. This'n's too young. And . . .' a face swam into view as Tom shook his head trying to get rid of the suffocating hand, 'he don't look half mad enough, by my reckoning.'

The hand clutched harder. 'That's just their cunning, Nat. Just their cunning. They makes you think they's normal and – bang! It's a swede in a stocking upside the head and next thing you know is they're all out the winder and away.'

Nat peered closer. 'I'm sure this isn't ours, though,' he said, still dubious.

'Do it matter?' Jack was pinioning Sledd's arms behind him with his other hand. 'Three groats old Sleford pays us for every runaway – and he don't often ask questions. They all look alike, don't they? Here, Nat, tie this, will you? Then this rag over his mouth. Bag over the head and we're done. Head count all right at dawn and nothing amiss.'

Sledd fought with all his strength but the two madhouse keepers were too much for him. He went slack in their hands and began quietly weeping inside his all-enveloping hood, with its stench of despair and fear soaked deep into the weft. The gag tasted foul in his mouth and his screams and cries for help were all in his head. Someone – his money would always be on Jack – kicked him in that head for good measure and, finally, thankfully, everything went a merciful black.

Marlowe unsheathed his knife and quickly cut sections of the shroud according to Dee's instructions. Then, he looked up and nodded at the other two. 'Let's get this good gentleman underground again, shall we?' He covered Greene's face with gentle hands. 'We weren't friends, Dominus Greene,' he said softly to him. 'You rarely missed a chance to do me down, to rob me when you could. But you didn't deserve this, an early grave in a dank, dark corner.' Shaxsper crossed himself and Frizer gave a cursory nod. After a silence, the three squared their shoulders and manoeuvred the coffin back into the earth.

'We haven't nailed him down,' Shaxsper suddenly realized, as the earth was thudding down on the lid from their flailing shovels.

'Are you afraid he'll walk?' Marlowe asked, drily.

'No.' Shaxsper managed a brittle laugh. 'No, of course not. It's just that . . .'

'I don't think Dominus Greene will mind a little draught,' Marlowe said. 'He'll sleep just as soundly without nails as with. Sounder, perhaps, if we can avenge his death.'

'Avenge? How?'

'By finding out who killed him.'

'Murder?' Shaxsper patted the soil down neatly over the dead Dominus Greene.

'Yes,' Marlowe said, pulling his mask back into place. 'Murder, most foul.'

THREE

Leaving Frizer and Shaxsper to tamp down the grave and make it look as much undisturbed as was possible, Marlowe crept quietly to the gates of the churchyard and looked left and right. The Pieto gardens were silhouetted in silver; the old Roman wall, crumbled now and broken, still stood to remind the world how the city had grown. From somewhere, perhaps Fynnesburie Field, a dog was barking at the night. There was no sign of Tom Sledd and Marlowe tutted. He had sent him to watch for the Watch, not hightail it home. But he allowed the man some latitude. He was scared witless of the Pestilence himself, though he tried not to show it; Tom had a family to think of and so a little discretion over valour was allowed. Just this once.

Frizer and Shaxsper clattered up behind him, their pattens loud on the cobbles. So much for being silent as the grave.

'Where's Tom?' Frizer said, loudly.

'Sshh!' the playwrights, real and imaginary, both turned on him and he pulled a wry face.

'Sorry,' he said aloud, then again, in a whisper, 'Sorry.'

'Keep it quiet,' Marlowe breathed. 'We're not safe until we are well away from here. I think Tom must have gone home and the Watch aren't here, so he has done us no harm. Now . . . no more talking. Goodnight and thank you both.' Coins clinked into Frizer's hand but Shaxsper's remained empty. He decided to take it as a compliment, one artiste to another.

Keeping their beaked masks firmly pulled down over their faces, the three men parted at the crossroads, two to their beds, to sleep as best they might, Marlowe to the Strand, to the rooms of Dr John Dee, the Queen's Magus. The streets of Shoreditch were strangely empty – Pestilence will do that to a city – and he made good time, without seeing a soul. He was almost at his destination among the great houses of the Strand that backed onto the river, when a shadow detached itself from a wall and he almost cannoned into the man who made it.

'Good morning, Brother.' The voice was smooth as honey, as soft as silk, and as reliable as thin ice over a bottomless lake.

'Brother?' Marlowe had been called a lot of things but never, until now, that.

The man turned his face sideways, a silhouette against the setting moon. The beak of the plague doctor cut the air like a scimitar.

'Oh, I see. Brother. Yes. Good morning.' Marlowe made to pass by but he was stopped by a surprisingly burly arm.

'Where are you off to, Brother?' Now the voice had steel under the silk, the honey dripped from a honed edge that could kill in a trice.

Marlowe's hand crept to the dagger in the small of his back. 'On my own business,' he said, keeping his voice light.

'May I ask your name?' the man said, leaning in close.

Above the scent of his own herb-packed snout, Marlowe could smell other things. Asafoetida, which he recognized from his many visits to Dee's sanctum. Attar of Roses; that would be to please the ladies, it certainly had no place in warding off the plague. And something else . . . something that made his nostrils wrinkle and the hairs stand up on the back of his neck. He didn't move or answer.

'May I ask your *name*, sir?'

Marlowe smiled. This was better – whoever this plague doctor was, this man who smelled of death, he was getting angry and angry men were easy to beat.

'Yes.'

The man stepped back, his eyes dark and glowering through the eyeholes of his mask. 'What is it?' he hissed.

Marlowe stepped back too, giving himself room to swing his blade, should it become necessary. 'Oh, I *do* see now what you are asking. You don't want to know if you can *ask* my name. You want to know my name.'

'Correct.'

'I don't choose to give it,' Marlowe said, making as if to step round the man, who sidestepped to match him. 'Although, of course, should you choose to tell me yours, I may change my mind.'

The man in the mask was clearly amazed. He swept an arm down his body, as if that were answer enough. He wore a long cloak, with strange swirling letters, shooting stars and moons, picked out in silver thread against the velvet which was blacker than night. Beneath it, he wore another gown, gathered onto a yoke, which was embroidered thickly with cut-glass brilliants and hung with crystal drops so it shimmered like mercury under the last rays of the moon. The sleeves were gathered in at the wrists by crisp white linen cuffs and it didn't take a genius to guess that this was one plague doctor who didn't do much visiting of the poor and sick.

'How can you not know who I am?' Outrage took the place of amazement. 'I am . . .'

Marlowe realized in a sudden flash of inspiration who this popinjay was. 'Simon Forman,' he said.

The beak swept forward and almost knocked into Marlowe's own. 'The *great* Simon Forman,' the man hissed. 'The greatest protection from the plague, or any other of the thousand natural shocks that flesh is heir to.'

'Hmm. "To which flesh is heir" would make you sound rather more believable, but I do get your general drift, Master Forman. Well, I am the great, I suppose I might say, Kit Marlowe.'

'*That* Kit Marlowe?' Forman was puzzled. 'You're a playwright, not a plague doctor.'

'Can a man not be both?' Marlowe asked. 'I daresay the theatres will be closing soon, if this Pestilence stays upon us.' He wasn't quite sure why, but this man was making him sound like someone posturing on a stage.

Forman struck a pose, a querying finger to his chin. He thrust out one leg and put a hand on his hip.

Marlowe smiled. Now he knew who this man reminded him of. Ned Alleyn, at his most pompous, playing some despot in overdone costume. He tapped Forman on his embroidered chest, with the tip of his dagger. 'You must excuse me, Master Forman,' he said. 'I do have places to be and you are in my way.'

At the sight of the blade, Forman threw his head back and laughed. 'Blades do not frighten me, Master Marlowe. No blade can pierce my carapace of magic.'

Marlowe cocked his head and his great, herb-packed nose made him look like an inquisitive magpie, eyeing up its dinner. How he would have loved to prove this man wrong. But he really did have places to be, and no time to explain away a dead magus on the highway. With a smile and a wave, he stepped past Forman as he stood there, still posing, and slipped down an alleyway and out of sight before the cock-of-the-walk had even noticed he had gone. As he walked, he couldn't help wondering how long the popinjay would stand there before noticing he was alone in the Strand and without an audience. His best guess was that it would be well and truly dawn before that happened.

Marlowe was out by half an hour or so, but it was a very disgruntled magus who finally clambered into bed in Philpot Lane with his long-suffering wife, putting his cold feet into the heat of the small of her back. She grunted and shuffled further to the edge of the great feather mattress, but he followed her, keen for warmth and, if he could wake her just about enough, a little more. He had not had a good night. He could usually fool most of the people most of the time, but some of his failures were coming home to roost and he had had a rather difficult interview with a widow who had suddenly realized that rather than have Simon Forman glittering and posturing in her bedchamber, she would prefer a husband, alive and bringing home the bacon. Even the doves had let him down; when he tried to release one to depict the soul of the dear departed, it had fallen to the floor with a sullen clunk, its eye dead and glazed. The woman had had hysterics which even his special massage could not assuage – and his massage was usually *very* special. He lay there, mulling it over, and decided to try it out on his wife – perhaps he had lost his touch.

'Get off me, Simon,' she muttered, elbowing him neatly in the head. 'Keep it for your silly widows. I've got to get up soon and tend to the house.'

'But . . .'

'No buts.' She turned over and kneed him neatly where he least expected it. She heard the air leave his lungs with a tortured groan. 'If I've told you once, I've told you a thousand times. That kind of thing isn't for a decent marriage bed. If it gets stupid women to part with money to keep bread in my children's mouths, so be it. And with them out of London to escape the Pestilence, they cost even more. But I don't like it, though I accept it's your calling. But don't think you can bring your nasty ways home with you.'

Forman was still trying to get his breath, through the red haze of pain.

'And, while we're on the subject, the laundry maid has been complaining again. You left a couple of dead newts in your lawn sleeves yesterday. She screamed so loud I thought she was going to be sick. You have to be more careful, you really do. It's bad enough having to clean those gowns of yours, all those beads and furbelows. Can't you be a proper doctor instead of all this nonsense? A clever man like you, surely . . .'

Forman lay in his warm feather bed and tried to block it all out. In the streets of Westminster, in the houses of the Strand and, yes, it was no exaggeration to say the palaces of Nonsuch and Placentia, he was a king, lauded and rewarded with every step. Here – here, he was nothing. What his wife's knee hadn't achieved, his misery completed and he lay there, limp and bruised in more ways than one. He began to drift away when he was aware of his wife's voice getting louder and nearer to his ear.

'But you're not a bad husband, by and large and you are certainly a good provider. So as long as you're quick and pull my nightdress down when you're finished, you may have a go at me.'

Opening his eyes just a little, he turned his head. His wife was lying on her back, her head averted and her fists clenched at her side. Her nightclothes were bunched up under her chin and her knees were splayed wide. Her lax stomach folded almost down to her pudenda, which, even in the half-light, was uninviting. He swallowed hard and thought fast. Giving vent to an almighty snore, he fell back on the pillows and was soon, quite genuinely, asleep.

* * *

His tap at the door was answered instantly. John Dee had been waiting on the settle in his hall since before dawn and now the morning was well advanced. 'Kit,' he breathed. 'I thought . . . well, I don't know quite what I thought, but I had expected you long before this.'

The Queen's Magus was nudging sixty, but his body and mind were as agile as ever – and if Kit Marlowe needed access to his vast store of knowledge, well, that was all to the good.

'My apologies.' Marlowe swept off his grey cloak and threw it down on the settle, following Dee into the kitchen where the best fire was burning. 'My plans have had a tendency to go awry since we spoke last. I suppose asking a stage manager, a would-be playwright and a walking gentleman to help me in the exhumation was my first mistake, but I was in a hurry and they were what came to hand. Then, I met Simon Forman on the way here – do you know him?'

Dee turned and spat neatly onto the fire. 'Sadly for me, I do. He considers himself a magus, though he is but a conjuror. The oaf was apprenticed to a merchant whose stock-in-trade was herbal remedies. Somehow, he smarmed around the authorities and got himself a place at Magdalen – Oxford, of course, not the real one. He specialized in medicine and astronomy but had to leave. There was some trouble with the bedders, by all accounts. He got to Utrecht, but for about ten years now he has been pretending to be a doctor. He hangs his shingle in Philpot Lane.'

'So what was he doing in the Strand, I wonder?'

'Those sleeves of his hide all manner of things,' Dee went on, 'though he uses his hands cleverly, I will concede that. The rumour has it that he fills them with doves and frogs and all manner of livestock every day, so he can amaze people as he goes about his business. Before the next morning, he empties out their poor, dead bodies, if he hasn't had the need to release them. He'll have been fawning around the more idiot of the wenches down the road, I'll wager.'

That at least explained the smell and Marlowe nodded. 'I can't believe his fame will last, Doctor,' he said, sensing the old man's sadness. 'Folk will see through him and his glitter and glamour, surely?'

Dee nodded. 'Of course they will,' he agreed. 'But until then, what harm might he do?' He looked into the flames for a while, as if he could see clearly the death and destruction that capered in the wake of Forman's stupidity and cupidity. Then, he clapped his hands. 'But enough of him! Did you get what I asked?'

Marlowe ferreted in his jerkin front and brought out the waxed packages. 'Yes. I got clippings from the shroud.' He handed them over one by one. 'Some of the liquid at the bottom of the coffin.' Dee nodded, pleased. That was the one he least expected to receive. 'And some hair from his beard and from his head and also some nail trimmings, as you asked.'

'And how did he look?' Dee leaned forward, his eyes bright and excited. It had been a while since he had had a real puzzle to solve and he was looking forward to it. For too long he had been worrying about his finances. The Queen was not as forthcoming as she had been and her Magus was only as successful as his last prognostication. As the old girl's years advanced, perhaps she was nearer to God and the answers to all things than John Dee would ever be. The puzzle had brought Kit Marlowe back to his door too, so he was a happy man, for once.

Marlowe looked thoughtful. 'He looked . . .' he smiled at the thought, 'he looked well, since you ask. Better than I have seen him look when he was still breathing. Not so anguished. Nothing like as angry. Peaceful, I suppose I would say. Yes. Peaceful and content.'

Dee pursed his lips and pulled a parchment and a piece of charcoal out of a pocket of his voluminous gown. He crossed through a word at the top of what seemed to be a long list, then another, lower down. 'Was he bent at all? Were his limbs displaced?' He twisted his arms so his palms faced outwards, as examples.

'No. But of course, he may have been laid out neatly before they buried him.'

'True. Though sometimes, the poison will fix the limbs.' Dee whistled soundlessly for a moment and crossed out another couple of words. 'Bloated?'

Marlowe shook his head.

'Discoloured?'

'No more than you would expect in the circumstances.'

Dee gave him a quizzical glance. 'Circumstances? Do you know something?'

Marlowe laughed. 'You are suspicious of everyone, Doctor. No, I mean the circumstances of having died and having been buried. He was . . .' he shrugged. 'A bit on the grey side. But otherwise, normal.'

Dee nodded once. 'I see.' He crossed off one more word and then looked down his list and frowned. 'I fear I must tell you, Kit, that your man may have died a natural death.'

Marlowe sat back in his chair and looked at Dee from under his lashes. 'I'm not usually wrong,' he said at last.

'Nor am I. But let's do an examination or two on these interesting pieces,' Dee shook the waxed bags in the air, 'and see which of us is proved right, shall we?' He levered himself up from his chair. 'Do you want to come and watch, or could you do with some sleep? You certainly look a little . . .' he leaned forward and smiled, 'dishevelled.'

'Dishevelled?' Marlowe was horrified. 'In what way?'

'Oh, nothing much. A little loam here,' Dee touched his own chin. 'Some gravestone lichen here.' He brushed at his chest. 'Perhaps a hint of . . .'

'Yes, yes, you've said enough,' Marlowe laughed. 'Perhaps I might adjust my clothing and have a wash and then join you. Can that be arranged?'

'A bed and water are already set for you,' Dee told him, ushering him to the door. 'Jane?' he called to his wife and was rewarded by scurrying footsteps in the hall. 'Ah, there you are, my dear.' He looked fondly as his wife embraced his friend. 'See Kit to his room, will you? And I will see you later. Jane will show you the way.'

Jane Dee was years younger than her husband, a pleasant woman with a broad smile. She worried about her old man, and worried even more when a man with Kit Marlowe's reputation came calling. What did they call him? Machiavel? The Muse's Darling? Jane Dee's husband was sometimes frightening enough, but Marlowe had a danger about him, a way of going that scared her. She saw beneath the curls and melting eyes to what lay beneath and it wasn't half as pretty as the exterior.

He bowed as she entered and kissed her hand. In all Dee's other houses, it had been easy enough to find his laboratory by sound and smell alone, but Marlowe allowed himself to be led off by Jane, as Dee shuffled off down the flagged passage, humming to himself and waving his little waxed packages happily in the air.

Simon Forman was not a man who was down for long. He had woken after an hour or two to find his wife gone about her business and the house buzzing happily along, as it always did. All he had to do was bring in the money to keep it buzzing and everyone was happy. He delved into his memory for a moment, trying to remember what had made him so introspective when he got home. The widow, yes, that had been a rare failure, but . . . something else. What was it . . .? Suddenly, it all came back to him and he shrugged on his workaday robes, less sumptuous than his walking-out attire, but still with enough beads to make the laundry maid weep, and he went in search of his apprentices.

They were where they always were, in his chamber in the shadow of the abbey, busy with retorts, mirrors, liquids and herbs, always with the background noise of the tame doves which cooed and wheeled above their heads, sometimes depositing their own very special additions to the brews below. Tanks of frogs and newts, green and slimy and pulsating with life, were along a shelf near the high window. Pots of herbs grew in even the smallest space. There was something of the countryside about Simon Forman's laboratory, were it not for the smell of brimstone, which was the subtle underscore to it all.

When they heard their master's step, the apprentices sprang to attention. Forman liked to have lackeys around him, but he preferred his lackeys to be clever and so he paid wages to garner the best rather than get the sweepings of the streets for free. He even gave them a week of paid holiday a year, beyond the wildest dream of any other apprentice in the land. Indeed, they had just come back from their annual visit to their families, bearing gifts for their master according to custom; the packages lay on his desk, as always, but he knew what they contained. Two would be new editions of some arcane Greek text which he never admitted he couldn't read. The other would be a dozen new-laid eggs and a pot of honey, much more to his taste.

Two of his apprentices were scholars, one from Cambridge, the other from Oxford. Their natural enmity kept them keen to impress. The other was not a scholar. He was an unschooled boy from the Weald of Kent but knew more about herbs and the creatures of the wild than the other two would ever know. He had learned to read and write with lightning speed and Forman knew that, if one of the apprentices would usurp their master, it would almost certainly be him. He dressed them in garments of his own design and would have been mortified to know how much they hated wearing them. He had chosen a deep blue, almost black, which reminded him of a dark winter sky, moonless and cloudless. To enhance the effect, there were specks of cut glass scattered here and there, more at the shoulder and less at the hem. He thought it made them look just mystical enough to act as a background for his own magnificence. They thought it made them look like tarts fallen on hard times. But he paid them well and he paid them promptly, so a bit of name-calling as they went about their business was a small price to pay.

He walked slowly past them as they lined up just inside the door. Matthias was the tallest of the three, well-made as to shoulder and calf and with a profile a Greek god would die for. His flaxen hair fell over the glittering shoulders of his gown in the style Forman favoured, in artless curls which took him half an hour at least every morning to achieve. He was the Oxford scholar and he bore it lightly. He had attended the College of the Holy and Undivided Trinity, though he hadn't had a holy thought since he had been about seven. He didn't talk much about his days among those hallowed halls where, it was whispered, Papists still held sway. He had not quite been sent down, but it had been a near-run thing. Oxford had so many things to interest a young man of frisky habits but, in the end, it had been dice which had been his downfall; not the game so much as the very substantial debts that his bad judgement had led him into. He had a pretty way with a retort, however, and could extract oil from anything that was handed to him. He had not yet managed to get blood from a stone, but there was yet time.

The next in line was the Cambridge scholar, Timothy. He only reached Matthias's shoulder and was little and weaselly generally, with very scant dark hair and a tendency to sniff. Surprisingly, he did rather better with the ladies of the district than Matthias did, having spied often on his master when the great magus was practising his massage on widows far and wide. He had not found it a hard technique to master and, once he had used his clever words to get close enough, there was never any demur from the girl in question. He was dishonest, not too keen on washing his hands no matter how unpleasant the experiment he had been engaged in and, generally, Forman passed over him with as much speed as was civil. He had also gone to Trinity – the real one, as he constantly called it, though it predated Matthias's alma mater by less than a decade. Extraction was not his skill. He wanted to deconstruct everything that crossed his path until he found that tiny spark that made it unique of and to itself. Only Forman could see that Timothy was as dark and weaselly inside as without – but the man had his uses and so he let him stay.

The country boy, Gerard, was Forman's pride and joy. His own sons were young yet but he knew that, when they grew, he wanted them to be like this. Gerard's frank, open face was smattered with freckles even after two years in London, mostly closeted in the distillery making tinctures from all the herbs he grew. He could make any plant flourish just by making a hole in soil with his thumb and then sticking it in, with a prayer and a gentle pat such as a mother will give to a sleeping child. The plant would grow, Forman always thought, just to please Gerard, because when he was upset a cloud would pass across his face and it would seem that God was crying to see his distress. In height, he came between the scholars and was neatly made, being neither skinny nor stout. He wore his gown as though he loved wearing it and indeed, of the three, he hated it least. He had had fourteen years of hand-me-downs, often from his sisters, so to have clothes that were his own was still a pleasure he cherished. He smiled at Forman and said good morning, with the soft burr of a true Man of Kent.

Forman stepped back from his apprentices and opened his arms in a distant embrace. 'Gentlemen,' he beamed. 'A new dawn. A new day.' He raised his arms and they all smiled and tried to look enthusiastic. Only Gerard managed it to any convincing extent. 'Sadly, we had a loss last night. Master Templeton, despite our best efforts, succumbed to the Pestilence and his wife . . .'

'Widow,' Timothy, who had a literal turn of mind, corrected him.

'Yes, yes, of course, widow . . . has not taken it well. I tried to comfort her . . .' Timothy looked at his shoes and smirked '. . . but it is perhaps too soon. However, we will not forget her in her time of sorrow. Matthias.' The apprentice perked up and adopted the look of a man eager to please at any price. 'Make a note to go and visit the dear, good woman in . . . shall we say one week? Yes. One week.'

Matthias went over to a desk in the corner and jotted something down.

'But . . .' Forman's scowl became positively Saturnine. 'On my way home from the sad home of Mistress Templeton, I met a man. A man wearing the mask of a plague doctor.'

The apprentices were stuck for an appropriate response. The city was full of men dressed like plague doctors. It was the employment of choice at the moment. As long as you chose your patients well and didn't actually go near anyone with plague, there was big money to be made. Eventually, Gerard, who hated anyone to not get an answer, even when they hadn't strictly asked a question, spoke. 'Who was it, Master?'

'A good question, Gerard. A very good question.' The great magus hitched his gown up on his shoulders and leaned forward. 'Now, boys, I want to tell you that I will not be angry whatever answer you give to my next question. What I want is honesty, no more, no less. Have you ever been to the theatre?'

The apprentices shuffled their feet. Of course they had been to the theatre. When the theatre was prohibited in no uncertain terms, as it was early in their indentures, it obviously became much more tempting than it otherwise would be. They had seen plays so sublime they would make their way back to their lodgings with wings on their feet; these were usually written by one Christopher Marlowe, though the spelling on the playbills varied widely. They had seen plays so appalling they had been funny and they had rolled home holding their sides; Ralph Roister Doister was always good for a laugh. And they had seen a play by Will Shaxsper. But admitting as much to Forman was another thing altogether. Matthias looked at Timothy. Timothy looked at Gerard, who had nowhere to hide.

'I have been to the theatre, Master,' he said, looking the magus squarely in the eye.

Forman nodded. 'I am glad to see that I have one honest apprentice,' he said, smiling grimly. 'Do you know a playwright named Christopher Marlowe?'

'I know his *work*,' the country boy acknowledged.

'But him. Have you ever seen him?'

'Once, when I went to see one of his plays, he was at the apron, watching and making notes. He rewrites all the time, men say. He seeks perfection.'

Timothy was aghast. 'There is no perfection but God,' he blurted out. The others looked at him. Religion was rare within these walls. 'Or . . . at least . . .' he blustered, 'so they say.'

'Well, anyhow,' Gerard picked up his tale with a sideways glance at his flustered colleague, 'I suppose therefore you can say I have seen him.'

'About so high,' Forman held up a hand, 'curls,' and he sketched them round his own close-cropped head. 'A rather handy man with a dagger.'

'So far, that sounds like me,' Matthias laughed.

Gerard grinned and nodded. 'And like Master Marlowe, too,' he said.

'Then it may well have been him,' Forman said. 'Why would he be dressed like a plague doctor? He has no medical training, has he?'

'Who has?' Timothy muttered in his throat, but fortunately no one heard him.

'I don't see how he would have had the time,' Gerard said, continuing in his role as theatre aficionado. 'He can't be more than the middle twenties and he came straight to London from Cambridge.' He looked at their stunned faces. They had not known that he was quite such an expert in the theatre and its people. 'Or so men say.'

Forman looked at Matthias. 'Make a note,' he said.

'What note, Master?' he asked, stepping over to the desk and dipping the pen.

'Just a note,' Forman said, low and level. 'A note not to overlook Master Marlowe.'

FOUR

Marlowe was still asleep in John Dee's second-best bed when the magus came trotting in, all smiles. He stood and watched the playwright sleeping. He loved and worried about the man in equal measure. Children had come late to the magician and, before they had come, had been Kit. He slept as though he hadn't a care in the world, which Dee knew to be untrue. But if there was one place he felt safe, it was under Dee's roof and so he lay on his back, one arm curved above his head, the other flung out across the empty side of the bed. With his eyes closed and his face turned to the faint rays of the sun coming through the lattice, he looked hardly half of his twenty-eight summers. After a moment, as if he felt the gaze touch his cheek, the man stretched and opened his eyes, treacle-brown and unfathomable, letting himself wake slowly, an indulgence he rarely allowed himself.

'Doctor,' he said, with a slight nod and laced his fingers together behind his head.

'Playwright,' Dee returned, before hitching himself up onto the foot of the bed and unfolding a paper he had had tucked up his sleeve.

It was an old joke, if joke it was, but it made them both smile.

'Do you have an answer for me?' Marlowe asked.

'I do. And I don't.'

'Very enigmatic.'

Dee looked down his nose and crossed his eyes slightly. 'I find enigmatic goes down well with the customers,' he smiled. 'I like to keep in practice.'

Marlowe looked fondly at the old man. 'You don't do yourself justice,' he said, hitching himself up in the bed and rearranging the pillows at his back. 'You need no tricks to do what you do. You are no Simon Forman nor Edward Kelly.'

'Thank you.' A shadow passed over Dee's face. There had been many who had sought to usurp him and some had almost succeeded, the charlatan Kelly among them. His house in Mortlake had been burned down. His beloved Helene had been murdered. And yet, here he was, still. And here he would remain.

'And, so . . .?' Marlowe lifted a quizzical eyebrow.

Dee cleared his throat and shook out his paper. He settled his wire-framed spectacles on the end of his nose and began to read, in a rather high-pitched and rapid style. 'I was made cognizant of the death of one Robert Greene, of Kyroun Lane in the County of—'

Marlowe held up a hand. 'Stop. Stop,' he said. 'This is not the Coroner's Inquest. There is no First Finder here. Just tell me what you found.'

Dee took a deep breath but was forestalled.

'In your own words, please. Don't read. Just tell.'

Dee looked a little crestfallen but nonetheless put away his paper. 'As you wish.' He looked a little wistfully at Marlowe. 'Shall I tell you about my tests?'

'Perhaps later. For now, just tell me what you found.'

'Very well. It was unexpected, I can tell you that.' He took off his eyeglasses and polished them furiously on a corner of the bedsheet. 'I was expecting one of the metallic poisons, mercury, that kind of thing. Taken in large enough quantities, mercury can be quite dangerous you know. My scrying mirror has enough in it to kill the whole of the Court, had I a mind.' He blinked up at Marlowe. Perhaps he had said enough. 'However, it was quickly obvious that it was a vegetable poison we were looking for.'

'You were sure it was poison, then? From the start?'

Dee looked surprised. 'Did you have anything else in mind?'

Marlowe shrugged. 'Suffocation?' he suggested.

'No. I was sure that was not the case. No discoloration. No sign of linen fragments or feather in the exudate from the nose and mouth. No blood, either. No, it was poison, I am certain.'

'What?' Marlowe had known a good many adroit poisoners in his time and none had used the same element. It made it at once easier and more difficult to solve. Poison was not a random thing, like a dagger in the back or a cosh across the head, nor yet a wire around the throat in a dark alley. Poison was planned. Poison was administered by stealth by someone who could be three counties away before death struck. Poisoners were cruel and cold; no one poisoned in the heat of anger.

'Vegetable, of that I am certain. It could have been put in his food or drink.'

'I understand he had been in his room, taking very little by way of sustenance for some time before he died.'

'It wouldn't need to be much, but I take your point.' Dee sucked his teeth and thought carefully. 'It would need, therefore, to be something that had little or no taste. Or something that is, in itself, food.'

'For example?' Marlowe ate to live and wasn't really that interested in food for its own sake.

'Mushrooms, for instance.' Dee got up and left the room, coming back minutes later with a book under his arm. 'See, here, the shaggy ink cap, as the country folk know it. It is edible, though I am not that fond of mushrooms myself, so cannot tell you how good it tastes. And here, on the next page, the death cap.' He handed the book to Marlowe, who flicked from one page to another.

'They look the same.'

'Precisely. Are we sure that his landlady did not make a mistake?'

Marlowe flopped back on his pillows. 'She didn't strike me as a woman who would cook anything special for her lodgers. They would have what she was having, and like it, I would guess.'

'In that case, if it was mushroom, it would have to be done on purpose. This is the season for them, of course. Though . . .' again, Dee paused in thought, 'I wouldn't have thought that Dowgate was awash with mushrooms, edible or otherwise. And you wouldn't say this lady would waste her money on bringing up delicacies from the country?'

Marlowe laughed, remembering the mean little house. 'No. I would say definitely not. But, are you saying it is mushroom, then?'

'Not for certain. I am simply giving an example of something which would not arouse Greene's suspicion. It could be a soporific, given in enormous doses. But then, you have the problem of the victim becoming drowsy before the full dose was taken and then waking up. And, of course, valerian and other herbs with that effect would have to be taken by the bucketload to actually kill anyone. By the way, some of the stains on the shroud were from bone broth. No poison in it, but I was puzzled.'

'Apparently, Dominus Greene was in the habit of sitting in his shroud while he worked. He was obviously a messy eater as well as more than usually eccentric.' Marlowe was beginning to feel almost sorry for the man; he cut a sad and lonely figure.

'Well, that explains that, at least. I'm sorry I can't be more precise, Kit. But I think that the poor Dominus was poisoned by a friend's hand. A stranger coming to his room with food would be unusual, surely.'

'A friend.' Marlowe swung his legs over the side of the bed and slid to the floor. 'Thank you, Doctor. That may be the answer we have been looking for.'

'Did Robert Greene have a large circle of friends?' Dee asked. 'From the little I have heard, he was rather a recluse, to say the least.'

'He was,' Marlowe said, slipping on his jerkin and lacing his Venetians. 'He was a man with rather a lot of lukewarm enemies, myself included, and one very hot friend.'

'Do you know who?'

'Indeed I do,' Marlowe said. 'And I know just where to find him; Paternoster Row, if memory serves.'

'He's gone.' The secretary had a mouthful of quill at the time and was staggering down some stairs under a pile of books.

'Anywhere in particular?' Marlowe asked. The house in Paternoster Row had four floors, linked by creaking stairs and the secretary was glad to reach the ground and put the books down. He took the quill out of his mouth and peered at Marlowe. 'Who did you say you were?'

'I didn't,' Marlowe said. 'I was enquiring after Dr Harvey.'

The secretary produced a pair of spectacles from his gown

and attached them to his rather beaky nose, making much play with winding the side pieces around his protuberant ears. He looked up at Marlowe, squinting. 'You'll forgive me,' he said, 'if I make the point that this conversation is going in circles.'

Marlowe gripped the man by his narrow shoulders. 'Let's get it on a straighter path, then,' he smiled, icily. 'Where has Dr Harvey gone?'

'I cannot give out information of that sort,' the secretary shook himself free and wriggled his shoulders to settle his clothing.

'Really?' Marlowe frowned. 'What a pity.' It was the work of a second to flick the dagger from its sheath in the small of his back and the blade's tip was tickling the secretary's throat.

'Cambridge,' the man spluttered, afraid to move. 'Pembroke Hall. He's staying with the Master, Dr Andrewes.'

'There, now,' Marlowe beamed. 'That wasn't so hard, was it? When did he leave?'

'Yesterday,' the secretary said, through clenched teeth. He knew he had a tendency towards a rather wobbly Adam's apple and he couldn't be too careful.

'By the North Road?'

'Yes, sir.' In the nick of time, the secretary stopped an incipient nod.

Marlowe stepped back and the dagger had vanished. He nodded at the man, whose nose was dribbling, and turned to the door, the one that led out to the weak sunshine of Paternoster Row.

'Who shall I say was calling, sir?' the secretary managed.

'Machiavel,' Marlowe said without turning. 'But I'll see Harvey before you do.'

It had been nine long years since Kit Marlowe had seen the spires of Cambridge and there had been a lot of Granta water under Magdalen Bridge since then. The university term had just begun and the town, from the old castle to Trumpington, was crawling with scholars in their grey fustian, carrying weighty tomes of leather and vellum, their fingers blue already with cheap ink, their linen beginning to grow as grey as their gowns, their hair wispy, without their mothers' care.

For old times' sake, the playwright sampled the ale at the Eagle and Child and looked across the narrow, cobbled lane to Benet College, the Corpus Christi which had been his home for nearly seven years. And what an apprenticeship that had been. He still felt the blood run cold in his veins at the memory of it, pushing against the bitter winds in the court; the winds that blew, men said, from Muscovy, without so much as a hillock to slow their passage or to warm their savage breath. He felt the whips of the proctors, their bone-ended thongs slicing through the skin of his back and shoulders. One man only had shown him kindness – Michael Johns, tutor in Hebrew. Where was he now? Where were any of them? They had all but vanished, the men who were boys when he was a boy. Matthew Parker would be in a rich incumbency some-where, dining out on the fact that his grandfather had been the Archbishop of Canterbury. Henry Bromerick wouldn't have gone into the Church, though old Dr Norgate, the time-honoured Master of Corpus in Marlowe's day, had assumed they all would. The law perhaps? Yes, he was certainly stupid enough. And Tom Colwell? Now, Tom Colwell, Marlowe knew about. He had gone of the sweating sickness not long after he left Cambridge. Already, the ranks of the golden lads were thinning.

He remembered other things too. That slippery bastard Robert Greene toadying up to him, watching over his shoulder as Marlowe rewrote Ovid, trying out the mighty line that one day would make his name. Greene was a stranger to iambic pentameter, not to mention plot and character, and he knew that Marlowe could help him with that. What could be easier, Greene had thought, than to creep into Corpus Christi one dark night and steal the outpourings of a greater man?

And who had helped him in this? Marlowe remembered *him*, too, only too well; Dr Gabriel Harvey, the dubious don who had hated Marlowe from the start. He had pretensions, did Gabriel Harvey. And he recognized a threat when he saw one. He had made it his personal business to do Marlowe down. The son of a cobbler had no place in Cambridge at all. Why not unleash Greene to carry out his mischief and use Harvey's undoubted power if Marlowe complained?

He watched them now, the scholars of this new generation. Had he *ever* been that young? Here he was, a Master of Arts of the greatest university in the world, and not yet thirty. Where had the years gone? He downed his ale and said a silent farewell to the Eagle and Child. Enough of yesterday. A man must live for today. And Pembroke Hall called.

The College of Valence Mary was the smallest in Cambridge and the third oldest. It nestled, grey and medieval, along Trumpington Street, its Gothic gatehouse adorned with ogee arches and the arms of Pembroke, the scarlet martlets on the blue and silver field. There were proctors lurking there, as there were at the gate of every college, waiting to catch the tardy scholar, late for dinner or in his cups. Kit Marlowe was neither of these things; nor was he a scholar in the current sense. But the proctors stopped him anyway.

'Can we help you, sir?' one of them asked. He had the shaved head and thick neck of a fairground wrestler and it sounded as though the word 'sir' cost him dear.

'I doubt it,' Marlowe said, breezily.

But the second man blocked his path. 'What my brother-proctor means,' he said softly, 'is that you cannot merely walk into a college of the university, without so much as a by-your-leave.' This man was half the size of his colleague, wizened and bent from years of peering round corners and listening at keyholes. His hands were white and gnarled, his legs bowed. He looked as if he couldn't blow the froth off a frumety yet, of the two, he was by far the more frightening. He had the look of a man who would stop at nothing when it came to doing what he thought was right. No matter how wrong that might be.

'As a matter of fact, as an alumnus of this university, that is exactly what I can do.'

'Oh?' The first proctor loomed behind the second. 'Which college?'

'Corpus Christi. In Dr Norgate's time.'

The proctors exchanged glances. 'Never heard of him,' the smaller one said.

'Your loss, pizzle,' Marlowe shrugged. 'Now, are you gentlemen going to let me pass or am I to tell Dr Andrewes the reason for my lateness?'

The proctors shifted uneasily. 'You've got an appointment?' the shaven-headed one growled.

'I have. As of . . .' Marlowe waited for the college clock to strike, 'Now. Good morning gentlemen,' and he was already striding across the court.

'Good God!' Gabriel Harvey was looking out of Lancelot Andrewes's leaded window onto the courtyard below. 'I don't believe it!' His London fashions looked out of place in this scholar's sanctum, and, truth be told, his ruff was killing him.

'What is it, Gabriel?' Andrewes had given up waiting for his steward. The buffoon never answered the Master's bell; he would have to go. So the Master was reduced to pouring his own wine. He passed a cup to Harvey.

'Either your Rhenish is particularly powerful stuff, or that is Christopher Marlowe.'

'What is Christopher Marlowe?' The Master was busy mopping up the spilled wine. It wasn't as simple a job as it at first appeared.

'There. Crossing the quad.'

'I asked what, not where.' The Master had a tendency to literalness which drove even those who liked him to distraction.

Harvey turned to his friend, keeping his voice level. He was, after all, this man's guest. It hurt him to even think it, but how could anyone not have heard of Christopher Marlowe, for good or ill? 'He's an ex-scholar of Corpus. Although for the life of me, I don't know how he ever reached that status. I remember, when we were both here permanently, as it were, there was some kerfuffle over his Masters degree.'

'That's right,' Andrewes dredged his memory. 'Didn't the Privy Council intervene on his behalf? He has some powerful friends, does young Marlowe.'

'He's a string-puller, that's for sure. The question is, what's he doing here?'

There was a rap at the door, short, sharp, that brooked no waiting.

'Attempting to gain entry, I shouldn't be at all surprised.' Andrewes bent his gentle, innocent gaze on Harvey, who managed to stay smiling, though only just. 'Come in.'

The door swung open, oiled by the sweat of generations of fearful scholars oozing past its hinges.

'Dr Andrewes?' Marlowe bowed; not the casual, rakish gush of London and the Court, but the formal bob of a Convictus Secundus to a Master that no man forgets.

'I am Lancelot Andrewes,' the Master agreed. 'Who are you?' Marlowe took in the man. He was shorter than Harvey, older and with greying hair. His scholarship was renowned, his Puritanism legendary. The plain white collar and the black doublet spoke volumes. 'Dr Harvey will have told you who I am,' he said, 'watching me cross the quad as he did. I apologize for barging in, *relatively* unannounced, Master, but it is Dr Harvey to whom I wish to speak.'

No one was fazed by the immaculate Queen's English. All three of them knew that Marlowe could have delivered it in Latin or Greek – even Hebrew, at a pinch. Andrewes looked the man up and down. 'Do I take it, Master Marlowe,' he said, 'that as an ex-alumnus of Corpus, you did not take the cloth?'

'There is cloth and cloth,' Marlowe smiled. 'These simple sleeves will answer my calling. No, I did not take the cloth in the sense that you mean.'

Lancelot Andrewes was not a kind man at heart and many were the things which riled him; one of them stood before him now. He narrowed his eyes and put down his goblet. 'You are a playwright, sir,' he hissed. It was all coming back to him now. 'A writer of fornication who fabricates for the delight of the unwashed. All Cambridge knows my views on the theatre.'

Marlowe chuckled. 'So does the Master of the Revels. And Her Majesty, I am told.' He clicked his tongue and shook his head. 'Enjoy your time here, Dr Andrewes. There'll be no advancement for you beyond this.'

'How dare you!' Andrewes bellowed, his face and neck purple with rage. Marlowe looked on with interest – it was always a revelation to see a mild man come to the boil. He thought that the citizens of Pompeii had probably seen something not unlike this when the top blew off Vesuvius, all those years ago.

'I'm sorry, Lancelot,' Harvey intervened. 'My visit here has caused us both embarrassment. On behalf of Master Marlowe, I apologize.'

'I do my own apologizing, Doctor,' Marlowe said, 'as and when it becomes necessary.'

'May we use your library, Lancelot?' Harvey asked. 'Master Marlowe clearly wants a word in private.'

'Private or public,' Marlowe said. 'It makes no difference to me.'

'Make it public, then,' Andrewes said. 'Let's all hear what this popinjay has to say.'

Harvey said nothing, so Marlowe crossed to the window and leaned forward, resting his elbows on one of the Master's spartan chairs. 'Robert Greene,' he said.

Andrewes looked blank.

'What of him?' Harvey asked.

Marlowe looked at the man. He was greyer than when they had last met, this arrogant Fellow of the university who had set himself up as a critic of critics. His face had a permanent sneer, born of showing contempt for the talents of men who were far greater than he was himself.

'He is dead, Dr Harvey,' Marlowe said simply, 'as you well know.'

'A tragedy.' Harvey leaned against the oak panelling, folding his arms. 'A pity he never wrote one. Or anything else of note, come to that.'

Marlowe stood up. 'He deserves better at your hands, Doctor,' he said.

Harvey roared with laughter. 'You couldn't stand the man, Marlowe. He used to try to steal your fire; fumbling efforts, if memory serves. There was a time when you'd have cut your throat.'

'But *I* wouldn't have poisoned him,' Marlowe said softly.

'Poison?' Harvey blinked. 'Greene died of a surfeit of pickled herring and . . .' he chuckled at the cup in his hand, 'Rhenish wine.'

'And you know this because . . .?'

'I went there!' Harvey said. He saw Andrewes looking at him, but he had said too much to backtrack now. 'To his foul lodgings in Dowgate. Spoke to that trollop of a landlady.'

'Why?' Marlowe asked.

It was a while before Harvey answered. 'I once had a certain respect for Dominus Greene,' he said finally. 'Scholar of St John's, after all.'

Andrewes nodded approvingly. It wasn't Pembroke Hall, but it wasn't at all bad.

'When did you see him last?' Marlowe asked.

'I saw his corpse, Marlowe, lying on his bed in a shroud.'

'You just happened to be passing?' The playwright would not let it go.

'In a manner of speaking.'

'There is the Pestilence in Dowgate, Dr Harvey. Are you telling us that you would risk all that to visit the body of a man you had lost touch with?'

'I don't have to tell you anything,' Harvey blurted out. 'This is not the Inquisition and you are no Torquemada. Lancelot, this man has tried my patience long enough. Not content with reading the filth of Ovid when he was a scholar here, he has become Machiavel; dabbling in the occult, sleeping with the Devil himself, I shouldn't wonder. And here he is, accusing me of . . . what, Marlowe? Murder?'

Marlowe could play the Biblical scholar when he had to. 'The words are yours, Doctor,' he smiled.

Andrewes lurched forward, eyes bulging in his head, but Marlowe raised a hand. 'Forgive me, Master,' he said. 'I have outstayed my welcome. Gentlemen,' he bowed again, 'I'll see myself out.'

For a long moment, neither man spoke after the door had slammed.

'Once again, Lancelot,' Harvey said, calmer now, 'my apologies. Here I am, visiting an old friend and garbage like that follows me from London.'

'Proctors, Gabriel?' Andrewes was looking out of the window as Marlowe strode for the gate.

'I'm sorry?' Harvey didn't understand at first.

'Proctors of colleges are inestimable fellows, aren't they? Good, for example, at clearing up such things as garbage that follows one from London.'

Harvey was not a little shocked. He had never seen this

side of Andrewes before and had had no idea what depths lay beneath the benign scholarly surface. He found himself hoping he never had to delve any deeper. For now, a simple grunt of assent seemed to be all the Master needed, so he gave it. Andrewes smiled icily and remained, staring out of the window, until he knew Marlowe was no longer in the purlieus of the college. Then he raised an eyebrow at Harvey and walked over to the table. 'Rhenish?' he asked.

Kit Marlowe had not finished with Gabriel Harvey. There were too many unanswered questions. Even so, he would bide his time. It would be a week or so before *The Massacre at Paris* was due to open at the Rose and Philip Henslowe was always at his grouchiest in the run-up to an opening.

But a certain nostalgia had hit Marlowe, one of those sorts of mixed emotions that playwrights and poets found useful. He watched the willows trailing in the Cam, the ducks squawking and flapping as the punts passed by, carrying casks of wine and boxes of paper between the colleges. He sat for a while in the peace of King's, the magnificent beams soaring above him and he listened to the choir.

Like all grown choirboys, he liked to think that it was not a patch on any of the choirs in which he had sung, but he really had to admit it wasn't at all bad. There was a boy treble in the mix somewhere who would be a marvel in six months or so, as long as his balls didn't drop too soon. Marlowe had been one of the rare ones; his voice hadn't broken, just mellowed and matured until the day when he could simply gather up his music and move from the treble decani to the alto cantoris and then finally to the tenors. He closed his eyes and allowed the music to invade what was left of his soul. Sometimes, choir practice was better than the service; it came without all the claptrap that Marlowe tried to avoid.

Then, something invaded his brain that couldn't be avoided and reminded him of why he was there. 'I know that my Redeemer liveth,' soared the voice of the almost-perfect treble. The burial service. Morley, unless he missed his guess. So, in the midst of life, he was yet again in death and some poor soul was waiting, wrapped in his linen, for these young voices to speed him on his way. Outside the dark was gathering but, for one man at least, the dark had come to stay.

Dusk was late to be out and about looking for lodgings. It made landladies nervous, to open the door in the gloaming to see a figure dark against the fading sky. He wandered the lanes, hoping he would find a welcoming house soon and, as he walked, he thought about tomorrow. He would visit Harvey again, this time without the pompous Puritanism of Andrewes in the background and do some straight talking. He was crossing Parker's Piece now, the field that Trinity College had bought to feed its sheep and the setting Fall sun was gilding the turret tops of the colleges around him. Bells were tolling, summoning scholars to dinner in their halls, and Marlowe knew that the various butteries would be loud with the chatter of voices and the clatter of pewter on polished oak.

He saw the man ahead of him, indistinct in the half-light but wearing the unmistakeable gown of a proctor. As he got closer, he noticed that the heraldic device was gone from the man's sleeve; he clearly had no wish to advertise his college this evening. He also saw the club in the man's right hand. Kit Marlowe was no stranger to the smock alleys of London, the murky depths by the river where the lanterns of the night Watch never shone. He felt his dagger hilt at his back and slowed his pace.

What he did not see was the man behind him and he had no idea what happened next. He felt a sickening blow to the back of his head and he went down, his dagger half out of its sheath, blood trickling over his collar. He felt a boot thud into his ribs and another into his back. He grabbed a swinging foot and threw its owner over so that the proctor hit the hard ground with a crunch which echoed as his head made contact. He cursed, so he wasn't knocked out, but down was half the battle. Another club came down, this time from directly above and for Marlowe, there was nothing but blackness over Parker's Piece.

Tom Sledd was not chained to a wall and, as far as he could tell, nor was anyone else. That was the good news. Other than that, even with his normally resilient nature, he couldn't really see anything to be pleased about. All around him were men and women in varying degrees of starvation, filth and degradation. They were wearing clothes, presumably the clothes they had been wearing when they entered the Hell that was Bedlam. Far above him, the roof was open to the sky and he heard the tolling of a bell. That would be All Hallows on the Wall, he guessed. Or it could have been a death knell. Sledd tried to keep his mind off his undoubtedly parlous situation by trying to work out how long each one of his fellow inmates had been incarcerated by the degree of raggedness of their clothes. It depressed him to discover that he could tell how long some of them had been there by whether their clothes were out of fashion. For instance, he asked himself, looking at a man in the far corner who was talking animatedly to a chair, who has worn a collar like that in the last thirty years?

When Jack and Nat had hurled him through the door, he hadn't been too worried, being sure the mistake would soon be rectified. After all, he was perfectly sane. True, he worked for Philip Henslowe for what other people might describe as a pittance. True, he worked with actors who drove him to distraction on any given day; making them do as they were asked was like herding cats. Worse, probably. But, those things aside – and the fact that for some years he had stood in front of crowds of people whilst wearing women's clothing – those things aside – and the fact he spent at least half an hour a day talking to Master Sackerson, who happened to be a bear. *Those* things aside, he was perfectly normal.

But now he had had a chance to look more closely at his companions and he was less sanguine. The man who had the straw mattress next to him was sitting calmly with his legs crossed and his back against a wall, writing on a tablet with a tattered quill pen. He had ink in a small bottle, which he held crooked in his little finger in the manner of scribes every-where and he seemed oblivious to the chaos around him. His clothes were looking grubby but were of recent cut and his hair had not yet become long and bedraggled. Tom had engaged him in conversation when they were eating their gruel that first morning and he had been very civil and not a little amusing. But sane, certainly.

'Good morning,' Tom had begun. Not an original greeting, perhaps, but it was all he could come up with, given the circumstances.

The man had looked up at the high window where the late Fall sun was trying its best to shine through the grime and cobwebs. He had turned to Tom and flashed a lovely smile, one which transformed his face, if only briefly. 'It seems to be,' he said. 'It's sometimes hard to tell in here.'

It was nine coherent words in a row more than Tom had heard since he had arrived, so he persisted.

'May I ask why you are here?' he said, politely.

'Oh, no,' the man had said, sipping his gruel as if it were finest consommé. 'We don't ask that sort of thing here.'

'Ah. But . . .' How did one say 'but you don't seem mad' without giving offence?

'I suppose you're thinking that I don't seem mad,' the man said, solving the dilemma. 'I didn't think I was but,' he shrugged, 'my wife thought otherwise and so, here I am.'

Sledd and Mistress Sledd occasionally did not see eye to eye. But to think of her having him put in Bedlam – impossible. 'Your *wife?*'

Again, the man shrugged. 'I suppose I can be a bit annoying at times. Poets are.'

And there the conversation had ended. The attendants came round to collect the gruel cups, kicking and slapping as they went when anyone got in their way. When it was Tom's turn, he tried to explain, but just got a cuff around the head for his pains. He fell back on his lice-crawling mattress, stunned. From his left, he heard the poet murmur, 'And that's the other thing we don't do here. We don't say it's all a mistake. Only madmen say that, or so Master Sleford tells us.'

Tom covered his head with his arms and wept. A sane man in Bedlam would soon be as mad as the rest.

FIVE

When Marlowe started to come to, he had no idea how long he had lain there. The sky was darker, but that could mean it had just been a few minutes; sunset didn't last long in Fall, even across the big skies of the Fens. From long practice, he lay still while he assessed the damage. He took a deep breath. It hurt, but not enough to suggest a broken rib. He tried a cough and the result was the same. He gingerly extended one leg and then the other. Not broken, though one thigh would have the mother and father of a bruise when he checked, of that he was sure. His arms likewise. The proctors had been careful to avoid his face; they didn't want him to be wearing the badge of their encounter around the streets. This was a loudmouth, they knew, and he probably had friends in high places. His sort always did.

He rolled onto his hands and knees and stayed there for a moment, head low, waiting for the spinning sensation to stop. As the ringing in his ears subsided, he heard footsteps approaching, breaking into a run. A hand came down on his shoulder, making him wince. Then a voice, a voice he knew.

'Kit? Kit, is that you?'

He turned his head and a familiar and beloved face swam into view. He closed his eyes tight and then opened them. There, in the faint light from the lantern that the man had laid on the ground, was the worried face of Michael Johns, late of Cambridge, London, and anywhere else that learning was to be found.

Marlowe coughed again and struggled to his feet. He was still muzzy and he staggered against the man who had so often had his back. Johns laid a gentle arm across his shoulders and picked up his lantern. 'Don't try to talk,' he said, gently. 'My lodgings are nearby. Let's get you there and we can find out what the damage is. Slowly, now. Slowly. You're safe now.' He looked left and right. 'Whoever did this to you has gone

now. In fact,' his voice was reassuring, 'I am sure they have
been apprehended. As I came around the corner, I saw two
proctors running in that direction.' He pointed ahead. 'They
will have the miscreant in their hands by now, I'm certain.
You remember how the proctors always get their man, I'm
sure.'

'Well, where the bloody hell is he?' Philip Henslowe had
not shaved this morning. He hadn't washed either. And his
breakfast was a pint of Bastard.

Will Shaxsper looked at him. 'Are you talking about Tom?'
he asked.

'Of course I'm talking about Tom,' Henslowe growled.
'Do they have this at the Curtain? The Theatre? No, only at
the Rose could the stage manager disappear days before an
opening. When did you see him last?'

The Warwickshire man thought fast. Today he was the
Prince of Condé, cousin to the King of Navarre. He owed
Marlowe a favour and the costume *was* rather fetching. Nobody
would notice his Midlands accent – the groundlings would
just assume they spoke like that in Condé. Was that a place?
Shaxsper didn't know. He wasn't a University wit and, beyond
the leafy fields of Stratford and the stews of Southwark, he
didn't have much of a clue. What he *did* have a clue about
was that he had last seen the missing stage manager near the
New Churchyard by Bedlam, keeping an eye out for the night
Watch. What he also had a clue about was that digging up
bodies at dead of night, with no authority whatsoever, was
against the law. He couldn't name the statute, but he knew it
was all in there somewhere of the Thirty-First Something-Or-
Other of Elizabeth, By the Grace of God, Etc. Etc. and it was
probably a hanging offence.

'Well?'

Shaxsper's thought processes were never swift and Henslowe
was losing patience.

'A couple of days ago,' Shaxsper lied. 'Chatting to Master
Sackerson.'

Henslowe threw his cup, contents and all, across the stage.
It hit a flat and sprayed red all over the painted Bastille that

had taken two days to build. 'We've got a play to put on and Tom Sledd is talking to a bloody bear?'

Shaxsper looked affronted on Master Sackerson's behalf. After all, he *was* Henslowe's bear.

'Morning all,' a cheery voice called. The Duke of Anjou had arrived.

'Good of you to call, Burbage.' Henslowe was thundering across the stage in the opposite direction to the second greatest actor of his day.

Richard Burbage pulled a face at Shaxsper. 'Somebody's got his Venetians in a twist this morning,' he muttered. 'Where's he off to in such a hurry?'

'I heard that!' Henslowe bellowed. 'If you must know, I'm going to check whether that bloody bear has eaten my stage manager. And while we're talking about worthless layabouts who don't earn their keep . . .'

'Were we?' Burbage mouthed at Shaxsper, who shrugged.

'Where in Hell is Kit Marlowe?'

Johns's rooms in Jesus College were not palatial, but they were clean and quiet. The walk there had not reached Marlowe's conscious memory and, had he known how gruelling it had been, he would be glad. At the end, Johns had been all but carrying him, no mean feat for a man whose heaviest load on any given day was a quill; but love and fear will always find a way. Marlowe was now reclining in the only comfortable chair, a cushion in the small of his back to ease the bruise there, a cup of warm ale within reach of his uninjured arm.

'Is there any point in my asking what happened?' Johns asked.

'I'm not sure I really know,' Marlowe said. 'I imagine that Dr Andrewes may be behind it somehow, or Gabriel Harvey. Both? I don't know.' He turned his smile on Johns. 'I annoy a lot of people, Michael.'

'But, Kit, you say you had only been in Cambridge for one day!' Johns had not forgotten Kit Marlowe, not for one lonely second, but he had forgotten how he could drive a person mad with his insouciant way of looking at things.

'One day is plenty,' Marlowe told him. 'But, yes – it was

clearly Andrewes or Harvey. I had come here to ask after Robert Greene . . .'

'Greene?' Johns remembered him too, but with no fondness. 'What is he up to these days, other than stealing other men's work?'

'He's up to being dead,' Marlowe said, bluntly. 'Poisoned, or so John Dee believes. And what Dee believes, so do I.'

'I'm sorry,' said Johns, and men like him meant things like that, 'but I wouldn't have thought that Greene's death would interest you in so far as you would come all this way,' Johns pointed out.

'In the normal run of things, no.' Marlowe winced and shifted as his back stabbed him. 'But he sent me a letter before he died.'

'What did it say?'

'I have it here. Could you just look inside my doublet, there? That's right. The inside pocket.'

Johns fished out a much-folded piece of cheap parchment and handed it to Marlowe.

'No, no,' Marlowe waved it away. 'You can read it, if you like.'

'May I?' Johns unfolded some wire spectacles from inside his gown and perched them on his ears.

'Out loud, if you would, Michael,' Marlowe said. 'I can interrupt at the relevant places, then.'

Johns cleared his throat. '"To Christopher Marlowe, Dominus of Corpus Christi College, poet, playwright, friend to the afflicted . . ."' Johns looked up at Marlowe, his eyes big and round behind the lenses. 'That's laying on the flattery a little, isn't it, Kit?' he asked. 'I thought he hated you.'

'He did. So that's why I carried on reading.' Marlowe waved a hand and Johns continued.

'"Kit, I know we have never been friends, but you are the only man in London, nay, in the country, to whom I can write and be understood. I know someone is trying to kill me. Don't ask me what brings such a thought into my mind. Some will tell you that I am mad, but I am not or, at least, no madder than erstwhile. But sometimes, I lose time. Sometimes but a minute or two, sometimes a day. And in that time, a demon comes to me, grinning at me and asking if I have spoken with God. I know that you will say that no one can send a demon; that demons are not at the behest of man. But this demon comes, Kit, I know he does, and he is sent by man. You know I have not been a good man, Kit. My wife has left me, my beloved Doll, and Fortunatus looks at me as if I were dead to him. My life is reduced to one room, my company to my landlady and what family she may have with her at any time. They come in droves sometimes, Kit, and all but drive me insane, with their whispering outside the door."'

Johns broke off. 'He is – was – just mad, Kit. He was always unbalanced, even when he was a scholar here. It was well known that he walked a razor's edge.'

'He wasn't mad like this, though, Michael,' Marlowe pointed out. 'He was a fraud and a liar and had no morals. But this letter is that of a man frightened by his own shadow. And whatever else he was, I never knew Robert Greene to be afraid.'

'"Kit,"' Johns read on, '"I know you know all the workings of men's minds, of how one man can make another see things that are not there. If you can stop this madness, I beg of you, although we have never been friends and never can be now – for I fear I am dying – come to my lodgings and save me if you can. Yours, in God, Robert Greene."' Johns let the paper drop into his lap. 'Kit . . . there was nothing you could have done.'

Marlowe shrugged and looked at him levelly. 'Nothing?'

'He died. People die. I heard there was Pestilence in Dowgate.'

'News travels fast.' Marlowe was impressed.

'News of the Pestilence travels fast. We just have to hope the news is ahead of the plague. I don't know where I heard it . . .' Johns tapped his temple to try to dislodge the memory. 'It doesn't matter. But could that not be the reason for his death? For his dreams, too? Because they have to be dreams, Kit. Everyone knows that demons don't visit men like that.' He crossed his fingers, for luck.

'He didn't die of the Pestilence.'

'How do you know for sure? People lie, especially a landlady with a living to earn. Especially one with a large family.'

Marlowe laughed, gently so as not to hurt his back and ribs. 'The large family is something of a misnomer,' he told Johns. 'Mistress Isam has a house full of young ladies, but they are not family, if you catch my meaning.'

Johns looked blank for a moment, then blushed. 'Oh, I *see*. But surely, Dominus Greene would have known that.'

'If what I hear about him is correct, he not only knew, but took advantage of the fact. He was rambling, I am sure, in his letter. But somewhere, there is a kernel of truth in it.'

'And you thought Harvey could help?'

'He was the nearest that Greene had to a friend once; although I believe they had had a falling out.'

'With friends like Harvey, a man doesn't need any enemies,' Johns remarked.

'I agree.' Marlowe knew that only too well. 'And yet, he had at least one. The man who poisoned him.'

Johns looked at Marlowe with a steely gaze. He was not the boy who had come to Cambridge all those years ago, still wet behind the ears and with the voice of an angel. But then, Michael Johns had seen some things, heard some things that had made him less gullible too. 'You're very sure it was poison. You say Dr Dee says it was poison. But how do you know? Did you see him before he died?'

'No.'

'Before he was buried?'

'No.'

'Then . . . when?'

Marlowe shrugged and, for once, couldn't meet his old friend's eyes. There were people who he wouldn't mind knowing that he had gone out at dead of night and dug up a man in a lonely churchyard. But Michael Johns was not one of them.

'Kit . . . when?'

Marlowe finally lifted his head. 'Best you don't know.' He carefully got up out of the chair. 'It's time I moved about. I'm getting stiff. I heard the choir at King's practising Morley's Burial yesterday. Is it for anyone special, or just to keep in trim?'

Johns knew a change of subject when he heard one and followed along obediently. 'In himself, the poor boy wasn't

special, but he died in an accident on the river and so the
college are giving him a funeral. He was also in the choir, as
is his twin, who survived the accident. So, you can see, the
circumstances are a little unusual. I shall be going. Every
college is sending someone and I am the choice for Jesus.'

Marlowe had lost a friend to the river and, although it
was what seemed a lifetime ago, he felt the pain again. 'May
I attend?'

'The chapel is large. I will be sitting in the choir, but of
course you are welcome to come. I happen to know there is
no family, so someone on that side of the nave will be
welcome.'

'What time is it?'

Johns went to the window and craned out, to see the clock
on the college tower. 'If we leave now, we needn't hurry. Are
you sure you'll be all right? The seats are not the most comfortable, as I am sure you remember.'

'I'll manage. If I need to, I can walk about. I'll sit towards
the back. In any case, I want to hear the Morley all the way
through. They have a very promising treble in the choir.'

'I forget your ear,' Johns said. 'They all sound the same to
me.' He shrugged on his gown. 'It's getting chilly, don't you
think?'

Marlowe laughed. 'I had almost forgotten the wind from
Muscovy,' he said. 'I've been in the caverns of London lanes
for too long, perhaps.'

'You'll never leave London,' Johns laughed. 'London
suits you, as you suit it.'

'When I am an old man,' Marlowe said, softly, 'I will retire
to Kent, back to where my bones belong. I shall plant an
orchard and sit in the evening and listen to my trees grow.
And when I am gone, people will sit under my trees and
remember me.'

'You don't need an orchard to be remembered,' Johns
said, with a catch in his throat. 'Your mighty line will live beyond
any tree.' He cleared his throat. 'We're getting maudlin.'

'It's the funeral,' Marlowe said, following Johns to the door.
'A funeral will do that to a man.'

*   *   *

The choir was perfect. The treble was sublime. The Burial had never sounded more wonderful. The dean gave a sermon which was moving in its simplicity, full of regret for a young and promising life cut short. Marlowe, who could write a pathetic line like no other, gave a small nod of recognition for another's talent. The man's poetry rang out in the chapel and could have made the angels weep.

The boy sitting at the far end of Marlowe's seat was weeping too. He didn't sob and gulp and make much of it, as many scholars were doing in the foremost seats. A girl sitting alone at the front wiped her eyes from time to time and kept looking behind her. The boy, though, sat like stone, the tears running down his cheeks and dripping from his chin, unheeded.

At the end of the service, Marlowe went over to him. 'Can I help you?' he said. 'Can I take you for a drink somewhere, while you collect yourself? It was a very moving service.' Half of Marlowe's motivation was pity, the other was curiosity. Why was he not with the others and why was his grief so all-encompassing, not made for common show as it was with all the scholars at the front?

The lad seemed to notice his tears for the first time and wiped them away with the sleeve of his fustian. 'That's very kind of you,' he said. 'I think I will just go back to my rooms. Roger's . . . friends . . . will give him a good send-off.'

'Are you not a friend?' Marlowe asked, kindly. 'You certainly seem upset.'

The boy looked at him and searched his face to see if he could recognize him. 'Who are you?'

'Christopher Marlowe. I am an alumnus of Corpus Christi, but . . .'

'Christopher Marlowe the playwright?' The boy's eyes, the lashes clogged with tears, were wide.

'Yes, but I—'

'Roger would have so loved to meet you. We went to one of your plays, once, when we were in London visiting an aunt. *Tamburlaine*. It was wonderful. Isn't Ned Alleyn a marvel?' Even in his grief, the boy's eyes shone at the memory.

'Hmm.' Even to be kind to the bereaved, Marlowe couldn't agree that Alleyn was a marvel. 'Who are *you*?'

'I thought you knew. I am Richard Williams. I am Roger's brother. His twin, actually.'

Marlowe was surprised. 'Why are you sitting so far back?' The boy tossed his head towards the scholars, who were still crying noisily. 'I didn't want to sit with them. They are just here because . . . well, I don't know if you know this, but my brother drowned. As did I, nearly. It made us quite famous for a day or so. The Inquest, and so on. They weren't Roger's friends. Any more than that trollop sitting over there was his paramour, on any level. But you know how it is, I suppose, being in the theatre. People just want to be part of the show.'

Marlowe was impressed. Not many scholars his age would have the insight of this boy.

'Where are my manners?' The lad gave a final sniff. 'I would be pleased to show you my rooms and perhaps we can share some wine, or ale or something. I . . . it's a bit lonely, now. I don't like going in by myself. I haven't been by myself since I was born, until last week.' The tears welled up again.

'That would be very pleasant,' Marlowe said. He thought about Johns, making his way out of the Choir and decided he could always find him later. 'Lead on.'

Marlowe took note of the leather-bound tomes on the high shelf. Bale was there, along with Fortescue's *Foreste*, Munster's *Cosmography* and Ramus and Aristotle for good measure.

'I'm impressed by your light reading, Master Williams.'

'I know them off by heart, sir,' Richard Williams said. He sat in his room with his brother's empty bed beside him, hunched and pale as though it was the dead of winter.

'That's as maybe,' Marlowe smiled. 'But do you *understand* any of them?'

The boy blinked. That thought hadn't occurred to him.

'No Ovid,' Marlowe said, still scanning the shelves. 'No Machiavelli.'

'Those volumes are banned by the university, sir.' Williams was clearly a lad who played things by the book.

'Indeed they are,' Marlowe remembered. Cambridge was no freer in its thought now than it had been in his day. 'By the way, don't call me "sir". My name is Marlowe.'

Williams tried a grin. It didn't suit him.

'This was your brother's cupboard?' Marlowe held open the little wooden door. 'May I?'

The boy nodded.

It was much as Marlowe expected. More books; nothing untoward. Another fustian robe with the roses of King's embroidered on the sleeve, a pair of pattens and two shirts. Not so much as a dagger.

'Where are you from, Richard?' he asked.

'York, sir . . . er . . . Master Marlowe. Or, at least, a village nearby. Poppleton.'

'I didn't see your parents at the service.'

'They're dead, Master Marlowe,' the boy said. 'The sweating sickness two years ago. We just have our aunt, in London. I mean . . .' his face crumpled briefly, '*I* just have *my* aunt in London.'

He checked the lad's status. 'And you are Convictus Secundus?'

'Yes.'

'The Church? As a career, I mean?'

'The law. The Inns of Court. What do you know of them, Master Marlowe? Our father was a lawyer, but he never went to London.'

'Begging your father's pardon, Richard, I know well enough to avoid them. Men in my profession usually do.'

Williams smiled bleakly. Laughter wasn't something that came easily to him now. It would probably take a while. The boy was . . . what? Sixteen? Seventeen? Without a mother, father or brother, alone in the chill winds of Cambridge, his clothes rough and lacking a mother's care, his hair cropped short to mark his status.

Marlowe sat down next to him. 'Tell me,' he said, 'what happened to Roger.'

Williams looked long and hard into those deep, dark eyes. 'I told you,' he said with a shrug. 'He drowned.'

'Where?'

'Paradise,' the lad told him.

Marlowe knew it well, that stretch of the Cam that curved towards the Fens, with its innocent surface, its deadly current. Many was the hapless scholar and drunken shepherd who had missed his footing on those deceptive banks where the dog rose and honeysuckle bloomed in the summer sun.

'You mistook the mood of the water,' he nodded.

'No.' Williams was suddenly sure, his eye clear and his voice steady. 'No. Roger and I were water-babies. We were swimming in the Ouse before we left our hanging sleeves. There was more to it.'

'What?' Marlowe waited.

'I don't remember.' Suddenly, the boy who would be a lawyer was a child again, not looking Marlowe in the eye, squirming on the bed as though the mouth of Hell was opening up before him.

'Try,' Marlowe said softly. 'You were on the banks of the Cam, you and Roger. When was this? A week ago?'

Williams nodded. 'Thursday. Our half-day. The Master gives us leave.'

'And you went swimming?'

'Yes. It will be too cold, soon, so we thought . . .' the lad looked down and knotted his hands together, 'we thought it would be the last one for a while.' The enormity of it all was sweeping over him yet again and his voice faltered and stopped.

Marlowe knew at this point it was important to be work-manlike, though he could feel the boy's pain. 'Just the two of you?'

'Yes.'

'Right. You're on the bank at Paradise. Was anyone else there?'

Williams looked up, remembering. 'No . . . yes.'

Marlowe waited, but there was no more detail to come. 'Yes or no, Master Williams?'

'I . . . I didn't tell them at the Inquest,' the boy muttered, the weight of the thing heavy on his heart.

'What? What didn't you tell them?' Marlowe was like a dog with a bone. But the last thing he wanted to do was to frighten the lad still further. He sensed that with one slip, one step in the wrong direction, he could lose him.

Richard Williams frowned, trying to concentrate, trying to remember. 'Roger went in first,' he said. 'I was . . . this sounds ridiculous . . . I was having trouble with my pattens. Couldn't get them off. Roger called out it was cold . . . something like that . . . then he swam a little way . . .'

'Go on.'

'I heard a splash. Well, a series of splashes. There are tall reeds where we were and I couldn't see Roger. He was splashing around, I suppose. It had to be him. That's when I saw him.'

Marlowe tensed. 'Saw who?' he asked. 'Roger?'

'No. No. Someone else. Tall – no, not tall, but he loomed over me as I bent over. Dark. He had the sun at his back, shining directly into my eyes. He grabbed me, by the arms. I struggled. Then, I was under the water.' The boy began to shudder, his mouth hanging open. He fell forward against Marlowe who caught him and held him tight. 'Oh, Lord,' Williams went on in a croaked whisper, 'I felt the pain of drowning, Master Marlowe. Such a noise in my ears. Such a pain in my chest. I went down, twice, three times. I don't know. Each time I went under, it all began again. Blackness. Deep, impenetrable blackness. I wanted to die, God help me.'

Marlowe felt the boy's tears soaking into his doublet and he patted his shoulder and stroked his hair until the lad felt well enough to sit up again. Williams wiped his eyes with his sleeve and went on, 'How long I was in the water, I don't know. When I woke up, I was on the bank again, with shepherds fussing round me. They may have saved my life. But Roger . . . Roger was gone. They found his body later that day, floating downstream.'

'Roger, the strong swimmer?' Marlowe had to check.

'Yes,' Williams said, sniffing back the tears. 'A better one than I, that's for sure.'

'This man,' Marlowe said, 'the dark one, who loomed over you with the sun behind him. Was there anything else about him that you remember? Did he speak?'

Williams blinked, trying to focus his tortured mind. 'Yes,' he said as the memory came back to him in a flash. Yes. He said . . . he said, not once, but twice, more than that even, over and over. "Have you seen him yet?" he said. "Have you seen him?"'

Marlowe frowned. 'Do you know what he meant?' he asked.

Williams shook his head. 'I haven't the faintest idea,' he said.

'Is this wise, Kit?' Johns knew his man. There was a wildness about Marlowe. He would walk through the fire just to prove he could and cut cards with the Devil at the end of it.

Marlowe looked at his old tutor and smiled. 'Is what wise, Professor?' he asked.

'What you're planning to do,' Johns said. 'You may have a broken rib for all you know, not to mention the blow to your head.'

'I've had worse,' Marlowe said, 'but there are some things that have to be answered.'

'You couldn't take it to law, I suppose? Find a constable? A magistrate?'

Marlowe laughed and shook his head. 'Don't find me again, Michael,' he said, clapping a hand on the man's shoulder. 'Whatever happens. You've already chanced your arm by doing what you've done. Keep out of it now.'

Johns opened his mouth to say something but he couldn't find the words. The path that Marlowe had taken since the days of Corpus Christi was dark and winding. Probably, the poet-playwright was right; better he should travel it alone.

SIX

K it Marlowe was no student of tactics, but he had an instinct about these things. He also understood the nature of trees and walls. He hauled himself up both, despite the pain in his side and the throb in his head, ducking under the branches with their dying leaves and dropping silently onto the stones of the court. It was broad daylight and scholars making their way to lectures looked at him with astonishment. True, it was the way some of them got into the college after dark, dodging the lanterns of the proctors, unsteady with ale and with their hearts in their mouths. But here was a gentleman, a roisterer by his doublet and Collyweston cloak, doing the same thing in the middle of the day. Why didn't he just walk through the gate? As they watched, spellbound, all became clear.

The proctor with the bull neck was lounging against the medieval stone. He would nip indoors in a minute to light his pipe and put his feet up, but there were drovers prodding their cattle along Trumpington Street and the proctor wanted to keep an eye on them. Riff-raff from the town he knew all about; nomads from God-knew-where took some watching.

Marlowe tapped him lightly on the shoulder and the man spun round. Nobody, not even the Master, laid a hand on a proctor of Pembroke Hall.

'How . . . how did you get in?' he blurted out.

'Back wall,' Marlowe told him. 'Third tree on the right.'

Before the proctor could say anything else or even move, Marlowe smashed his face with the pommel of his dagger and the man went down, moaning, with blood pouring from his nose. There was a roar of appreciation from the scholars and, from nowhere, a little crowd had gathered, clapping and laughing. Marlowe could have done with them at the Rose. He crouched and ripped the embroidered college badge from the man's sleeve. Then he stood up and aimed a careful kick into the man's ribs.

The proctor lay there, curled up and half insensible and Marlowe leaned back against the inner doorframe. Sure enough, within seconds, the second proctor emerged. He saw the crowd first and bellowed at them, 'What's going on?' Then he saw his brother proctor lying by the gateway.

'That's what I wasn't ready for,' Marlowe smiled at him. 'A *second* arsehole in the night. I must be getting old. And you,' he looked the man up and down, 'you're not as old as you look, are you?' He reached out to squeeze the man's bicep. 'Still wiry. Strong. And as handy with a club as your friend here. You swung it pretty well from behind. Let's see how you do from the front.'

Marlowe crouched in a duellist's pose, the dagger blade flashing in his hand. He threw it in quick succession from one hand to the other and the proctor lost his nerve, stumbling backwards until he collided with the scholars, who pushed and jostled him, revelling in their chance.

'Now, lads,' Marlowe shook a disapproving finger at them, 'I'm sure the proctor here has your best interests at heart.' And he was drowned out with guffaws. Marlowe lunged forward, the dagger sheathed now and he kicked the proctor into the street. It was more bad luck that the man landed in a freshly deposited cowpat and this gave rise to more applause and laughter from the scholars.

'What is all this noise?' A voice from behind them brought quiet.

Marlowe turned and bowed. Not, this time, as a Convictus Secundus to a Master, but as a London gentleman who could have this man for breakfast. 'Ah, Doctor Andrewes,' he said, unsmiling. 'This, I believe, belongs to you.' He threw the woven badge at the man.

'What's this?' Andrewes frowned, catching it cleanly.

'Don't you recognize the coat of arms of your own college, sir?' Marlowe asked. 'Specifically, it comes from the robe of this oaf at my feet. He didn't wear it the other night when he met me on Parker's Piece and attempted to knock my head off. Now,' he closed to the man as the scholars watched in silence, their eyes wide, 'answer me one question. Whose idea was it to send these two? Harvey's or yours?'

For a moment, Andrewes toyed with brazening it out. His proctors were out of it, one barely conscious, the other out on the road covered in shit. He knew all too well that the scholars of his own college hated his guts, so he'd get no support there. 'I don't know what—' he began, but he got no further.

Marlowe had him fast by his Puritan collar and hissed into his face, 'Out of respect for your learning, Master,' he said, 'and your position in this university, I will not subject you to the punishment you deserve. I will be in Cambridge for a day or two longer. And if, in that time, I see you again, I will cut off your *membrum virile*, as scholars of your status say.'

For a moment, there was silence. Then Andrewes tore himself free of Marlowe and stumbled backwards, running towards his lodgings as though the fiends of Hell were after him. And in a sense, they were, because the scholars were racing him to the door. And they all got there first.

Lancelot Andrewes slammed the door of his private chambers shut. The college bell was tolling the scholars to their classes, so one of the proctors at least must have been back on his feet. He heard the clamour die down as the scholars drifted away. This was a day to remember.

'One thing more.'

Andrewes spun round, clutching his gown against his throat. Kit Marlowe stood there, looking for all the world as if he had just walked through the wall.

'How . . .?' but the Master of Pembroke Hall was lost for words.

'Gabriel Harvey,' Marlowe said. 'Where is he?'

'Gone,' Andrewes gasped. 'Back to London. Urgent business, he said.'

Marlowe smiled. 'I'm sure he did.'

There was little chance that Edmund Tilney would see fifty-seven again. His piggy little eyes were flashing fire that morning as he passed the Queen's guards patrolling Whitehall. His brain, his tongue, his self-importance were as active as

ever; it was just his knees that were letting him down. There
had been a time when he would have bounded up Burghley's
stairs with the speed and grace of a hart. Now, he stopped
and grumbled on every riser. Finally, he reached the inner
sanctum, which he swore got higher every time he went there
– typical Burghley, the weasel.

'Is this true?' he screamed, waving a piece of parchment in
the face of Her Majesty's Secretary of State.

Burghley looked up at him and quietly put down his quill.
'Good morning, Master Tilney,' he said. 'Is what true? I can
read many languages. I can read things upside down. Cyphers
I can either read or have a man who can. But things waving
about are beyond even my skills.' His acid smile could have
etched glass.

'This . . .' Tilney was almost speechless with indignation,
'this decree. It's all over London, pinned to any wall and tree
your vandals can find.'

'It's how we spread the news,' Burghley told him, spreading
his arms as if to demonstrate.

'But . . . but you've closed the theatres!'

'Of course I have,' the Queen's Secretary said, folding his
arms. 'And if I could, I'd close every alehouse, church and
bawdy house, too. I have the Lord Mayor's backing.'

'Bugger the Lord Mayor!' Tilney snapped. 'What you and
he decide to do with the rest of London is up to you, but the
theatre is *my* domain. *I* am Master of the Revels.'

'Indeed you are,' Burghley sighed, 'and as such, it is your
responsibility to provide entertainment for Her Majesty and
to censor such dramatic material as might give offence. The
actual opening and closing of theatres is a civic issue beyond
your jurisdiction.'

'But, why?' Tilney ripped off his feathered cap and stood
there like a petulant schoolboy.

Burghley frowned, looking up at the man. 'It may or may
not have reached your delicate ears, Edmund, but the
Pestilence is abroad in London. I have consulted with Dr
Dee *and* with Simon Forman. All right, they don't agree on
the *cause* of said disease – that would be too much to hope
for – but they *do* concur that theatres are the most dangerous

means of spreading the damned thing. Let's confine it as best we can.'

Tilney frowned. 'Do you know what Alleyn's going to say? Burbage? And don't get me started on Philip Henslowe.'

'He's done what?' Philip Henslowe had turned a rather nasty shade of purple.

'Closed the theatres.' Will Shaxsper wasn't the Prince of Condé this morning. He was just a glover's son from Stratford who was beginning to think that the forest of Arden suddenly had a strange lure. He tentatively passed what ironically looked like a playbill to the theatre manager, afraid that Henslowe might snatch his hand off at the wrist.

'Pestilence, my arse!' Henslowe growled. 'We've had the Pestilence in London all my life. And if it's not that, it's the sweating sickness. In my old grandame's day, you hung a dead bloody rat around your neck and got on with it.' He glared at Shaxsper, who opened his mouth to speak, but Henslowe hadn't finished. 'The trouble with Lord Kiss My Backside Burghley is that he doesn't have to work for a living.' Henslowe strode around the Rose's stage, kicking Tom Sledd's flats and slapping a practising hautboy player around the back of the head. 'And stop that bloody racket!'

He spun around and marched back to Shaxsper. 'Kit's going to go spare, Will,' he muttered, his mind racing with the complexity of the problem. 'No stage manager. No playwright. And now, no bloody play.' He whirled away, hands on hips, fingers tapping on his Venetians. Then he was back to the Warwickshire man. 'How are you at organizing petitions?'

'Petitions?' Shaxsper repeated. He didn't like the sound of this. He had a feeling, tucked away at the back of his head where he kept all his kneejerk fight-or-flight reactions, that a man wandering the streets with a page full of signatures was going to attract the attention of Richard Topcliffe or one of his minions at the very least. The Tower was full of nasty contraptions just waiting for men who signed petitions.

'Yes, you know. Thousands of useful idiots complaining about something. In this case, depriving honest Londoners of their culture. We need names, signatures, crosses, I don't care.

And,' the impresario was creating a plot every bit as mighty as one of Marlowe's, 'we'll take it to the Queen. March on Whitehall. Or Placentia. Or Nonsuch. Wherever the rancid old bat is living at the moment. You . . . Frizer, isn't it?'

It was. The walking gentleman had seen the posters too and was just contemplating a return to his old day-job of fleecing strangers in town. Though . . . his mind was whirring, they might be few and far between right now, what with the Pestilence and all . . .

'Master Henslowe.' Frizer touched his cap.

'Who's this?' The theatre manager noticed a taller man next to him.

'Nicholas Skeres, Master Henslowe,' Skeres said, a little hurt. He had been at the Rose exactly as long as Ingram Frizer. 'I was Alexander the Great in *Faustus* . . .'

'Yes, yes, marvellous. Marvellous. How are you boys at raising a few likely lads? River types, you know. Boatmen, hauliers, sailors. Lads who don't mind mixing it and won't ask too many questions.'

Frizer and Skeres looked at each other. 'It's not the company we usually keep, of course, Master Henslowe,' Frizer said, 'but I think we could manage that, for the usual considerations, of course.'

'Of course,' Henslowe grinned, clapping an arm around each of them. 'Of course. Get me fifty. No . . . better make it a hundred. Tell them there's free tickets for a play in it.' He caught the expression on the walking gentlemen's faces. 'Oh, all right. Three groats a head. *If,*' he insisted, 'they bring their own clubs.' He looked up. 'You still here, Shaxsper?'

The place was like a mortuary. Even Master Sackerson, in his pit, lay like a dead thing, the mist of October lying like a pall over his tree stump and the half-eaten vegetables somebody had thrown him. There was no flag over the tower, no stage-hands drinking smoke outside the gate. The doors were locked and barred, and what was left of an official notice hung forlornly from a single nail.

'Kit! Thank God!' The playwright turned at the mention of his name to see a distraught-looking Philip Henslowe hurrying towards him, his ruff knocked askew, his gown flapping. 'Where in Hell have you been?'

'Reliving old times,' Marlowe said, smiling, 'one way and another.'

'Riddles!' Henslowe threw his arm towards the leaden sky. 'The man gives me riddles!'

'What's the matter, Henslowe?' Marlowe asked. He tapped the heavy padlock. 'What's this?'

'This,' Henslowe hit the man with his fist and instantly regretted it. 'This is Tilney, the overpaid pocky. Not content with squeezing the life out of great literature with Puritan blinkers, he's now closed the bloody theatres. All of them. Burbage is furious. Alleyn's demanded his head.'

'The plague?'

Henslowe nodded. 'Spreading from Dowgate like a spilled inkwell. Even so, Marlowe, it's nonsense. The disease is passed by jakes seats, that's well known. And we don't have a jakes at the Rose, as you know; not for the public, anyway. I think the Curtain has got one, but that's the Lord Chamberlain's Men for you.'

'No *Massacre at Paris*?'

'No *Massacre at Paris*. No proceeds. No profits. No pay. Does Tilney offer any compensation? Does he, my arse!'

'It's not Tilney,' Marlowe said, 'it's Burghley.'

'Really?' Henslowe hadn't considered that. 'Well, if you ask me, it's a bloody conspiracy. They're all in on it.' The theatre manager became confidential. 'Look, Kit, you've got friends in high places. Muse's Darling and all that; all air and fire. You *know* people; people in Whitehall, I mean.'

'Do I?' Marlowe gave Henslowe his wide-eyed look.

'Don't come the innocent with me, Kit Marlowe. There's talk you worked for Walsingham.'

'Walsingham's dead,' Marlowe reminded him.

'As we'll all be, of bloody starvation, unless the theatres reopen. Pull some strings, Kit. Have a word.' Henslowe was nudging Marlowe in the ribs, the ones that still ached from his visit to Cambridge, and he moved away.

'I'll see what I can do,' he said, turning back down Maiden Lane, where the Winchester Geese wandered, wondering where their next mark was going to come from. 'No promises, now.'

Henslowe watched him go, hope and dejection flitting across his face in turn, like light and shade through sunlit leaves. 'And see if you can find Tom while you're at it,' he said. He would have died rather than admit it, but he was getting a little worried about his stage manager. He pretended to be angry, but had Sledd walked towards him now, he would have greeted him like a long-lost son.

Marlowe turned as Henslowe spoke, but didn't catch what he said. Henslowe had that habit and it drove everyone wild; just as you got out of earshot, he added a vital piece to the conversation. But this time, Marlowe was not playing that particular game and just waved a hand and walked on.

'Look, I feel for you, Marlowe, I really do.' Edmund Tilney had known this day would come. It was not a happy lot, being Master of the Revels. On the one hand, the Queen and her Court had to be entertained. On the other, said Queen didn't like spending money, so plays were cheaper than masques. On yet another hand, the Puritans believed that plays were an abomination in the eyes of the Lord. And before he knew it, the Master of the Revels had run out of hands. For the past two days, he had been bombarded by actors, playgoers, musicians and set-builders. Everyone, it seemed, with an interest in the drama wanted a word with Edmund Tilney. Richard Burbage had stamped on his foot. Ned Alleyn had threatened to tie his testicles to the cart's tail. Even the clown, Will Kemp, had hit him with a pig's bladder. No one could ever accuse Kemp of being subtle. Tempers were short.

But no one, until today, had actually produced a weapon. Kit Marlowe slowly drew the dagger from the small of his back and proceeded to shred Tilney's cloak with it; not angrily, but carefully and delicately. Luckily for Tilney, it was hanging behind the door at the time, but it nicely demonstrated Marlowe's skill with a blade.

'It's not me!' Tilney all but screamed, watching the velvet reduced to rags. 'It's Lord Burghley. I am merely a cypher.'

'Knew you were,' Marlowe winked at him and turned to

go. 'Oh,' he flicked the ruins of the man's cloak at him, 'send His Lordship the bill for this, would you?'

Philip Henslowe had been under the impression that Johanna Sledd was a dear little thing who wouldn't say boo to a goose. This was partly because he hardly ever took any notice of anything not happening on his stage or in his coffers, and partly because she always dipped a little curtsy and lowered her lashes whenever he went by; she knew on which side her bread was buttered and who did the buttering. So her arrival like a whirlwind in a temper was somewhat of a surprise.

'Where is he?' she snarled, nose to nose with Henslowe, who had his back to the wall. Literally, the wall of Paris, made of canvas, wood and spit, but it held out against the onslaught, just.

'Who?' As his lips parted to say the word, Henslowe knew this was a mistake.

Her eyes narrowed and her teeth bared. 'Who?' she hissed. '*Who?* My husband, your stage manager. The man who does everything for *everybody*. Thomas Sledd, that's who.' She backed away, her arms cartwheeling to encompass the entire Rose. 'None of this would happen without him. No scenery. No rehearsals. No audience.' She poked Henslowe in the chest. 'No *money*.'

Henslowe reeled as if she had slapped him. Money wasn't coming in at the moment and that was worrying enough. But really no money, no more money *ever*. He might have to return to the grocery business. That actually made him feel a little sick. He took a deep breath. 'Mistress Sledd,' he began. He never could remember the dratted woman's name. 'Please believe me, he isn't here.' If he had meant to be comforting, he realized at once he had misspoken.

'Not here?' She looked frantically from left to right. 'Not here? But he's *always* here!'

'We thought he was at home,' Henslowe hedged. After his first annoyance at Tom's absence, he had hardly given it a thought, what with the closure and everything. 'Or . . .'

'Or?' The woman's eyes were steel.

'No or. Come on . . .' What in the name of Hell was the

woman's name? 'Come on, my dear woman, you know that Tom is either here or at home. There is nowhere else he would be.'

'But . . .' the tears sprang to her eyes. 'But . . . where *is* he?'

Henslowe risked a punch by gathering her into his arms. He wasn't a demonstrative man, but, in his own way, he loved Tom Sledd too and he needed comfort as much as she did. 'We'll find him for you, never fear.'

She wiped her nose copiously on his already dishevelled ruff. 'Where's Master Marlowe?' she muttered. 'He'll find Tom.'

'Um . . . I don't know where he is either,' Henslowe had to admit. 'He went to see if he could sort out this little misunderstanding about closing the theatres and who knows where that will take him. And of course, with the theatres closed, he has no need to be here, no rehearsal, no rewrites . . . not that he does rewrites anyway . . . where was I?'

'Where were *you*?' Johanna Sledd was beginning to gather speed again. 'You're here, you useless lump of dung. Where is Tom? Where is Kit? They are the only people I want. And you've lost them.' She wriggled out of Henslowe's embrace. 'And let me go, you . . . you . . . you *creature*, you!'

Then, she punched him. It was a long time coming and he almost welcomed it as he sank to the floor, winded. If there was one thing Philip Henslowe couldn't bear, it was hanging about waiting for the worst to happen. It was always something of a relief when it did. And today he was finding that when sorrows come, they come not singly, but in battalions.

'He can't see you,' the secretary said, trying to reach the door to the inner sanctum before Marlowe did.

The playwright clicked his fingers. 'I *knew* I shouldn't have worn my cloak of invisibility today.'

'What? No, I mean . . .'

But it was all too late. Marlowe was already in the inner chamber, looking down at the diminutive Spymaster hunched at his desk.

'You should get yourself a better gatekeeper, Sir Robert,' Marlowe said. 'This one isn't fit for purpose.'

Cecil waved the man away. He had been thinking that

himself for a while now. Marlowe had simply confirmed it. 'It's been a while, Master Marlowe,' he said. 'What can I do for you?'

'I was hoping to see your father.' Marlowe lounged in a chair, unbidden, 'but he, it seems, has better gatekeepers.'

'Of course he has.' Cecil almost smiled, but strangled it at birth. 'He is the Secretary of State, when all is said and done. Well, then, what could *he* do for you?'

'Open the theatres,' Marlowe said.

'Well,' Cecil's eyes widened. 'I should come right out with it, if I were you.'

'I'm not concerned for myself, Sir Robert. I'll get by. But I have friends at the Rose, not to mention the Curtain and the Theatre; good, honest men and women. Close the theatres and they'll starve.'

'Keep them open and they'll die of the Pestilence,' Cecil said. He had put down the quill he was using and was sipping from a cup of Bastard on his table. He had not offered one to Marlowe.

'If that is God's will,' Marlowe said.

Cecil looked up sharply, searching the man's face for signs of sarcasm, contempt, even, but found none. He wiped a dribble of wine from his chin and thought carefully before continuing. When Marlowe mentioned God, it was wise to keep your wits about you. 'Speaking of which,' he said, at last, ferreting among his papers, 'this has recently come to my attention.' He moved a sheaf of papers in Marlowe's general direction.

'What is it?' Marlowe asked.

'Various documents belonging to the late Dominus Robert Greene, of Dowgate.'

'Really?' Marlowe sat upright, intrigued. 'And what is your interest in Greene?'

Cecil turned puce. 'May I remind you, Marlowe, that you work for me? In this chamber, *I* ask the questions.'

'As you wish, Sir Robert. I was merely wondering why you would mention the man to me at all.'

'You knew him, didn't you? At Cambridge.'

'I did.'

'And since?'

'I have heard *of* him from time to time. He was a pamphleteer latterly and wrote some appalling tosh called *Alphonse, King of Aragon.* I think it was supposed to be a parody of my *Tamburlaine*, but it flopped badly.'

'As, I understand, did Master Greene. You went snooping in his lodgings.'

'I spoke to his landlady,' Marlowe said. 'Not quite the same thing.'

'Clearly not,' Cecil said, 'or you would not have left these behind. I assume this is you he's writing about.' He pointed to the first page and tapped it for emphasis. 'The "famous gracer of tragedies".'

'I'm flattered,' Marlowe smiled.

'Don't be,' Cecil snapped. 'Here, on page two. It urges you to, and I quote, "turn from diabolical atheism". And here, "pestilent Machiavellian policy". What does he mean, Marlowe?'

The poet shrugged, spreading his arms wide. 'I've no idea,' he said. 'I understand from Greene's landlady that he became unhinged towards the end. Between you and me, Sir Robert, he was never exactly balanced in the first place. Fame has been kind to me. It was not to Dominus Greene.'

'His mistress was a woman whose brother is a cutpurse, it's true.' Cecil was reading another sheet in a different hand. 'His wife had left him. What brought you to Dowgate?'

'The man wrote me a letter shortly before he died,' Marlowe said. 'He believed he was being murdered.'

'Murdered?' Cecil frowned. 'How?'

'The letter didn't say.' Marlowe was not about to discuss with the Queen's Spymaster the intricacies of an exhumation at dead of night, nor the post-mortem diagnosis of Dr Dee.

'Your best guess, then?' Cecil worried it like a dog with a bone. 'Poison?'

'It's possible,' Marlowe said. 'It's hard to think of another method of murder which gives a man time to write a letter about it.'

Cecil nodded, agreeing. But there were more things in heaven and earth that could kill a man than even Cecil knew. He took up his cup again and leaned back. 'I will assume for now,

Marlowe, that the allegations in Dominus Greene's papers are the result of jealousy. *For now*, mind. In the meantime, stay clear of Dowgate, Master Marlowe; there's Pestilence there.'

He waited until Marlowe got up.

'By the way,' he said, 'the theatres will remain closed. Good morning.'

'What was it called, then,' Ned Alleyn had to ask, 'this drivel of Greene's?'

'Luckily, the stationer who had it in his possession didn't know I could read upside down,' Marlowe said, without a blush at the lie. 'It was called *A Groatsworth of Wit*.'

The three men burst out laughing and Alleyn clicked his fingers for a refill of ale. Maiden Lane was not jammed to the gunnels with theatregoers but the taverns were full of theatre men drowning their sorrows, so the flocks of Winchester Geese pestering them with their wares were still busy.

'I am a "mad and scoffing poet" apparently,' Marlowe went on.

'There must have been something about me, surely?' Alleyn frowned. 'After all, he did ask me to play in *The Tragical Reign of Selenius* and I left him in no uncertainty where he could put all those copies of the rubbish.'

'Not that I saw, Ned,' Marlowe said; then, ever the diplomat, 'it must have been on the back of the sheet. You're there, though, Will.'

'Am I?' the Warwickshire man was actually astonished. After all, he'd only written the First Part of *Henry VI* and he'd had a lot of help with that.

'He uses the phrase "Shake-scene", whatever that means, and refers to you as "the upstart crow".'

More laughter. This time from only Marlowe and Alleyn. Shaxsper was too busy bridling. 'Upstart crow?' he repeated, crimson with fury. 'Upstart crow? If Dominus Greene had wanted to bring in the bird world, I'd have thought . . . I don't know . . . Swan of Avon would have done the trick.'

And Marlowe and Alleyn laughed again, until Shaxsper got up and left in a huff.

SEVEN

Tom Sledd was taking his exercise, round and round and round. For a change, he sometimes went widdershins, until he got giddy. Finally, he slumped against the wall, next to the incarcerated poet, who was reading back through his work and making the occasional change, accompanied by a quiet 'Tut'.

'How can you bear this?' Sledd asked his neighbour.

'Hmm?' The poet held up a finger for quiet. He was checking his metre. With a nod to himself, he turned to Sledd, marking his place with an inky finger. 'Bear what?'

Sledd spread his arms and rolled his eyes. '*This*,' he said. 'The smell. The noise. The . . .' he nodded to a couple across the room, who had been making the beast with two backs, relentlessly, lovelessly, for hours now and showed no sign of stopping. He had no word for what they were doing. 'That.'

The poet smiled softly and laid a hand on Sledd's arm. It was the first human contact other than thoughtless blows that he had received since coming to this awful place and he felt a tear crawl down his cheek. 'I am not given to handing out advice,' the poet said, 'except what you need to survive in here. This is something you may not be able to do but, if you can, it will keep you sane, if sane you are.'

Sledd leaned forward. That was just what he needed, something to tell him he was sane, because sometimes, he was beginning to wonder. 'I'll do anything,' he said. 'Anything I can.'

'Then, try this,' the poet said. 'Close your eyes. Lean your head back on the wall. Feel the wall, hard against your head. Think of nothing but that wall. Then, when you have a mind as empty as it can be, when all the sounds, the smells, the fears have gone away, put back into your mind some happy things.' The poet's eyes snapped open and pierced Tom Sledd where he sat. '*Don't*,' he said, 'on any account think of your old life. That will surely send you mad. Think of something else, something of your imagination. Hmm . . .' He looked the stage manager up and down. 'When you were a lad, did you dream of being a knight? A knight in armour?'

Sledd looked at the man kindly. They had clearly had very different childhoods. All Tom could remember dreaming of was where his next meal was coming from and whether they would be tenting or sleeping under the wagon with the dogs. But the poet meant well, so he nodded.

'Well, there you are then,' the man said, with his gentle smile. 'I would put it in verse, because I just can't help myself. You might want to conjure up pictures. But the main thing is, fill your mind with it and the rest will fade away.'

Sledd looked doubtful. The couple across the way were still keeping to their own rhythm, the woman to his right was picking over a plate of cockroaches which she was keeping for a feast for later. How could anything block this out?

The poet closed his eyes and spoke in a singsong voice to the air. 'With a host of furious fancies whereof I am commander, with a burning spear and a horse of air, to the wilderness I wander. By a knight of ghosts and shadows I summoned am to tourney. Ten leagues beyond the wide world's end; methinks it is no journey.'

Sledd felt a tingle go up his spine. He closed his eyes and pressed the back of his head to the wall. He felt the heavy armour wrap itself around his limbs and the crested helm bowed his head with its weight. The warmth of the horse between his thighs was tangible. The smell of herbs and bright, cold water stung his nostrils as he wandered along, waiting for a call from a man of ghosts and shadows. The mad cacophony fell away and he hefted his lance under his arm, looking for battle.

Beside him, the poet smiled and turned again to his manuscript. If he could keep just one man sane in this insanity, his life was not, after all, in vain.

There was no sign of the plague the next morning as Kit Marlowe padded along Knightrider Street. He could see the toppled tower of St Paul's to his right and the ruins of Baynard's castle to his left, its curtain wall shored up by the wooden hovels of the dispossessed. If the Pestilence didn't strike there in a day or so, it would be a miracle.

At the sign of the kettle, Marlowe dashed under an archway and found himself in a maze of passages, each darker and more menacing than the last. The sun never shone here and rats scuttled in and out of the gutters that sloped down towards the river.

'Mistress Jackman?' Marlowe had left his Colleyweston at home today and had put on his second-best doublet. If it wasn't exactly possible to blend with the inhabitants of this abyss, at least he wouldn't stand out like too much of a sore thumb.

The girl was probably twenty, but years in these alleyways had hardened her features and it was too early in the morning for her to have dressed in her finery, breasts above her stomacher rouged and powdered. 'Who wants to know?'

'I was a friend of Robert Greene,' Marlowe told her.

'Robyn?' She raised an eyebrow. 'Nah, he didn't have no friends.'

Perspicacious one, this, Marlowe thought. 'Plenty of enemies, though,' he said.

She tilted her head. She'd never seen this man before, with his dark eyes that burned into whatever passed for a soul in her. 'Some,' she agreed. 'What do you want?'

'I want to know who killed him,' Marlowe said, watching her face for any sign at all. He saw nothing.

'That's not the sort of question you ask around here, pizzle.' A rough voice made him turn. A huge man stood there with a pickadil hat perched on the back of his head.

Marlowe smiled. 'You must be Billy Jackman,' he said, 'this good lady's brother.'

'Good lady?' Jackman grunted, grinning at the girl. 'Somebody's been saying nice things about you, Fan.'

'Stow it, Billy,' she growled, looking under her eyelashes at him. 'I'll have you know—'

But Jackman wasn't interested in Fanny's pride. He was staring at Marlowe. 'Who are you?' he growled. 'What do you want?'

'My name is Marlowe,' he said, 'and I want the truth.'

'What about?'

'The murder of Robert Greene.'

Brother and sister looked at each other. 'What makes you think he was murdered?' Jackman asked.

'A lot of things,' Marlowe said, 'none of which need concern you, friend.'

'I ain't your friend, pizzle,' Jackman hissed, his lips curling. 'Now, bugger off to wherever you've come from and leave honest folk alone.'

'If there were some honest folk here, I'd be delighted,' Marlowe said.

Jackman checked himself, frowning. 'Are you saying we ain't honest?'

'Is the Pope a Catholic?' Marlowe asked.

'The Pope?' Jackman was finding the constantly changing subject a little hard to follow. Usually, his vocabulary was based around violence, sex and money, heavy on the violence. 'What are you? A bloody Papist?'

'My religion is my own business,' Marlowe said. 'Did you know Dominus Greene?'

'Dominus Greene? Dominus Greene?' Jackman mimicked Marlowe, then spat onto the cobbles. 'Stuck up, he was. Always spouting poetry . . .'

'Somebody else's, I'll be bound,' Marlowe smiled.

'I wouldn't know about that. It's all bollocks, that stuff. This theatre rubbish. What did Greene call himself, Fan? A University wit? What a load of bollocks!'

'Oh, leave him alone, Billy,' Fanny whined. 'He was all right, was Robyn. All right, he had a bit of a smell under his nose, but he did right by me. And I tell you what, Billy, he taught me some stuff, some stuff to bring me up in the world, save me having to work for a living at Mrs Isam's, that's for sure. De mort you is nigh hill nice I bone um, he'd say right now, wouldn't he, Master Marlowe? Don't speak ill of the dead.'

Marlowe had heard '*de mortuis nihil nisi bonum*' pronounced better, but never with so much feeling and his opinion of the girl rose.

Billy Jackman spat again. 'Did right by you? What, you mean he didn't knock you up? Couldn't get it up, more like. Stuck up . . .'

'Do I take it you weren't overfond of Dominus Greene, Master Jackman?'

'Overfond, my arse!' Jackman looked at Marlowe with his piggy eyes hard with hatred. 'Look, are you going, or what?' Marlowe spread his arms. 'What,' he said. 'At least until I have some answers.'

There was the ring of steel as Jackman whipped his dagger from the sheath at his back. Marlowe stepped back, his own knife in his hand.

'Come on, boys!' Fanny Jackman tried to appeal to the men's better natures. But, glancing at their faces, she knew that they didn't have any.

'This is not worth dying for, Master Jackman,' Marlowe warned.

'I was just going to say the same thing to you.' Jackman lunged, but Marlowe was faster. He caught the wrist and swung it upwards, driving the blade into the man's jerkin and arm. Blood spurted over the leather and linen and Marlowe swung the man round to force him to the ground.

'Never, ever,' Marlowe held his blade to Jackman's throat, gripping his hair with the other. The pickadil had gone. 'Never, ever try that move with a man who knows what he is doing,' he hissed. 'It can get you killed.' He hauled the man to his feet by his hair and shoved him forward, his knee in his back. The cutpurse turned, clutching his ripped arm, but still looking for a fight.

'Oh, go and get yourself cleaned up, Billy,' Fanny said. 'Master Marlowe and I are going to have a little chat.'

Simon Forman was in a quandary. He had advised against closing the theatres and he couldn't in all conscience believe it was wrong to do so. But he had noticed a falling off of calls for his expertise lately and he couldn't help but wonder whether preventative advice was really the way to make a living. Perhaps letting everyone mix hugger-mugger might be the better option. He, of course, and so by extension, his apprentices, would never succumb to the Pestilence. He wore his mask – copied now by every charlatan in London – stuffed with his special herbal mixture. He cast runes and sat in a pentangle every night, divining by the position of the stars the best amulets to wear the following day to keep him safe. He washed in water of the Nile and the Jordan – some may have considered he was hedging his bets, but his answer was always simple. He was alive. Many others were not. Ergo, whatever he was doing, he was going to keep right on doing it.

His wife was a thorn in his side and he was working on that. Whatever herbs he used for himself, Timothy, Matthias and Gerard, not to mention his more deep-pocketed clients, he gave to his wife as well. Indeed, she insisted upon it. But he made certain special changes to her mixture; for instance, he never gave her asafoetida and always added a nice dose of ransons instead. And yet, the harridan was still alive. It was a puzzle, but not one he had time for this morning.

Decked out in his best robes, newts, frogs and doves stowed safely in his sleeves, Forman burst through the door of his laboratory like an avenging angel. One day, he knew, he would catch his apprentices in some misdeed or other, but today was not that day. As always, they were standing to attention at their trestles, work well in hand, their hated robes clean and neat and a newly herb-stuffed mask slung across each shoulder. Forman hadn't prepared anything to say, so he made do with walking around, hands clasped behind his back, examining minutely everything on each table. He had to take care that none of the boys ever discovered that, actually, he knew far less than they did. For all he knew, they could be making soup, yet he trusted them to be working hard to find whatever it was they sought. Gerard, he knew, only used natural things; things that grew in wayside and hedgerow. Although he had tried to persuade the lad to forage in darker places, graveyards, under gibbets, he had never succeeded. Wholesomeness was Gerard's middle name. Matthias and Timothy were different – he knew that they each had a dark side. Eventually, one would eclipse the other and then it would probably be a fight to the death. If it were to be physical, Matthias would win hands down. Cerebral – it was too close to be able to predict, even with all the crystal balls and scrying glasses in the world. The trick would be to not be standing too close when it happened.

His examination finished, Forman turned to his apprentices and gestured for them to form their usual line, as they waited for instructions.

'As you all know,' he began, 'the theatres are closed and people are staying indoors as much as they can. This means, of course, that the spread of the Pestilence is slowing . . .'

Gerard raised an arm and cried, 'Huzzah!'

'. . . which is not, of course, unalloyed joy for us, welcome though the news must be to the populace at large.'

Gerard lowered his arm as slowly as possible, wishing that his cheer was not still ringing in the rafters.

'We are welcome in many houses, of course, with our healing and comforting words, but my request to you today is that you all pack a bag – a modest bag, because the universe will provide, as you all know – and go into the highways and byways, bringing succour and comfort where you may. Today is . . .' he looked up vaguely. He knew perfectly well what day it was, but it was better to be the vague magus than the whip-smart man of business, especially when sending his boys out on a wild-goose chase.

'Wednesday, Master,' three voices chorused.

'Thank you.' He beamed at them and rubbed his hands together. 'Don't let me keep you. I would like to see you back here at noon on Tuesday next.'

'But . . . where shall we go, Master?' Matthias liked his home comforts. Sleeping under a hedge wasn't really his style.

Forman waved an airy hand. 'Where'er you will,' he said. 'Let the air and spirits of the air guide you. Take a horse each from the usual livery – tell the ostler to put it on the account.' He beamed at them again and then grew serious. 'But if I find any of you have beetled off home to mother, auntie, be they who they may, it will go worse with you, I promise.' He clapped his hands and a newt fell gratefully to the floor and scuttled off. 'Now – off you go. Until Tuesday next.'

They made for the door, grabbing their bags from the hooks on the wall.

'At noon.'

And they were gone.

*   *   *

Marlowe and the girl swung into step with each other; to anyone passing, they would have looked like old friends. She kept her hands demurely at her waist and her eyes downcast. He waited patiently for her to begin her tale.

They were almost out of the abyss where she lived and into some streets with light, air and life before she spoke. 'He wasn't so bad, you know, Master Marlowe.'

'Dominus Greene?' Marlowe just needed to be sure she wasn't talking about her oaf of a brother.

'Who else?' she chuckled. 'I will never be heard to say that Billy is not so bad. Billy is about as bad as a person can be, but he didn't kill Robyn, that I know. Mrs Isam would never let Billy through the door. He scared the other gentlemen and none of the girls would let him near them. So . . .' She shrugged a grubby shoulder and then pulled modestly at her slipping bodice. All very well to allow everything to pop out pertly for money, but she didn't flaunt her wares for free.

'So, you are one of Mrs Isam's girls?' Marlowe needed to be sure.

'Was. Was one of her girls. She threw me out when Robyn died. Bad luck, she said.'

'Bad luck for Dominus Greene, to be sure.' Marlowe spoke mildly, but she was immediately up in arms.

'I never hurt him,' she said. 'I . . . I won't say I loved Robyn – he wasn't easy to love, poor man. But he was never cruel to me and, to be honest, he didn't bother me much in that way, if you understand me.'

Marlowe did.

'He said he liked to have me near him, to stop Death from talking to him. And he taught me some things. Some Latin, like I done before. And he was teaching me to read. But his books were hard, so . . . I can read a bit, though.'

Marlowe thought to himself how like Greene that was. Take a girl from the street, not use her for what she was made and then make her unsuited for her profession. But he could also see something in the girl – some spark, some deep, secret place – and that made him understand, just a little. 'Well done,' he said. 'Though I expect you keep that to yourself, do you?'

She laughed. 'You are very wise, Master Marlowe.'

'Tell me about Mistress Isam's house.'

'There is but little to tell,' the girl said. 'We are usually five or six girls, usually with regular visitors. Mrs Isam deals with anyone with . . .' she looked up under her lashes, '. . . special tastes. She feeds us well. We have some brandy wine at bedtime, though when that is can be anybody's guess, sometimes. That's why being Robyn's special girl was so nice. He kept very regular hours, bed with the sun, and wanted me to sleep beside him every night. So, you can imagine, Master Marlowe, it's hard to be back on the street again. I would never have harmed him. It would be like harming myself.'

Marlowe mulled it over. Mrs Isam was notorious, of course, but he would be interested to know who her special visitors were, nonetheless. He could get that list later. For now, he needed to know more about Greene's milieu before he died. 'I assume, therefore,' he said, 'that if you were otherwise busy, Dominus Greene did not avail himself of . . .'

She turned around, hands on hips, careless now of her slipping bodice, to the joy of passing apprentices. 'Robyn wasn't *like* that, I told you. He just wanted company. Yes, I was sometimes otherwise busy, as you put it. A girl has to live and he wasn't rich. But then, someone else from the house would sit with him. Mrs Isam, sometimes. Or her nephew, if he was there. She has a sister as well, a comfortable body and I would be willing to bet that had she been willing, Robyn would have preferred her company to mine. He was still in love with his wife, you know, Doll, though she treated him like dirt.' She looked pensive. 'Robyn rather liked being treated badly. Mrs Isam offered to treat him really badly, once, but he threw her down the stairs for her trouble. She almost broke her neck.'

Marlowe looked at the girl and smiled. Sometimes, he wondered what was the more extraordinary, fact or fiction. If he put that scene in one of his plays, it would be laughed off the stage as unrealistic.

'So, I think, Master Marlowe, that, miss the strange creature though I do, there is nothing to be gained in digging up Robyn's past.'

Marlowe's heart skipped a beat then steadied – her innocent words were close enough to the truth, in all conscience.

'Leave him to lie in peace. To rot, as he always said he would, and be food for the worms.' She looked up at him and, to the playwright's surprise, her eyes were bright with unshed tears. 'And please, just once, for me, call him Robyn. There is so much hatred in everyone's voice when they call him Dominus Greene. It's hard to hate someone called Robyn, don't you think?'

Marlowe smiled down at her and brushed a tear from her cheek with a gentle thumb. 'For you, Mistress Jackman,' he said, 'for you and you alone, I will let Robyn rest in peace.'

'Ress kwi ass ket in par chay.'

'I couldn't have put it better myself,' he said, and pressed a coin into her hand. 'Thank you for your company.' And he turned and was gone.

The three sorcerer's apprentices found themselves out on the street in a state of some confusion. They knew that times had become a little harder with real Pestilence stalking the land, but they didn't think they would be sent out into the land in question in quite so peremptory a fashion. Forman had always made it clear that he was training them for the day when they could go and spread his words among those not fortunate enough to live in London. They just didn't know that day would be today.

'So, where are you planning to go?' Timothy asked the others. 'Don't forget, we are not to go to family or friends.'

Matthias snorted. 'I don't see how he would know. I'm planning to go home for a day or two, perhaps talk one of my mother's friends into writing me a testimonial of some kind, then go back.' He looked at the other two. 'You?'

Gerard was shocked. 'He *will* know, Matthias. He will see you in the glass.'

Matthias raised an eyebrow. What an innocent country boy Gerard was. 'I don't think the glass is *real*, Gerard, do you?' he said, condescendingly. 'How can a piece of crystal tell him anything?' He gave a derisive snort.

'I think you should take all this more seriously, Matthias, I really do.' Gerard was getting quite upset. 'You know the master knows things that ordinary mortals can't know. He can speak to spirits, you know he can. We've all seen him do it.'

'I've seen him talking to himself, yes.' Timothy noted with an inward smile that, although Matthias was keen to show his disdain, he was still making sure that his voice was low and they were moving away from the door. 'It doesn't prove there were spirits though, does it? And what about all those poor creatures he puts up his sleeves every morning?'

'I asked him that,' Gerard said. 'I don't think that a sleeve is a healthy place for any of God's creatures. He said that he put them there in case someone unworthy expected a miracle. Then, he would use one of the animals. In case . . . in case a believer was nearby and . . .' Gerard was running out of excuses. They had sounded so convincing in Forman's mouth.

'Yes, well, if you say so,' Matthias said, clapping the lad on the back in friendly fashion. As a man with family money, a scholar of a University, he didn't really need Forman's apprenticeship. But for now, it suited his purpose. It was really a matter of waiting until he had the secret of the massage and he would be out of there, like a rat up a pipe. 'You, Tim? Where are you off to?'

Timothy looked thoughtful. 'I am going into the world, as the master asked. It will be a challenge I shall enjoy, I think. What I will be seeking is somewhere that the Pestilence has not yet reached. I will teach them about herbs, how to stop the sickness in its tracks. I will go from house to house; I think that gathering folk together is not a good idea. That's why they have closed the theatres and I won't go against that. I am not sure which way I will ride. I will let the horse decide.'

Matthias laughed. He had hired horses from Forman's livery before. 'In that case, you will be spending the week in a stall in a stable. None of those horses has the strength to go far or fast and they have even less will.'

'I don't think I will ride,' Gerard said. 'I just intend to walk until I find a meadow and a stream. There, I will put up a tent and wait for folk to come to me for healing.'

'That happens, does it?' Timothy didn't speak unkindly. He just wanted to know.

'I have never seen it done,' Gerard said, seriously. 'But if

I saw a tent pitched in a meadow by a stream, I think I would want to know who was in it. And if I was sick . . . or knew someone who was sick . . . I might . . .' The light of enthusiasm died in his eyes. 'But in any case,' he said, giving himself a shake, 'if I don't try, I'll never know.'

'And anyway,' Matthias chimed in, 'the master might be watching.'

Gerard looked at him sternly. 'Will be watching, Matthias,' he said. '*Will* be watching!'

They had arrived at the livery stable, perhaps not the best in town, but certainly the cheapest. And it did have commanding views of the abbey. Matthias stuck his head round the door and called for the stable boy, who shambled out, carrying a tangle of harness over his arm. He looked at them unenthusiastically. He had been told not to give Forman or his boys any more credit, but if he didn't send a few horses out soon, they would be out of hay. He would rather the beasts dropped with starvation on someone else's watch, not his.

'Three, no, *two* horses, lad, and make it quick,' Matthias said.

'Oh, sir,' the stable boy said, 'I can't let two of you gentlemen share a horse. T'ain't natural. It's like them Templars of olden days. Two on a horse, t'ain't—'

'No, I do know,' Matthias said, looming over the lad. 'My friend here is on foot. He has just walked with us to be friendly.'

'Oh. Ar. Two it is, then, sir. I got a nice grey here, if you'd like it. And a roan.'

'Is that the same grey I had last time?' Timothy asked. 'The one with one leg shorter than the others?'

'I wouldn't say *shorter* . . .' the lad looked shifty.

'What would you say, then?' Timothy had taken a nasty tumble and wasn't keen to repeat the experience.

'More . . . later. That's it, later.'

'I see,' Matthias said. 'One leg is slower than the others. Is that it?'

The stable boy smiled. 'Yes, that's it, sir. Easily fixed if you just give him a bit of time. Patient, that's what you've got to be with horses.'

'No.' Timothy was adamant. 'I don't want the grey. What else have you got?'

'Umm . . .' the lad didn't want to give them anything decent, not with the thick bundle of unpaid notes in the tack room. 'I've got a nice black. White blaze on the nose. Handsome beast.'

'Temper like the Devil,' Matthias said. 'What else?'

'This chestnut's a nice well-tempered mare. In foal, so a bit slow, but you will fit her nicely, sir,' the lad said to Timothy. 'You're nice and light. She'll give you no trouble.'

The mare looked huge. It would be like riding a barrel. 'When is she due to foal?' Gerard, the country boy, couldn't help but be concerned.

'When are you due back?'

'Next Tuesday.'

'Make it Monday and all will be well,' the stable boy assured them. 'I would imagine. Anyway, gents, I can't stand here all day. The roan and the chestnut?'

Matthias and Timothy shrugged and nodded. It was pointless standing here arguing when there was obviously nothing better on offer. The lad tacked the horses up and soon the three apprentices were off on their travels, to who knew where.

'So . . . what we gonna do, then?' Hal Dignam was wiping the grease from his fingers all over the curtain at the Curtain.

'You mean now,' Will Kemp asked him, 'or for the rest of our lives?'

'See, that's your trouble, Will,' Dignam prodded the man in the shoulder. 'For a comedian, you're the gloomiest bastard I know. Always looking on the dark side.' He nudged the man hard. 'It might never happen, you know.'

'It has,' Kemp all but shouted at him. 'They've closed the bloody theatres.'

'Yes, yes,' Dignam reached for his goatskin wine sack and took a swig, 'but that's just one of life's little ups and downs. Tilney will see sense shortly and it'll all be on again. You'll see.'

'Sense and Master of the Revels don't belong in the same sentence, Hal. I know; I've talked to him.'

'So, what we gonna do, then?'

Kemp sighed. He slipped a groat out of his purse. 'Call it,' he said, tossing the coin into the air.

'Heads,' Dignam said, as his partner in rhyme caught the coin.

'It's tails,' Kemp said. It was the story of both their lives.

'So, what are we gonna do, then?'

'Bedlam.' Kemp got up and tugged his jerkin down. 'Poke some lunatics.'

'Oh, right.' Dignam got up too and slung the sack over his shoulder. 'What would it have been if it had been heads?'

Kemp looked at him, stone-faced. 'We'd have gone to the Tower and asked that nice Master Topcliffe to pull our teeth out one by one.'

EIGHT

Matthias had an easy journey, in part because he knew where he was going and also because he was a reasonable horseman. His roan was unremarkable, except for being a bit short in wind but, with a journey of only just over twenty miles, she would suffice. Matthias's father had an ample stable, should the mood come upon his son for a ride. But Matthias's plan for the coming week was to eat decent food, sleep in a bed on his own – or not, as the fancy took him – and not get up until noon. He stretched in the saddle, just thinking about it. He let his mother's friends wander past his mind's eye. He wanted to give something in exchange for the testimonial but he wasn't about to waste what natural talents he had on any woman who was not deserving. And in Matthias's mind, deserving meant having a body which still had a bit of bounce in it and a face that didn't need to be covered by a pillow. With those criteria always in mind, there were a fair few to choose from. He had not yet managed to be present when his master's special massage was being performed, but from the garbled mutterings from Timothy when dreaming, he had a few inklings of how to proceed.

Matthias and his nag had different welcomes. The man's mother cried, hugged, yelled for the cook to make Master Mattie's favourite pudding. The groom took the horse and tethered it to a tree in the furthest paddock. But in their way, they both enjoyed their greetings. Matthias put up with the primping and kissing with good grace and the horse had grass instead of musty hay. It was going to be a good week, the last pampering before the Fall gave way to winter, some fattening up for the cold months ahead for both of them.

'You went to see the Lord Admiral?' Philip Henslowe couldn't believe his ears.

'I did.' Will Shaxsper was proud of himself.

'Hero of the Armada, one of the greatest men in England?' Henslowe was peering into the actor's face, trying to read signs of madness there.

'So he'd have us believe,' Shaxsper nodded.

'When I asked you to get signatures, Will,' Henslowe explained, 'I was rather thinking somebody below the rank of God.'

Shaxsper looked at the man, hunched in his attic room at the Rose, the coffers nearly empty, the hourglass run out. 'I thought you were serious about this petition thing,' he said.

'I am,' Henslowe assured him. 'I am.'

'Well, there you are, then. The Lord Admiral has his own troupe of actors, doesn't he? What are they called, now? Oh, yes, the clue's in the title, isn't it? The Lord Admiral's Men.'

'Don't be flippant with me, Shaxsper!' Henslowe snapped. 'It doesn't suit you.'

'I just thought he'd be the perfect figurehead to take the petition to the Queen. He's her cousin or some-such; he's rich; he's famous; and he's got a theatrical bent. Who better?'

'What did he say?'

Shaxsper hesitated. 'Told me to bugger off. Said he'd heard about me and if I crossed his path again, he'd have to bring up that nonsense about the deer in Charlecote.'

Henslowe frowned. 'What nonsense about the deer in Charlecote?'

'Nothing,' Shaxsper said, a little too quickly perhaps. 'Long story cut short, he wasn't interested.'

'Right.' Henslowe was chewing his lip, thinking on his feet. 'How many signatures have you got?'

Shaxsper pulled the rolls of parchment out of his satchel. They looked ominously blank. 'Er . . . twenty-three,' he counted, 'although I'm not sure "Doxy" and "Sidebollocks" are going to count.'

Henslowe nodded. 'As I thought,' he murmured. 'So it'll have to be the fallback plan.'

'The what?'

Henslowe looked the Warwickshire man up and down. 'How are you at carrying a flaming torch, Will?'

*   *   *

Gerard, horseless, wandered aimlessly along, his pack on his back, his trusty stick in his hand. He had spent most of his life in the countryside, and pavements still hurt his feet, whether they were smooth or cobbled. He had not lost his old skills and he navigated by the sun, not easy on this hazy, October day. Even so, he soon found himself on grass not stone, and could smell water which had not already passed through many bodies. He lifted his nose and sniffed – hopefully, the stand of willows ahead would mark a curve in the stream; where there was a curve, there was often a patch of dry shingle, where he could make his camp. A nice trout to add to his carefully stowed bread and apples and he would be a happy man. He was also looking for somewhere sheltered from Forman's all-seeing eye.

He walked through the damp grass, looking out for likely kindling for the fire he would light later. He was looking forward to curling up in his tent, without the mad dreams of Timothy or the basso-profundo snoring of Matthias to keep him awake. All he would smell would be the clean scent of crushed grass and the crisp tang of fresh water. His belly would be full of grilled trout and there would be no belching or farting to put him off his food. And if no one came, sick or well, he would have tried his best. And surely, even for Simon Forman, that would be good enough.

'Master Sleford.' Will Kemp bowed with a flourish only a professional clown could manage. 'It's been a while.'

Roland Sleford had been the Keeper at Bedlam for nearly half Kemp's lifetime. A clothier by trade, he made a pretty penny on the side from casual visitors like these two, unemployed actors or not. 'It has, Master Kemp, it has. I trust that Mistress Kemp and all the little Kemps are well?'

'As well as can be expected, Master Sleford, under the circumstances.'

'Quite, quite,' Sleford nodded sympathetically. 'Times are hard all round.' He held out his hand. 'That'll be a groat, please. Each.'

The men paid up.

'Anything good at the moment?' Dignam asked. 'New blood, I mean.'

'I've got a poet come out of nowhere,' Sleford pocketed the cash, 'who's quite interesting. There's some bloke who says he's a theatre stage manager.'

Kemp guffawed. 'Well, they don't come much madder than that, do they?'

'I'll have to search you gentlemen,' Sleford apologized. 'No weapons, pictures, anything that might inflame the senses.'

'Naturally,' Kemp said and both men extended their arms while Nat and Jack patted their clothes.

'Right, gentlemen.' Sleford himself slid back the heavy iron grille at the gate. 'You know the way. No bowling today, I'm afraid. One of my sweet souls brained another with a ball the other day. You can't be too careful.'

The visitors were ready for the stench because somebody, in their wisdom, had built Bedlam between two sewers, both of which lay open to the chill October air.

'Which of you wants me first?' an old crone enquired, demurely slipping off her sackcloth and prancing in the straw. Kemp and Dignam pointed to each other and went the other way. A man was rolling on the uneven flagstones, groaning, his eyes wild. He was tearing his hair and, when he saw Kemp, stopped dead and began counting his fingers, just to assure himself he still had them all.

'See any method in this madness, Hal?' Kemp asked. He was prodding a reclining girl to see if she reacted.

'Buggered if I do,' Dignam shrugged. 'I should be careful, Will; you'll catch things from her.'

'Will!' A voice brought them to a halt. 'Will Kemp. Thank God!'

They turned to see a face they knew. Tom Sledd was making his way towards them, stepping over the rolling madman and the sleeping girl. He had to fight off the old crone first but he reached them eventually.

'Do I know you, fellow?' Kemp asked haughtily, in the best tradition he had seen from Ned Alleyn.

'Of course you do, you old bastard!' Sledd nudged the man in the ribs. 'And you, Hal. How've you been? Get me out of here, will you? You're a celebrity.'

'Is this lunatic bothering you, gentlemen?' Jack asked, seeing the scene unfold before him.

'A little,' Kemp said. That was enough for Jack. His whip snaked and hissed through the air, lashing Sledd round the throat, and he shrank backwards, blood seeping into his crumpled collar.

'Don't hurt him, though.' Kemp stayed the gaoler's hand. 'He meant no harm.'

'That's what they all say,' Jack grunted. 'But whipping's all they understand. We have that from the highest medical authorities. That and darkness. If they can't see anything, they're not likely to eat it, or worse.'

'Will! Hal! It's me, Tom. Tom Sledd. From the Rose. Over here!'

Jack raised the whip again and Sledd shrank into the shadows. 'If you come this way, gentlemen,' Nat took over the role of guide, 'I'll show you a woman thinks she's the Queen of Sheba. Got an arse on her the size of Surrey.'

That sounded promising, and they followed the man down a dark, twisting passageway. 'What we gonna do about Tom, then, Will?' Dignam whispered in the echoing chamber.

'Nothing,' Kemp shrugged. 'Christ knows how he got himself in here but we're not going to be the ones who get him out. Knowing Sledd, he'll have himself branded as an Abram man and make more begging for the rest of his life than you and I have had laughs from audiences.'

'But even so, Will. We should tell someone, perhaps . . .' Dignam was cruel, but never as cruel as Kemp; no one does cruelty quite like a clown.

Kemp wrinkled his monkey face. 'Perhaps,' he said. 'We'll see. We'll see.' Then, raising his voice, 'Where's this arse then, gaoler?'

Timothy's groins told him very quickly that riding a horse due to foal in less than a week when you were only five and a half feet tall would never be a good idea. He shuffled in the saddle, trying to get comfortable, but that only gave him cramp, so he released one stirrup at a time so he could ease his poor, stretched ligaments. This whole process was a complete waste of time. It was clear that Forman had sent them into the world to save him having to feed them for a week. If they managed to make any money out of it, it would be a bonus, but the saving alone would make it worthwhile. Timothy had noticed little cheeseparing economies in the last week or so and if literal cheeseparing had not yet happened, it could only be a matter of time.

Timothy came somewhere between Matthias and Gerard when it came to Forman's skills at scrying. That it could be done, he had no doubt. He had seen the great Dr Dee contact the dead on two occasions and each time had been chilled to the marrow. Dee had done it with no frills, no sparkle and glitter. He had simply sat at a table, a mercury mirror in front of him, and spirits of the long and recently dead had flocked around him, twittering like sparrows. When Forman raised the spirits or spied on distant lands or people far from home, there was gunpowder, there were explosions, the room rocked with eldritch cries. And yet, no spirits were seen, their messages made no sense, though Forman's audience went away happier than had Dee's. Sometimes, Timothy thought, he had chosen too hastily in becoming Forman's apprentice, but when all was said and done, a roof over your head and quiet in which to work was not easily got in London and it was well known that Dee was old and crotchety and didn't mix with the great and good much any more. No, Timothy decided, just in case the magus could see all, he would do his best to find a wealthy patron, preferably a widow whose weeds would blind her eyes to his obvious imperfections. He smiled to himself as he imagined the look on Forman's face when he poured the golden coins onto the table next Tuesday. He clicked his tongue at the mare who ignored him. Easing a groin, he settled down for a long, slow but hopefully ultimately successful ride.

Eunice Brown sat in the window seat catching the last rays of the October sun. Out of the wind and damp, there was still some heat in it and she stretched her hands out to greet the golden warmth as it crept through the leaded panes. She felt the joints unknot and, as long as she didn't look down, she could imagine her fingers long, slender, girlish again, not gnarled, dry and painful. She closed her eyes and tilted her head back. Hers had been a busy life, compared with many. Happy, compared with most. She had never known a man, so had never had the pains of childbirth. She had never known love and loss, except the love of God, which no one could ever lose. And now, as the end of her life was approaching on soft feet down the passageway of years, she could sit in the sun and bask like a cat, all because a great man had a great heart. She sighed and smiled. Life was good; it didn't get much better than this.

For the rest of his life, Philip Henslowe would rue the decision he made on Friday 13 October in the year of his Lord 1592. With no petition worthy of the name and no one of note to act as his spokesman, he met his followers at the appointed time at the Vintry, where the great cranes swung and creaked in the night air.

They were as ragged an army as any ever seen in London and they carried flaming brands, clubs and pikes. Frizer and Skeres had done their work well and every disaffected apprentice and out-of-work riverman who could be bought with Henslowe's coin shouldered along the river's edge, the lights of the palace of Whitehall bobbing ahead. Whitehall Stair was empty. There was no royal barge fluttering with flags and bright with the Queen's heraldry. There were no guards in their crimson livery and no one was looking up at the walls where Robert Cecil's men lay in wait.

The little man was wearing his usual Puritan black, his face pale against the roofs of the buildings behind him. He glanced to his left and to his right, turning briefly to scan the rabbit warren of lanes behind him. Whitehall was not a palace; it was a village, crammed with all the great offices of state and, tonight at least, bristling with pikes, halberds and guns. At his side, a long cloak over his armour, stood Sir Wentworth Astley, commander of the massed Trained Bands and he had been praying for this moment nearly all his life.

An ill-assorted rabble was making its way along the

lapping waters, armed to the teeth and growing more mutinous with every step. Astley could hear them now, growling their discontent, spitting their venom. He could almost smell them. They carried no banners, nothing to say who they were. But Astley knew who led them. And he knew because Robert Cecil knew. Robert Cecil made it his business to know everything. He also made it his business to drip the odd falsehood where it would do most harm. Everybody knew that the Queen didn't keep court at Whitehall until 17 November when the Accession Day Tilts were held, dashing young courtiers clashing with each other in ever more outrageous fancy dress. But this year, Cecil had leaked the information, the Queen would be in her Presence Chamber from 8 October onwards.

Cecil watched the army advance, coping as best they could with the rising river, stumbling over the anchor chains that held fast the Queen's ships and the galleys from the Levant. The watchers on these decks didn't move. They had extinguished their lights and all was blackness.

Philip Henslowe was yards now from Whitehall Stair. He had studied the plans carefully and had a good grasp of the tilt yard, the cockpit, courtyards, gardens and orchards. He knew where the Queen's chapel was and knew that he would find her in the Presence Chamber, playing her virginals most evenings if reports were true. He had no idea that those reports came direct from Robert Cecil, the Spymaster.

He was just about to give his orders for his men to split, one group to each side of the water gate, when a solitary figure strode out onto the planking alongside the Stair, his buskins ringing on the timbers. He stood with his hands on his hips and a rapier at his side. Then he folded his arms and waited.

Henslowe raised both arms to bring his rabble to a halt. There was an eerie silence now. Most of the men at Henslowe's back had expected trouble long before this. They had watched for the pikes and helmets of the Trained Bands, looked for the steady tread of the Watch. And they had seen nothing. Nothing at all. Surely, this one man was not going to deny them entry to the Queen?

'Kit,' Henslowe hissed, creeping forward. 'What in God's name are you doing here?'

'I might ask you the same,' Marlowe said, a little louder. He used no name because he knew that Whitehall's walls had ears.

'We've come to see the Queen!' a voice behind Henslowe bellowed. So much for secrecy. Marlowe walked forward, stepping down from the decking into the grey ooze of the Thames mud.

'Her Majesty is not at home,' he said.

There was a murmur in the ranks and a jostling broke out.

'You said she'd be here!' another voice called. 'Henslowe, you've shafted us.' So much for anonymity.

'Gentlemen,' Marlowe called out and waited for silence. 'Beyond these walls are two hundred matchlocks of the London Trained Bands. Beyond them are a further two hundred pikes and bills. Oh, and I should have mentioned, there is a demi-culverin pointing at the head of your column.' He stepped closer, standing almost alongside Henslowe and staring at the leading man behind him. 'Ever seen what a demi-culverin can do to flesh and bone?' he asked. 'The gulls will be feeding off you lads for weeks.'

There were murmurs and mutterings, followed by shouts and buffetings. Some men swung their clubs towards the wall, ready for an attack. Others stumbled into the water. Suddenly, the portholes of a dozen ships flew upwards with a rattle of chains and a thud of timbers and there were guns on both sides of Henslowe's army, their muzzles black as night, their hungry mouths open.

'Believe me,' Marlowe said, quietly, 'you don't want to hear the voices of the guns.'

'We only want . . .' Henslowe began, but Marlowe hushed him with a raised hand. For a moment, nobody moved.

'We only want,' another voice said, taking up the theatre manager's sentence, 'this popinjay on the end of a meat hook.'

He lunged for Marlowe, but the poet was quicker. His sword snaked out through the London night, the blade tip ripping through the man's throat as he fell backwards, choking in the slime at his feet.

'Go home,' Marlowe said, 'or that will be the fate of you all.'

It was Henslowe who blinked first. He spun on his heel and yelled at the mob, 'You'll get your money, lads,' he promised. 'You have my word. But you've done enough for tonight.' Slowly, they shifted, grumbling still and mutinous. Some spat at the ships, others bashed the palace walls with their clubs. But the fight, if there had ever been any, had gone out of them and they drifted away along the river bank like the flotsam they were. Philip Henslowe was the last to go.

'What price this, Kit?' he asked. 'Did you know about this?'

Marlowe sheathed his sword. 'Not until earlier today,' he said, 'when it was too late to warn you. Go back to the Rose, Henslowe and stay there. I'll do what I can to sort this madness out.'

He heard the rattle of bolts behind him and Henslowe was running through the mud, for the sake of his reputation if not his life. Wentworth Astley was at Marlowe's back, his sword-arm extended. 'Turn, Hell-hound, turn,' he grated. 'Who are you, sir, to interfere with the Queen's business?'

Marlowe turned as requested. 'That's a good line, sir,' he smiled. 'I am Christopher Marlowe, the playwright. Should I decide to use the line, I shall of course credit you with it, Master . . .?'

'Marlowe.' Robert Cecil had reached the landing stage now. 'This is Sir Wentworth Astley of the London Trained Bands.'

Marlowe bowed low.

'Do you know this man, Robert?' Astley growled, not at all happy with the way the evening had gone.

'After a fashion,' the little man said. He barely reached Astley's baldric, but he carried a gravitas all his own. 'What brought you here, Marlowe?'

'A little bird told me there'd be trouble,' he said, 'and you know, Sir Robert, that I can't abide trouble.'

'I'll have you in chains for this, sir,' Astley said. He had not sheathed his sword yet.

'For saving the lives of countless men?' Marlowe queried. 'I seriously doubt that, Sir Wentworth.'

The commander of the Trained Bands had turned purple

under his helmet rim but Cecil patted his arm reassuringly. 'Let it go, Wentworth,' his murmured. 'Leave Marlowe to me.' Astley slammed his sword home and thundered over the timbers, barking orders to his men.

'Who was their leader?' Cecil asked Marlowe softly.

'I have no idea,' Marlowe shrugged. 'Never seen him before.'

'Not Philip Henslowe, proprietor of the Rose, then?'

'Henslowe?' Marlowe looked horrified. 'Good Lord, no. I've never seen Master Henslowe get his hands dirty. If he is indeed behind this – and we don't know that he is – he will have sent somebody else, trust me.'

Cecil looked his man in the face. He would trust Kit Marlowe when Hell froze over, but for now, that would have to do.

Eunice always stayed awake late to see in the first few moments of the Lord's Day. She had never had the good fortune to be able to devote her life entirely to God, as the blessed sisters in France could do, but she tried her best to keep the services, if only in her head. She had heard the great clock in the hall strike the quarter before twelve and since then she had counted the seconds and minutes, so that at midnight she could be composed and ready to greet her Lord, who she knew, one day, would come for her in triumph. She lay on her back, her feet pointing to the footboard, her hands softly crossed on her breast. If tonight was the night she was to be called, she would give the layers-out no trouble. She said her version of a rosary, to count the seconds. She smiled softly to think that if her benefactor could hear her thoughts, perhaps he would not be so good to her. So, she didn't make a sound as the minute before midnight wound to a close. Sometimes, when the night was still, she could hear the clock beneath her chamber click its cogs before its mighty twelvefold strike, but tonight was windy and she could hear nothing but the sighing in the eaves and the tap of a branch at the window.

The hand over her face took her completely by surprise, therefore. She had heard not a step, not a creak of a board before, suddenly, her breath was stopped. Her eyes flew open and rolled madly in her head, but whoever it was who had his hand over her mouth and nose was behind her and she could see no one. Surely, her last thought came like an explosion in her head, surely, the Lord would not come like this, violent and cruel? Her eyes strained in the darkness, then the dark was absolute, a void as wide as the sky.

She couldn't tell how long she had been in the darkness, but she could feel what seemed to be rain on her face. She opened her eyes eagerly; was this Heaven? She had always liked rain, liked the way it made the gardens smell fresh, like a baby's skin. She put a hand out to feel the drops, but it wasn't rain. It was just wetness on her cheek. Someone was splashing her with water. She spluttered and struggled to sit up, but there was a weight on her chest, holding her down. Her eyelids felt swollen and she couldn't see, but darker against the dark of the window, she could see a shape, a heavy shape, sitting on her chest, crouching like a demon. She tried to cross herself but the demon had her wrist caught in its fist and she couldn't move. The demon leaned down until she could feel his hot breath on her mouth.

'Have you seen him yet?' the demon grated. 'Have you seen him?'

Eunice shook her head as far as she was able. The pain in her throat and across her jaw was the worst she had ever felt. The demon tucked her hands under his knees and used his claws to press on her throat, her mouth, her nose. She struggled to take one last breath. Could this be a test? Did the Lord test you before he let you into Paradise? If that was the case, she would try her best to pass, but she didn't know what the answer should be. As the blackness came upon her, she hoped this time to get it right.

There was no water this time, no gentle, healing rain. Instead, there was a stinging slap across one cheek, then the other. Eunice gasped, forcing air into her lungs past her tortured throat. Her eyes wouldn't open now at all. They were hot and sealed with dried tears. She felt the demon change position and again his hot breath seared her face.

'Have you seen him yet? Have you seen him?'

She couldn't really remember, but last time she thought she had shaken her head. This time, she tried to nod, but could scarcely move. Cruel hands grabbed her shoulders and shook her violently. 'Is that yes? Have you seen him? Did he speak? What did he say? Was his light too glorious? Tell me! Tell me!' A vicious slap rocked her and her brain – old, tired and frail – rebelled and she finally went into a darkness which would never fade.

NINE

M arlowe knew better than to hide from Cecil – he knew that it simply couldn't be done. He had become quite adept at keeping out of the way of Henslowe and all the importuning actors begging for roles, but from Cecil, no one could hide. He was at his breakfast table in Hog Lane that Monday morning, buttering the last crusts of a new loaf, when the hammering at the door alerted him to a more than usually determined visitor. He called through into the kitchen that he would answer the door and did so, still wiping buttery crumbs from his moustache.

'Master Marlowe?' Two men stood outside, between them blocking out the light. They were both well known to Marlowe and he to them but, clearly, today things were going to be kept on a formal footing.

'Yes,' Marlowe said, smiling slightly. 'And you are?'

This foxed both of his visitors. They had expected a bit of backchat – they knew him too well for it to be otherwise – but this was a difficult one. Finally, after some thought, the slightly larger of the two spoke. 'It's us, Master Marlowe, Sir Robert's bodyguard. You know us.' He pointed to the *Sero, sed Serio* woven into the pleats at his shoulder that was the Cecil motto.

'Do I?' he asked. 'I only ask because Sir Robert's guard know me well and yet, here you are, asking me my name.'

The two looked at each other in confusion. 'We were just making conversation, Master Marlowe. Being pleasant, like.'

'I see. Well, in that case, come in while I finish breaking my fast, if you would be so good. Would you care for a little something? Bread? Ale? I believe there may be some posset from yesterday, if the kitchen maid hasn't finished it up?'

'Er, no thank you, Master Marlowe, kind of you to offer. Sir Robert did say that we had to bring you to him with all speed.'

'Is that what he said?'

'Not in so many words, Master Marlowe, no. But he did seem to be in a bit of a state, if I'm honest. His old dad's in a bit of a stew as well. They're both there, waiting for you.'

Marlowe could hardly suppress a smile to think of Lord Burghley, the Queen's Secretary of State, being anyone's old dad, but he supposed that, taken literally, the guard did not misspeak. 'Lads,' he said, throwing his cloak over his shoulder, 'do you know if this is about last Friday?'

'Friday?' The shorter guard had a face devoid of expression. 'Did something happen on Friday, Master Marlowe? I know it was the thirteenth, but I am not superstitious, myself.'

Marlowe nodded. Right – well, that was something. Henslowe might be safe after all. 'Something else, then,' he murmured, half to himself. 'Expect me when you see me,' he called over his shoulder into the kitchen, and was rewarded by a vague yell. 'I don't know why I even say that,' he said to the guards. 'They hardly seem to notice I'm here anyway. Sometimes, I wonder who employs who.'

In the kitchen, the cook looked at the kitchen maid and they both suppressed a giggle. They knew right enough who was in charge in the house in Hog Lane – and it certainly wasn't one Master Marlowe, the Muse's darling and ex-scholar of Corpus Christi.

Robert Cecil knew that he didn't measure up physically to most men, so he had learned at his nursemaid's knee to make his presence felt in other ways. He had never bothered trying to be louder either; the bigger children could always just shout him down. So what he did was make stillness into an art form and he was practising that art when Marlowe was shown in by Cecil's new secretary.

Marlowe sat in his usual chair in the rabbit warren that was the Palace of Whitehall and waited for the Spymaster to take notice of him. The little man sat behind his desk like a spider on a web, still but watching, feeling every twitch of the silk, no matter how delicate and slight the movement. After a moment, he looked up.

'Do sit down, Master Marlowe,' he said, with a wintry smile.

'Thank you,' Marlowe nodded and settled back against the cushion. 'I don't mind if I do.'

Cecil bent to his papers again but this morning his heart was not in his usual mind games.

'I have called you in to see me, Master Marlowe, because I need someone of your . . . shall we say, special talents?'

'I do write a mighty line,' Marlowe conceded. 'It's not like you to sponsor a play, though, is it?' His smile would not have disgraced a choirboy.

'Not that special talent,' Cecil said. Marlowe pricked up his ears. That Cecil did not take him up on this sally said far more than any words. 'I need your skills in discovering a murderer.'

It wasn't often Marlowe was surprised, but he was now. 'Surely, Sir Robert, you have men at your disposal more worthy than I . . .'

'No false modesty, Marlowe, please. And this is not a murder which threatens the safety of the Queen, or at least, my father and I don't think it is, so . . . you would seem to be the better choice.'

'Your men did say your father was . . . upset.'

'My men said too much.'

'He is here, though.'

'He is.'

Marlowe was getting testy. He could tell when something was being withheld from him and it wasn't fair for Cecil to ask him to solve a mystery when he didn't even know what the mystery was. 'Is he to join us?'

'I think not. He is, as my men told you, upset. And there are also, as always, affairs of state.'

Marlowe cast his mind quickly over the Burghley family. Cecil's mother was dead, he knew, his grandparents long gone to their reward. Of Burghley's sisters he knew nothing. It could only be one person and he blenched at the thought of investigating that particular murder. 'Is it . . . Thomas?'

Cecil gave a shout of laughter. 'I'm not sure whether my brother's murder would upset anyone very much, Master Marlowe,' he said. 'No, it is someone much more important than that. It is his nursemaid. And mine. Eunice – Noo-Noo, we all called her. She was found dead in her bed yesterday morning.'

Marlowe blinked. The thought of Burghley in hanging sleeves going for walks with his Noo-Noo was something that even his vivid imagination baulked at. He tried to come to the point. 'She must have been a considerable age,' he said.

'She was elderly, yes. She came to the family when she was twelve, so she is . . . was . . .' Cecil did some quick calculations, 'eighty-three, -four, something like that.'

'And so,' Marlowe was uncertain how to put this delicate question to a man clearly grieving. 'Could she not have simply . . . died?'

A door hidden in the panelling burst open and the Queen's Secretary of State burst in, the hair unruly without the ubiquitous cap and the beard stained and yellow. 'Don't you think we have thought of that, Marlowe?' he yelled. 'We're not *idiots!* Noo-Noo – I mean, Mistress Brown – was found dead in her bed with clear signs of foul play.' The old man's eyes filled with tears. 'She had never hurt a soul, in all her life. She was devout, she was loyal . . . Master Marlowe, she was a woman who made the world better by being in it. And yet, someone . . .' He pressed a kerchief to his mouth and signalled Cecil to continue, flopping into a chair.

Cecil cleared his throat. 'Mistress Brown was found by one of the maids. Since she had ceased to be a nursemaid, she had been a pensioner of the house, with a bedroom on the nursery floor, where she had spent so much of her life. She kept to her room of recent years, reading devout tracts, doing some mending, embroidery, that kind of thing. My father visited when he could, as did I when visiting Hatfield. She . . . she was happy, I hope, in her retirement.'

Marlowe was touched by the devotion of the men who, between them, ran the nation. 'What did the maid find, that makes you think of murder?'

Burghley was in control of himself again and took up the tale. 'I was in Hatfield myself. I try to get there when I can and it was politic that I was not in London on Friday.'

A glance went between father and son that Marlowe didn't miss.

'The maid was hysterical. She ran out of Noo-Noo's bedchamber and woke the whole house with her screams. I was next on the scene and it was truly dreadful. The look on her face . . . I have seen some sights, Master Marlowe, but she looked as if she had seen the Devil himself.'

Marlowe had also seen some sights. He had seen people who died peacefully in their beds who looked terrified; he had seen people chased and hunted down and killed who looked as peaceful as a saint. 'That alone is no proof of murder,' he told them.

'Alone, no, I agree,' the Secretary of State said. 'But her face and throat were a mass of bruises.'

'That's different.' Marlowe knew that evil stalked the world in every place, but when it struck at an old and defenceless woman, it was evil indeed.

'I do not have your expertise,' Burghley told the playwright, with unaccustomed modesty, 'but it seemed to me that someone had gripped her face hard, like this.' He moved towards his son. 'May I, Robyn?' Cecil lifted his face up to the only man in the world he trusted. Burghley pinched the Spymaster's nose between finger and thumb, at the same time pressing up under his chin with the heel of his hand. With the other, he gripped around his throat.

'I have seen that done,' Marlowe nodded.

'Sadly, haven't we all,' Cecil agreed, quietly grateful that the old man had let go of him. 'But the odd thing, Marlowe, was that this had happened not once, but several times. The bruising showed it clearly.'

'Especially around the throat,' the Secretary of State agreed. 'The thumb marks were particularly clear.'

'I assume that Mistress Brown was not unusually strong.' Marlowe could not somehow conjure up an old lady known as Noo-Noo being built like a wrestler.

'If anything, rather frail,' Cecil confirmed.

'So, there was unlikely to have been a struggle.'

'Very unlikely. Also, she was in her bed, so she was taken as she slept.' Burghley's voice was thick with sorrow. 'I daresay you think me a maudlin old man, Master Marlowe, but my nursemaid is the last person who had known me all my life.

It was into her arms I was put on the day I was born. Her mother was my wet nurse. Now, there is no one to remember me as a child.' He smiled wanly. 'I did not know how lonely that would be.'

Cecil looked at Marlowe, a question in his eyes, and Marlowe answered it.

'If you would permit me, my Lord,' he said, 'I could go up to Hatfield and ask questions. The servants. The tenants. If, as you say, your old nurse was beloved by all, it shouldn't take long to run the murderer to ground. Someone will know who he is and won't stay quiet for long. No one would shield a man who could do that to a defenceless old lady.'

Burghley nodded and blew his nose again. 'I will send to my man of business to make sure no one interferes with your questions, Master Marlowe. In the meantime, please excuse me, I need to go and pray for Noo-Noo's soul.' He turned and opened the door in the panelling, turning as he did so. 'No candles or any popish idolatry, of course.'

Marlowe inclined his head. 'Of course.'

'Just a simple prayer.' Burghley cleared his throat again. 'A simple prayer, for a simple soul.' And the door closed softly behind him.

There seemed to be nothing else to say. Marlowe got up and was almost out of the room when Cecil called him back.

'Just because you are helping with our little family trouble, Master Marlowe, I do still want to remind you that I have not forgotten Master Henslowe's involvement on Friday last. It isn't over. Perhaps you would be good enough to tell him as much.'

Marlowe bowed but this time didn't speak. Sometimes, the least said was the soonest mended.

'How are things at the Rose, then, Will?' Hal Dignam was wringing out his pickadil now that October was here and a driving rain had added to London's woes.

'Hello, Hal.' Shaxsper was as close to the fire as his feet could bear, a pint of ale in front of him. 'As bad as the Curtain, I'll wager.'

'At least,' Dignam waved to his host, miming the downing of a cup of his best, 'we haven't driven our stage manager mad.'

'How do you mean?'

Dignam looked at the Warwickshire man. 'Well, Tom Sledd. He is still *at* the Rose, isn't he?'

'As much as any of us are,' Shaxsper muttered. 'I'm seriously thinking of going home.'

'Where's that, then?'

'Stratford.'

'I always thought you was from the north.'

'Stratford is in the Midlands, Hal.' This was not the first time that Shaxsper had had this conversation with a Londoner. '*Bradford* is in the north.'

'Where?'

'Never mind.'

'You see,' Dignam became confidential, leaning over the table and dripping rainwater into Shaxsper's ale, 'and I'll come clean about this – I always thought Stratford was east London.'

'That's at Bow, Hal,' Shaxsper sighed. No wonder this man was a clown. 'I'm talking about "on Avon". Different thing altogether.'

'Ah, right.' Dignam was still waving at various serving wenches, seeing as how his host was ignoring him altogether. 'So what's this with Tom Sledd, then?'

'What?' Like a large number of people, Will Shaxsper was easily confused by the circles of Hal Dignam's conversation.

'He's in Bedlam. But then, I s'pose you know that.'

'In Bedlam?' Shaxsper's mind was racing. The last time he had seen Tom Sledd, the stage manager had become a trifle green at the resurrection of a dead man and had gone off to watch for the Watch. 'Are you sure?'

'Will Kemp and I saw him, clear as day. He was as close to us as we are at this very moment.'

'What did he say?'

'Asked us to get him out.'

'And . . . did you?' Shaxsper needed to know. Closed theatres or not, men like Tom Sledd didn't grow on trees. They were the lifeblood of the theatre, men who made the wooden

O, O. In fact, so many metaphors were whirling in Shaxsper's head, he felt he ought to lie down.

'Nah,' Dignam shrugged. 'Well, let sleeping dogs lie, ain't it?'

Shaxsper grabbed the man's shoulder. 'But, he's one of us, Hal!' he bellowed. 'Well,' he dropped his voice because people were starting to stare, 'not one of you, exactly, but when a man's chained to a wall, surely we can forget little theatrical rivalries.'

'Oh, he wasn't chained,' Dignam was at pains to explain, 'and to be fair, I wanted to help him, but you know what a double-dyed shithouse Will Kemp is. Wanted to see the Queen of Sheba instead.'

'Don't we all,' Shaxsper muttered, but his mind was elsewhere.

'Well, there we are then. What's a bloke got to do to get a drink around here?' he shouted. Still nobody was listening. He looked at his fellow actor. 'So, how are things at the Rose, then, Will?'

Gerard was the first of Forman's apprentices to reappear at the house under the walls of the abbey. Mistress Forman was the first person he saw as he pushed open the door.

'Oh, you're back,' she grunted. 'Hungry, I suppose.'

'Not especially,' Gerard said, politely. 'I ate quite well while I was away. Largely fish, but very tasty. In fact,' he rummaged in his pack, 'I have some for you. Fresh caught this morning.'

She took them and sniffed them. 'These don't smell of fish,' she said. 'Is it some trick?' Being married to Simon Forman tended to make a person suspicious.

'They don't smell because they are fresh,' Gerard told her. 'I have some vegetables here as well.' He had another rummage and brought out some roots the woman couldn't immediately identify.

'Black sticks. Thank you.' She sounded dubious.

'It's salsify,' Gerard told her. 'It tastes of oyster. Just in season now. And some carrots.' He handed them over. Carrots, she could recognize and she smiled for once.

'Did you have a good holiday?' she asked him, just to be polite.

'It wasn't a *holiday*, Mistress Forman,' he said. 'I was *working*.'
'And how did that go?' she asked, with no interest evident
in her voice.
'I pitched a tent in a clearing by the river. It took a day
or two, but finally, a few people found their way to me and I
think I . . .'
But the woman had wandered away.
'. . . made a difference.' Gerard sighed. Perhaps making a
difference was putting it rather strong, but one ingrowing
toenail less in the world could only be a good thing, surely.

If truth were told, Will Shaxsper missed Warwickshire, the
green fields, the shaded forests, the babbling brooklets.
One day, he had promised himself, he would write a play set
there. It would be about fairies, nothing heavy, nothing too
serious; one for the ladies, essentially. So here he was, that
wet, chilly afternoon, slushing through the mud of Moor Field,
making his way to Bedlam.
A solitary donkey, with ears like errant wings, looked at
him, taking a moment off from chewing the grass. Sheep
moved to one side, not caring for the man's determined stride
at all. The rain had done little for the sewer that ran under
the old Roman walls, except to make it overflow and smell
even worse. Rats played on its banks, so somebody in London
was happy.
'You on your own?' the gaoler challenged him.
Shaxsper looked to each side. He hadn't realized that the
keepers had to be mad to work here as well. 'Yes,' was the
best the playwright could manage. All the way here he had
kept telling himself that Dignam had been joking. The man
was a clown, after all, famous for talking in riddles and tipping
over non-existent stumbling blocks for the amusement of the
crowd. Every year, on Twelfth Night, handbills would appear
announcing the sale of the Rose and every year a furious Philip
Henslowe would tell would-be buyers where they could stick
their paltry offers. Such playbills were written by Hal Dignam;
everybody but Philip Henslowe knew it for a fact. But Tom
Sledd was Tom Sledd and Shaxsper counted him a friend. He
couldn't let it – or Tom – lie. So, here he was.

'Anything special?' Jack asked the actor. 'Queen of Sheba? Dick Three-in-One?'

'Just browsing,' Shaxsper said cheerily.

'Right you are.'

The noise in the Hell-hole was deafening. A woman was banging a tray against a wall to a rhythm known only to her.

'For the love of God,' a sallow-faced man intoned, 'alms, alms, good sir.'

Shaxsper was the son of a glover and he had inherited his father's lack of giving ways. He carefully removed the man's bony fingers from his sleeve and swept on.

'Wanna see what I got?' an old crone asked him coyly, swaying her hips and fluttering what passed for eyelashes.

'Nobody wants to see what you've got, Bessie,' Jack was at Shaxsper's elbow. 'Oh . . . unless the gentleman . . .?'

But the gentleman had already turned a corner and there he was; Tom Sledd, as large as life, if a little sallow.

'Will!' Sledd shrieked, leaping on him and wrapping his arms around his neck. 'Will, thank the Lord!'

Jack was like a leech, if only because he sensed in Shaxsper someone who was looking for something specific and might be prepared to pay for it. 'Do you know this gentleman, sir?' he asked.

Again, Shaxsper's mind whirled. Nobody was committed to Bedlam for no reason. Whatever had happened to poor old Tom, Shaxsper wanted no part of it. 'No,' he said, a shade too quickly, perhaps. 'No, I don't.'

Sledd was gripping Shaxsper hard, his knuckles white as he clawed at his doublet. For a moment, the visitor stood rooted to the spot, at a loss as to what to do. Jack, as usual, read it wrongly. 'Would sir like a little time with this madman?' he asked. 'Get acquainted, like?' Jack didn't judge. He had a family to feed and clothe and, without his little extras, they would be on the streets.

Shaxsper's mouth hung open. He'd seen enough for one day. If ever he wrote a play for real, he vowed then and there, there wouldn't be a madman in it.

*   *   *

Matthias was some hours behind Gerard and managed to get into the house without encountering Mistress Forman, who was busy in the kitchen trying to work out how to cook salsify, which still didn't strike her as looking very edible. Carrots she was at home with, but they weren't the makings of a meal. And now, these gannetting boys were back – she could hear the great clodhopping one trying to creep up the stairs.

Matthias was anxious not to make too much of an entrance until he had changed his clothes. His mother had insisted that he had a complete wardrobe as a gift and before he could leave the house she had decked him out in every latest fashion. He had a feeling that he looked a bit of an ass, but as he was built like a privy, most people had laughed behind their hands and behind his back. He also needed to choose which of the testimonials to show to Forman. He had earned them all – especially the one from Mistress Flambeaux, the French governess at the big house in the next village. She had not needed Forman's special massage, but she had taught Matthias a thing or two which he would never forget, especially in damp weather. In the end, he chose three, two from grateful widows, and one from a lady who expected to be brought to bed of a healthy child thanks to Matthias's good services. The date of the confinement was something she had fortunately left out. Matthias folded the testimonials neatly and put them with the allowance from his father in a pouch. Master Forman would be impressed, Matthias had no doubt. Even if his scrying glass worked, he wouldn't turn his nose up at gold coins, Matthias knew well.

'It was him, Kit. As God is my witness, it was Tom Sledd.'

The Angel was crowded that evening; in fact, it was so full that the muttered conversation between the two men went unnoticed. Shaxsper was still trying to calm his nerves after Bedlam earlier in the day. He had been propositioned by an old crone and leapt upon by a mad stage manager; someone had ripped off his codpiece as he left and was last seen wearing it on his head. Jack had found it all very amusing.

'What did he say?' Marlowe asked. Nobody had mentioned Tom Sledd for days and Marlowe's days had been full recently, one way or another. He would be leaving for Hatfield in the morning and another iron in the fire was something he could really do without.

'Asked me to get him out . . . well, not in so many words. He just seemed *so* glad to see me.'

Marlowe nodded, frowning. If Tom Sledd was glad to see Will Shaxsper, things were very bad indeed. 'You left him there?'

Shaxsper knew Marlowe all too well. The man could fill you with guilt one moment, even without resorting to his mighty line. The next, he'd have you shouting from the roof-tops at the joy of his company. Kit Marlowe could drive men mad as surely as Bedlam did. 'It must have been Greene,' the Warwickshire man said. 'Well, you know, the exhumation. It's unhinged him.'

'Don't talk bollocks, Will,' Marlowe growled. 'Bedlam. How do I get in?'

Timothy was the last of the apprentices to get home. It was pitch dark and late as his key scraped in the lock and Forman whisked the door open before he had had time to turn it.

'And what time do you call this?' Forman hissed. 'Where have you been?'

Timothy was in no mood for this. If it cost him his apprenticeship, he would speak his mind. 'Firstly,' he said, not bothering to whisper, 'I am not late. I am still in fact a day early, as midnight has not yet struck to bring in Tuesday, which I believe was the day we were to return. Secondly, my horse decided to give birth yesterday.'

Forman's eyebrows shot up, disbelievingly.

'Yes, that's right. Your damned scrying glass didn't see that, did it? In the middle of the highway, there we were, ambling along, when suddenly, a wave went through the creature as though she had been shot and she lay down, right there in the road, screaming and kicking. We were in some Godforsaken village in the middle of nowhere but, believe it or not, within minutes we were surrounded by yokels all scratching their heads and mumbling at each other. And all the while, the mare was screaming and she looked fit to explode.'

'Nasty for you,' Forman muttered.

'Nasty for you,' Timothy spat. 'Because, in the middle of all this, some old bat appears out of a cottage and everybody falls back. T'was old Gammer Gummy or some-such name and she was the local wise woman, or so they said. She walked up to the mare, put a hand over her eye and then, when the creature was still, walked to the other end, put her arm up . . . well, up there and pulled the damned foal out, just like that. And in a minute, the foal was suckling, all the village maidens were going "aw" and that was that.'

'Why nasty for me?' Forman had got a little wrapped up with the story and didn't remember to be angry.

'Because old Gammer Gummy had to be paid, didn't she? I offered her the foal, but she didn't want it. What she wanted was my purse and there were too many of her sons, grandsons and, for all I know, great-grandsons there for me to refuse. You may not have noticed, but I am not a fighting man. So,' and he pushed his way past Forman, 'if you'll excuse me, I have been a long way, I have had a trying day and I want my bed. Good night, Master.'

Forman stood just inside the doorway, watching his apprentice go up the stairs and disappear into the gloom beyond the candle's glow. The week's experiment had not been a complete washout. He had had a nice meal of trout and salsify, though one of the ingredients had given him appalling wind. He had a nice little purse of coin. And he had, if he played his cards right, a foal to offset against his credit at the livery. He smiled to himself. It could have been much, much worse.

Most men would have walked across the Moor Field or down Bishopsgate Street. But Kit Marlowe was not most men. Bedlam was locked until eight o'clock the next day, but Tom Sledd must have been in the seventh circle of Hell for days now, and time was of the essence. It may be that his mind had gone already – after all, he had been glad to see Shaxsper.

There was no rapier tonight, no plumed cap, ruff and Colleyweston cloak. Marlowe wore black with a plain Puritan collar. Only his dagger hilt shone silver under the fitful moon.

He knew this part of London well. His home in Hog Lane was not far away, with a second home at the Curtain closer still. He passed the gate of the New Churchyard where he had resurrected Robert Greene what already seemed a lifetime ago, and turned the corner, tight to the Wall. He heard the thud of the Watch on the cobbles and saw their lantern beams darting like fireflies in the night. He flattened himself against the wall and waited.

Bedlam's gates may have been locked, but Bedlam's roof was not. It was open to the sky as it had been for months now and the rain of the previous day had brought down more tiles to lie sodden with the straw of the chamber below. Marlowe edged his way across the roof, feeling the guttering fragile and fragmenting under his buskins. Years of bird shit had encrusted the tiles and no amount of rain would soften that again. He felt it scrape against his back through doublet and shirt. Then he caught an upright and swung himself across so he was face to the roof now, looking down into a pit.

There were one or two candles down there, too high on the rain-dribbled walls for the inmates to reach. He could make out bodies lying on the straw; men, women? Who could tell? From somewhere, there was a rattle of chains, snoring and crying in the half-light. The drop was . . . what? Fifteen feet? Twenty? But there was nothing to break his fall and no other way into the hospital that had become a gaol. He had to risk it. And he, who never prayed at all, prayed that the ground was soft.

He hit the straw hard and rolled upright. Three or four faces peered at him, eyes wide, mouths open.

'Are you an angel?' he heard a voice croak. 'Are you from God?'

'If it pleases you,' Marlowe said and backed into the shadows.

Most of the inmates still slept, including one who lay against a wall with his mouth open, snoring with the best of them. Marlowe knelt beside him and clapped a hand over his mouth. 'Hello, Tom' he said.

Sledd jerked awake and swivelled his eyes. Before Marlowe lowered his hand, he was crying. He threw his arms around the playwright. 'I knew it would be you, Kit,' he sobbed. 'I knew it.'

'I don't see why not,' Marlowe smiled, as if he were having a casual conversation in the street with a passer-by. 'Are you all right?'

'How long have you got?' Sledd hissed. 'First that arsehole Kemp, then that bastard Shaxsper. They both saw me and looked right through me. I . . . Kit?'

But Marlowe was standing up, staring at a man half hidden in the shadows.

'Oh, Kit,' Sledd struggled to his feet, but the beating that Jack had given him had taken its toll and he staggered a little. 'Kit, this is . . .'

'We don't have names here,' the man said. His hair was straggly and his beard was alive with creatures.

'This is the poet,' Sledd was unfazed. 'He's a bloody good one, too. He—'

'I must be going, Tom,' Marlowe said. 'I'll be back.'

'Kit? Kit? No, you mustn't go. I can climb.' Sledd watched Marlowe clawing his way up the rough stones of the wall. 'I can make it . . . Kit. Kit?'

But the poet had Sledd firmly in his grip and the playwright had gone, back the way he had come, the wailing of Bedlam ringing in his ears.

TEN

Kit Marlowe was packing his saddlebags for the road before dawn the next morning. The bay was as unused to this hour as he was, but the animal was of a stoic disposition and took it well. It would take the pair of them half a day to reach Hatfield by the North Road and he wanted to be away before the drovers began to clog the lanes.

'Master Marlowe?' The voice made him turn, hand near his dagger hilt as it always was at moments like these.

'Johanna.' The hand relaxed and he reached out to take her hand and kiss it. 'Whatever happened to Kit?'

The woman was struggling with her tears. She had left her children with her mother, a sure sign of her desperation as the woman was a meddling harridan who had thought her daughter had married beneath her and never forgot to remind her. She clutched at Marlowe as a drowning man will clutch at straws. 'Have you any news of Tom, Kit?' she asked.

With all that had happened in the last few days, Marlowe had completely forgotten about Tom's better half and how frantic she must be. 'He's safe, Johanna,' he said, smiling. 'Safe and well.'

'Where *is* he?' she blurted out, all but stamping her foot.

'That I can't tell you,' he said.

The Devil in Johanna Sledd wanted to slap Kit Marlowe, gouge his eyes out and throw his ravaged corpse onto a dung heap. But the angel in her remembered that this was kind Kit, the man her Tom worshipped nearly as much as he had worshipped his old master, Ned Sledd, whose name he had taken. She closed to him and laid a desperate hand on his chest, just above his heart. He was strong and safe and she needed that to calm her. She looked down for a moment, swallowing hard. Some questions, once spoken, could change a life forever, so it paid to take your time. 'Has he left us,

Kit?' she asked, her voice scarcely audible. 'Is there another woman?'

Marlowe couldn't help but smile. In Bedlam there were several, but none to whom Tom Sledd would give the time of day. 'No,' he assured her. 'Nothing like that. You've heard him use the phrase "the Queen's business"?' he asked.

She blinked. 'He's used it about you,' she said, 'but never about himself.'

Marlowe tapped the side of his nose. 'Enough said,' he murmured. 'There are more things in Heaven and earth, Johanna . . .'

In spite of her misgivings, the woman smiled. 'That's one of Master Shaxsper's lines, isn't it?' she said.

Marlowe frowned. 'No,' he said, 'it's one of mine.' When all this was over, he would have to have words with Master Shaxsper. He dipped into his purse and pressed two gold coins into Johanna's hand. 'You'll see Tom soon enough,' he said. He held up her chin, still wet with her tears, 'and I don't want to see any more of these.'

Simon Forman dressed with his usual care to hear his apprentices' stories and he went a step further, one he seldom took, and sat in his magnificent carved chair on the dais at the end of his chamber. He lolled there, one arm stretched out and the other bent, an elegant hand supporting a head too full of wisdom to be trusted to a mere neck. The image was somewhat marred by the faint scurryings in his sleeve and the occasional croak or coo, but the three apprentices were used to it now and lined up accordingly, to tell their tales. They were all, including Matthias, a little concerned about what the scrying mirror had told their master, but brazening it out was probably the best plan and they squared their shoulders in their ridiculous gowns and locked their knees to stop them shaking.

Forman looked at them through narrowed eyes. He was having trouble focussing at distance lately, but was far too vain to wear eyeglasses. Besides, being a little short-sighted made it easier to handle some of the more raddled widows in his portfolio, and certainly his wife. 'Well, gentlemen,' he said, smiling. 'I hope you all had productive weeks. Very different, all of them, I am sure. I myself have been extremely busy. After you had all gone, I thought to myself, "My lads have gone into the highways and byways and here am I, in comfort. This cannot be allowed to continue." So, I packed myself a travelling bag and set off myself, to seek my fortune, as it were.' He gave a light laugh, to show them that they were allowed to smile.

Gerard, always anxious to please, let out a guffaw, instantly stifled.

'Yes,' Forman closed his eyes and raised his face to an imaginary sky, 'I went out into the highways and byways, alongside you all in spirit. I took nothing but a crust of bread, some herbs for healing and my mask, so that the simple people I encountered on my way would know my calling.' He fell silent, a beatific smile on his face. After a moment, his eyes flew open and he pierced his apprentices with his special basilisk stare, practised over long hours in front of a mirror. 'They came to me in their hundreds. I was exhausted.' He dropped his head into his hand and shook it gently. 'They had nothing, but I gave freely of myself and of my healing.' He sat up straight and clasped his hands in front of him, to the particular relief of the dove which had been caught under his elbow. 'And so now, my boys, my brave boys, tell me of your travels. Matthias, you first, I think, as the senior among you.'

The apprentices all showed signs of relaxation. Just a crust of bread, some herbs and a mask – no mention of the dreaded mirror. All three racked their brains for a better story than the truth; the world was their oyster as long as they could remember what they said later and keep their stories straight. Gerard and Timothy glanced at each other, pleased that Matthias had to go first. The fact that he constantly flaunted his seniority usually annoyed them, when he had the washing water first, the softest pillow, the cleanest under-linen but, sometimes, the pendulum swung in their favour. They turned to him and made their expressions show their interest in his tale of derring-do and healing out on the road.

*   *   *

Mistress Forman's maidservant stumbled into the kitchen laughing like a banshee. She often did that, being a little soft in the head, but her mistress, being usually devoid of other amusement, never failed to ask her what was amusing her.

The girl wiped her eyes on a grubby apron and her nose on the back of her hand. 'Oh, Mistress,' she gulped, 'you would have laughed if you could have heard it.'

'Listening at doors again, Tab?' Sometimes, the lady of the house wished she could be stricter with her servants, but that would leave just her husband for company and, frankly, that would never do. He had a way with him, she had to give him that, but when he wasn't giving some poor deluded woman his usual flannel, or whatever he chose to call it, his conversation was less than sparkling.

'Not listening, Mistress, no. The master's voice carries, as you know. I was just stopped outside the door.'

Mistress Forman decided to say nothing. She had found out some very useful information this way before now.

'Well, the reason I laughed is that he was spinning such a yarn to those boys, 'bout how he was out and about sleeping under a hedge and whatnot all last week.'

The magus's wife raised her eyebrows. 'I don't think he even left his bed on Friday, did he?' she asked.

'No.' The maid shook out her duster determinedly. 'Unlucky, he said.'

'Superstitious rubbish,' her mistress remarked. 'He was out on Saturday, I suppose, but when I saw him next he didn't look like a man who had slept under a hedge to me. What time was that?'

'Cock-shut time,' the girl said, after a think. She was a country girl at heart and though woodcock were not exactly common in Westminster, old habits died hard.

'Or thereabouts,' her mistress agreed with a sigh. 'Sunday, I know that.'

The maid primmed up her lips. How the mistress put up with the master's filthy ways she would never know. Coming back all hours, reeking of Attar of Roses or worse. And the linen; she tried not to think of the linen, because it turned her stomach, it really did.

'Never mind about it, Tab,' Mistress Forman gave her a kindly pat to send her on her way. 'He'll just be trying to impress the boys, you know how he is. Have you put those sheets out, yet? We'll have rain before long and we need to get the worst of the wet out of them before then. The master does hate wet washing about the house, you know that.'

'Never mind,' the maid said, acidly, 'I suppose he could always go and sleep under a hedge somewhere.'

'One day,' his wife said, 'he may have to. Even a worm turns in the end, or so I have heard tell.'

The maid shuddered. Worms. Newts. Dead pigeons. This house would drive her to Bedlam before it was done, of that she was sure.

Tom Sledd had always been an early riser, but in Bedlam that way madness lay. As long as he could stay asleep, or at least feign sleep, he could pretend he was elsewhere. The knight on horseback story was wearing a little thin, but it was still something he could call on when the noise and smell got too bad. At the moment, though, his mind was like a nest of vipers and he couldn't forget how many people had denied him over the last few days. Will Kemp he would expect it of; the man was a total shit. Hal Dignam was better, but completely under Kemp's thumb. Shaxsper, though; Shaxsper was supposed to be a friend, but he had let him down as well. But none was as sharp as the viper's bite of Kit's exit last night, swarming up the walls and disappearing into the night, leaving him there, in the cold and dark, for what might be the rest of his life. He put his head down in his arms and curled up with his sorrow.

The poet stirred beside him and looked at him covertly through lowered lashes. He could tell that his best efforts were beginning to fail and he didn't want this innocent man to end up as mad as everyone else in this Godforsaken Hell. As mad as all but one, perhaps he should say. He lifted his eyes and looked around the room with a carefully contrived blank stare. As mad as all but two. He put out his hand and laid it gently on Sledd's shoulder, patting it absently. He knew what it was like to be lost, though fear had not been part of his life for many a long year now.

'Well, Tom,' he whispered, so low that only his own soul could hear it. 'Perhaps it's time I brought this madness to a close.'

'What was that?' A rough boot kicked his foot.

The poet crossed his eyes and raised his voice. 'The moon's my constant mistress,' he intoned. 'And the lowly owl my marrow.'

'Do what?' Nat was leaning forward, listening.

The poet spread his arms and shrugged, wagging his head from side to side. 'The flaming drake and the night crow make me music to my sorrow.' He smiled at the gaoler and dropped his head again.

Nat stood looking at the poet and the theatre manager for a moment longer, then spat neatly into the straw. He had got the feeling from time to time that the poet could tell a hawk from a handsaw, but this morning removed those doubts. The man was as mad as any man here, madder than most. His wife had seen the back of him forever, that was certain. He smiled at the memory. A pretty little piece she was as well. Too pretty to be tied to an old fool like this one. He gave the poet another kick for good measure and moved on. That was one thing about working in Bedlam – every day was different and every day was fun.

Matthias had missed his calling when he took up his apprenticeship with Simon Forman – the stage had lost a tragedian of some talent. He took a step forward and looked slowly around his little audience. Two of them would know he was lying. He knew there was a risk that the third man there would as well, but it was a risk he was prepared to take.

He addressed himself to Forman. 'As Timothy and Gerard both know,' he began, 'the mounts provided for us were not of the best quality.'

Timothy snorted and got an indignant glance from his colleague. Timothy made a rueful face and raised a hand in apology.

'Mine was slow and had a tendency to go lame. At the end of ten miles or so, I could hardly bear its halting gait and so I stopped under a sheltering tree – it had come on to rain

– and felt its legs, one by one. When I got to the stifle of its left rear, I knew I had found the trouble. It was hot and felt hard and bruised; a kick from another horse, most likely.'

Gerard laced his fingers together in distress. Any animal with an injury hurt him to the quick, even when it was entirely imaginary.

'I had no horse liniment with me or any other physick, so I laid my hands on the sore part and willed the pain into me. It was like a lightning bolt, straight through my body. I felt it leave the top of my head, blowing my hair about as it did so and making a crack like that of doom.'

Forman nodded. Having a horse doctor in his household might well pay dividends. Men had always been hard to attract and keep as clients, but everyone knew a man would pay good money to physick his horses that he wouldn't spend on his wife.

'My mount was grateful, you could tell. He nuzzled my shoulder as I walked back round to pick up his reins and, as I did so, a woman appeared from where she had been secreted in the hedge. She was of somewhat wild appearance and I must say I was dubious; I feared she had a rough companion who might do me harm.'

Timothy almost gave another snort, but managed to withhold it. Firstly, the whole tale was a tarradiddle. Matthias couldn't care less about another creature in the world except himself and, secondly, he was built like a brick privy, so any rough trade would come off the worst.

Gerard hardly dare breathe. His own adventures were as nothing compared to these. He forgot that he already knew that Matthias had spent the best part of a week being fed and pampered by his mother and sundry local ladies and allowed himself to be lost in the story.

'She was alone, however, and said that her mistress was ill in their house just over the hill. They had fallen on hard times and they could pay me but little, but she could see I had the healing in me and she begged me to visit her mistress, if only to bring her comfort.'

Forman nodded magisterially. He had had his doubts when he took on Matthias, but his trust was being repaid. This was how you got a foothold in new territory, grew a business. Timothy wiped the smirk off his face. He was rather impressed how Matthias wove small facts into the fiction, giving it an air of verisimilitude.

'A bit of the old special massage, I suppose,' he muttered out of the corner of his mouth and got a kick on the shin for his pains.

Matthias dropped his head modestly. 'I do not need to tell you, Master, how I proceeded. I remembered everything you have ever taught us about the administration of herbs and I am happy to relate that they worked to perfection. Within the hour, the mistress of the house was up and about and I was given lodgings for the night. By morning, the hall was full of the importunate sick of the countryside and – as you know from the modest purse I gave to you – they had little but they gave it gladly.'

Forman hoped that the importunate sick had not given their last groat. It did no good to bleed any area dry. 'And where was this place?' he asked.

'Umm . . .' Matthias looked at Timothy and Gerard, who were no help. 'We had decided to let our mounts lead the way. So I suppose . . .' he looked round again but they were still not meeting his eye, 'it would be north. Northish, in any case.'

Forman looked annoyed for the first time. 'You mean you don't know where this place is?' he asked, incredulously. 'Whatever is the point of going out into the world if you don't know where in the world you have been?' He tapped his hand on the arm of his chair, irritated with the great oaf. 'Would you know it again if you saw it?'

Matthias nodded enthusiastically. 'I'm sure I would, Master,' he said. He had been having some rather vivid dreams of the French governess, to the distress of the others who shared his bed and another week off would be very welcome. 'Shall I go and—'

Forman flapped a hand. 'No, no. Your work here is behind-hand. Perhaps in a week or so, depending on this dreaded Pestilence. I think now we will hear from Gerard. You brought us no gold, Gerard, but some food. Not what I was expecting, but roots tasting of oyster – now, that is surely a story?'

But it wasn't. Gerard was no liar and his story was more
or less exactly what had happened. Yes, he added a couple
of dozen grateful clients. Yes, he exaggerated where he had
been; as he saw it, it wouldn't help if he told Forman
that he had gone to the next bend in the Thames and stayed
there a week, surviving on the tag-end of berries in the
hedgerow and trout from the stream. Like Matthias, but for
a completely different reason, he couldn't say precisely where
he had gone, but he thought it, too, was north. North-east,
perhaps. Or thereabouts.

Forman was disappointed. He had had high hopes of
Gerard. He had never expected him to be a big earner, but
there was something about his country-boy looks and his
innocent demeanour that should have brought the rich
widows swarming like wasps to the honeypot. Too honest,
that was his trouble. Too straightforward. He made himself
a note to teach him the massage – it would be a difficult
conversation with one so unworldly, but with it under his
belt, so to speak, he would be unbeatable.

'Timothy?' Forman gestured his third apprentice forward.
'What of you and your adventures?' He held up a hand as the
lad drew a deep breath. 'Not the foal. We know about the foal.
Tell us what happened *before* that.'

'I went south,' Timothy told them. 'South-west, I suppose,
to be more accurate. I do confess I called in at my aunt's
first, but,' and he glanced at Matthias, 'I didn't stay there.
You had told us not to rely on friends or family, so all I did
was tell her I was not going to be in London and then I set
off. I didn't reach the coast, though. I came into a village – a
small town, maybe – clustered around a big house. A few of
the hovels were boarded up and the Pestilence was obviously
in the place. I had no luck knocking on doors until I thought
of my mask. I went round a corner and tied it on and then I
was welcome everywhere. Most people are still well there,
but they bought my preventative herbs with any pence they
had and were grateful.'

'Did you get into the big house, though?' Forman leaned
forward. Follow the money, that was his motto.

'After a day or so, I did,' Timothy confirmed. 'The cook

there was not feeling well. It turned out that having a waist measurement two yards round was not helping her and her liver was engorged.' He looked up to check on Forman's expression. He did not want to overreach himself. 'In my opinion. I could be wrong.'

Forman bestowed a gentle smile of condescension. 'If your tinctures did the trick, you may well be right,' he said.

Timothy basked a little. 'The cook rules that household. The master is often away – they didn't tell me what he did, but he has other houses, they said.'

Forman almost rubbed his hands together. He could all but feel the weight of gold in his lap. 'And where was this place?' he asked.

Timothy smiled. 'I'm sorry. Did I not say? The big house was called Barn Elms. I could take you there, if you want. But if I may be a little boastful for a moment, Master, I don't believe there is a person in the house or town who will need physick for a while. I was busy day and night when I was there.'

Forman sat back and beamed at his boys. 'I am very proud of you all,' he said. 'I had considered using my scrying glass but I said to my wife, "No, Mistress Forman," I said to her, "no. I can trust my boys. I know they will do their best." You had misfortunes, yes, of course you did. Gerard, you happened upon a poor place, but you were made welcome and that is the main thing. You, Timothy, lost your money when your mare foaled – Matthias!' A train of thought interrupted him. 'Make a note to speak to the livery stable about that; they must owe us money for the safe delivery of a healthy foal.'

Matthias went to his desk and made a note in the ledger.

'Where was I?'

'Me,' Matthias said, smugly.

'Yes,' Forman said, looking him straight in the eye. 'Well, clearly, your story is a lot of hogwash. Well told, but ultimately too ridiculous for words. Learn from your fellows and always tell the truth. But the purse was useful, so we will let that go for now. Also, a messenger has brought you a letter.'

Matthias blushed scarlet. 'A . . . letter?'

'In French. I don't read it myself, but it was easy to tell it was of a smutty nature. I will not have smut!' He beat both hands on the arms of his chair.

'May I . . . have it?' Matthias said.

'Mistress Forman put it on the scullery fire,' Forman told him. 'There is no room for smut in my house. I will not have it!'

The three apprentices stood in front of him. Even Timothy and Gerard felt admonished and they had done nothing wrong. Forman was like that – he could make you feel like a lark or a worm with a turn of a phrase.

'But on with the work. Umm . . . Gerard. Would you like to come through into my sanctum? I need to have a word . . .'

The tower of St Ethedreda's stood tall and square in the noonday sun. October was proving a tricky month and the almanacs were wrong again. It wasn't exactly warm, but Marlowe's bay was sweating by the time he took the rise to Hatfield's gates. The arms of Burghley, quartered and requartered, fluttered above the red stonework, and ancient carts creaked and rattled their way between the house and the town, laden with every conceivable provision that a great household would need.

There was another flag over the chapel. This one was plain black and hung at half-mast, drifting with the Hertfordshire breeze. A flunkey took Marlowe's horse under the arch of the gate and he was taken, saddlebags and all, into a vast library, of the type he had not seen since his Corpus Christi days. Huge maps hung on the panelled walls, worlds of faerie where sea monsters snorted in the oceans and anthropophagi watched him warily, their eyes in their chests. The coastlines were guesswork and Marlowe knew that men like Hawkins, Drake, Ralegh and Frobisher, who had actually seen those coastlines, would have something unpleasant to say about them. While he waited, he perused the leather-bound tomes, recognizing most of them and in awe of some. These were not the front of a parvenu, bought by the yard for the look of the thing. It was obvious from the worn spines and the faded gilding that Burghley actually *read* them, and more than once. Marlowe was impressed.

'Master Marlowe?' Another voice. Another place. But the hand hovered near the dagger all the same. A tall, courtly-looking man stood there, in Burghley's livery with a staff of office in his hand. 'Welcome, sir. I am James Cruikshank, His Lordship's steward.'

Marlowe bowed and Cruikshank did likewise. 'His Lordship has asked me to assist you in any way that I can. Would you care to take refreshment first?'

'Thank you, but I would like to see Mistress Eunice before I do.'

Cruikshank nodded and took Marlowe's saddlebags, passing them to a lackey who had appeared from nowhere. As the playwright surmised, Hatfield was riddled with secret passages that made a murderer's job easy and an investigator's a nightmare. He followed Cruikshank through a winding passageway almost devoid of light, until they came to an oak door set into solid stone. 'This was the Lady Chapel in the old days,' Cruikshank told him, 'named for St Etheldreda. You'll find Mistress Eunice in there.'

'You're not coming with me?' Marlowe asked.

Cruikshank blinked. He had been told by Burghley's messenger that this man had no fear of anything on earth, except perhaps the Pestilence. Did he baulk, then, at the presence of a corpse?

'I have servants to muster, sir,' the steward explained, 'and Lord Burghley's mule to walk. The animal gets tetchy when His Lordship is not here.' He bowed and left.

As it turned out, Mistress Eunice was not alone. The sun was flitting through the stained glass of the window where the saint herself glowed in reds and blues, throwing strange colours onto the already discoloured face of the Cecils' old nurse. Another woman sat beside her, in the weeds of mourning, a rosary in her hands which she quickly hid under her apron. She got up as Marlowe went in and bobbed a curtsey.

'Madam,' Marlowe said, 'I am—'

'I know who you are, sir,' she said, 'and your business. I was the Second Finder, if the law recognizes such a thing.'

It didn't. According to him, Burghley had been the Second

Finder after the maid, and it was the maid that Marlowe needed to speak to next. This was awkward. 'Madame,' he said. 'You'll forgive me, but I need to examine Mistress Eunice. Her body.'

The woman was horrified and clutched at her coif. 'That would be most unseemly,' she said.

'Perhaps,' Marlowe agreed, 'but if it will tell us how she died . . .?'

The woman reflected for a moment. 'Do what you must,' she said, through pursed lips. 'I shall wait outside.'

Noo-Noo looked as old as the stone on which she lay. What had once been an altar was her resting place now, before the funeral of the next day would take her to a better place altogether. Marlowe carefully untied the cloth around her head. The woman had been dead for three days now; the stiffness of death had left her limbs and the skin was mottled, especially around the throat. Burghley had been right. There was severe bruising here where someone had held her roughly, and a scratch on her cheek below the right eye. Three thumbprints were clearly delineated amongst the yellowing bruises on the right-hand side of her face and, on the same side of her neck, the indentation of one fingernail, left too long, was repeated, like a line of punctuation down her throat. Someone – or several someones, but Marlowe doubted that – had held her face and her neck not once but many times until she had died. He checked her fingernails. They were clean and unbroken with nothing under them to say that she had fought with her killer. Noo-Noo was small and old. A child could have silenced her. And she was silent still; Marlowe could learn nothing more from her.

Lettys was the First Finder and Marlowe found her waiting for him in the Great Hall, the reliable, solid frame of Cruikshank standing behind her.

'If I may talk to Lettys alone, Master Cruikshank?'

Everything about that idea, the steward disliked. These were *his* people; more, they lived under the roof of the most powerful man in England. But Burghley had spoken – Marlowe must be given his head, so there it was. He bowed curtly and withdrew.

Marlowe sat down on a settle and patted the seat alongside him to encourage her to sit too. She perched on the edge and looked at him anxiously. She was probably twenty and had been born on the Hatfield estate. She was still in shock, twisting her fingers together in dread of this strange, dark man and the questions he was going to ask. She had seen great men coming and going to Burghley's household all her life, but this one was different.

'Lettys,' he spoke softly, sensing her unease, 'it was you who first found Eunice?'

'Yes, sir.' He could barely hear her.

'Tell me, and I don't want to distress you, was she peaceful? Lying on her bed?'

Lettys blinked back the tears. Bad enough that she had seen it once. Now, because of this strange man, she had to see it twice. 'No, sir. She looked . . . she looked like she had seen the Devil. Or so I imagine. I've never seen him myself.' And she crossed herself, for all this was Burghley's household and the Queen they all served was head of the Protestant church.

'You're lucky, Lettys,' Marlowe murmured. 'Did it seem to you that anyone had been in her room, recently, I mean, before you found her?'

'I don't rightly know, sir,' she muttered, eyes flicking from side to side. 'Old Eunice didn't have no visitors as a rule, 'cept me and Betty. The master would go in when he could and of course, Master Robert – Robyn, Eunice called him – would visit. But mainly, it was me and Betty.'

'Betty?'

'The other maid who does for her. I have the days. Betty has the nights. We cross over at dawn. There was one thing, though.'

'Oh?' Marlowe was all ears. 'What was that?'

'Well . . . and I haven't told no one this, sir, but . . . well, I should have, but I thought I'd be laughed at. I thought I might tell Dr Parry, but I didn't.'

'Who's Dr Parry?'

'He's the vicar of Hatfield, sir. He holds services in the chapel sometimes. I thought he might be able to explain it, as he's a clever man and all.'

'Explain what, Lettys?'

'Well, old Eunice, she was a good woman. Worshipped the Lord all her life. If anyone should go to Heaven, it's her, sir, don't you think?'

'I'm sure she has, Lettys,' Marlowe said, soothingly.

'Well . . . if that's the case . . .' Lettys was feeling her way, searching for the words in a situation she found alien and terrifying, all at once, 'why was her face so stricken? If the Angel of the Lord came for her, why that? And then . . . then . . .' the girl was clearly wrestling with something inside her, 'what about this?' She pulled something out from a pocket of her apron, held fast in a closed fist.

Marlowe frowned. They were both staring at Lettys's hand, but the girl seemed loath to open it. Gently, Marlowe prised her fingers upwards and looked at her palm. A small gemstone twinkled there, like a frozen tear. 'Where did you find this, Lettys?' he asked.

'It was on her forehead, sir, like a star it was, shining in the early morning light. Now, I don't believe the Devil would leave that, sir; indeed I don't. It was an angel left that. So why was old Eunice so mortal feared? Angels are good things, ain't they?'

Marlowe forbore to remind her that Lucifer was once the morning star, son of the dawn, most beloved of all angels in Heaven. She didn't need to know that if the alternative gave her comfort. 'They are, Lettys,' Marlowe nodded. 'Do you mind if I keep this?'

The maid Betty was of little help. Older than Lettys and more a no-nonsense woman of the world, she had seen and heard nothing after cock-shut when she'd bedded old Eunice down and heard her say her prayers and had gone to bed herself. It was windy that night and that bloody dog of Harry Hawkins's hadn't shut up until way gone midnight and Betty was going to have words with him about it; but other matters intervened, what with the old girl dying and all. The master, he was very cut up about it and she, Betty, had had to slap that stupid girl Lettys around the head a few times to calm her down. But Betty slept along the passage from old Eunice and she'd have heard anybody going past her door; she was sure of that. When Marlowe thanked her, walked away and turned to whisper her name, Betty was oblivious, however, so Marlowe was unconvinced. As far as he knew, a whole legion of devils could have tramped past Betty's door and she'd have been none the wiser.

Yes, Harry Hawkins had a dog. In fact, he had forty of them. They actually belonged to His Lordship, of course, and, not being a keen huntsman himself, he kept the pack for visiting nobs, one of whom, the Earl of Rutland, had turned up only the other day, mighty put out by the fact that Burghley wasn't there. Not to be too put out, he had borrowed His Lordship's pack and gone hunting anyway. None of His Lordship's dogs ever barked after midnight and if that old besom Betty Horsemonger said they did, she was lying. Master Marlowe might want to have a word with Jem Layton, though. He formed a sort of unofficial night Watch at Hatfield. After all, His Lordship was the most powerful man in England, some said in the world. And you couldn't be too careful.

It turned out that Jem Layton couldn't be careful at all. Much of his time as commander of the Hatfield night Watch was spent dressing up in burgonet, breast and back. The four men who served as his company couldn't hit a barn door with their matchlocks and His Lordship only paid them because he was too nice not to and their presence had made the late Lady Burghley feel secure, even though she was a better shot than they were. No, there'd been nothing untoward going on at Hatfield the night old Eunice had breathed her last. It was her time, wasn't it? Jem Layton had no time himself for all this hysteria, with lions whelping in the streets. The sanctimonious old trout should have gone years ago. Jem had never liked her. He didn't like the vicar, either, so maybe Master Marlowe might want to talk to him.

He did, but not before he had talked to everybody else. The staff were utterly loyal to the Cecils; there could be no question of that. To each other now, that was a different matter.

Even so, Marlowe could discern nothing murderous in any of them. It was just the usual griping of any group of people forced to work together by circumstance. You can choose your friends but you can't choose your fellow-servants.

What concerned Marlowe more was the steady stream of visitors and hangers-on who were constantly in and out of Hatfield. The Muse's darling was horrified that none of them was a playwright or a poet or even a musician. And he remembered that, almost uniquely among the Privy Council, Lord Burghley did not have his own theatrical troupe to entertain Her Majesty. What Burghley went for were scholars, men like himself who spoke Latin, Greek and Hebrew and who read Cicero for laughs. The Earl of Rutland had arrived on the day that Burghley had left for London, distraught over the loss of his old nurse. The earl had brought ten or twenty hangers-on with him, all ambitious as the Devil and no doubt strangers to scruple. Days earlier, a team of acrobats had arrived but Cruikshank had given them their marching orders. There were lawyers, physicians, supplicants, merchants, knights of the shire, all traipsing over Hatfield as if they owned the place. There was simply no way to account for all of them.

So it was an exhausted projectioner-playwright who pushed open the vestry door of St Etheldreda as night fell.

'Dr Parry?'

'That's me.' A large, florid, almost cherubic man was folding away his chasuble. 'Ah, aren't you Christopher Marlowe?'

'I am.' Marlowe was impressed and suspicious, all at once. It was not for the first time.

'And I'm not him, by the way.'

'Him?' The vicar had lost him already.

'The Doctor Parry who is chaplain to Her Majesty. That's my cousin, somewhere down the line.'

'How do you know me?' Marlowe asked.

'The Muse's darling? Come, come, Master Marlowe, no false modesty. You are the greatest playwright in England.'

'Have you seen anything of mine?' Marlowe had long ago stopped blushing at flattery like that.

'*Dido*,' Parry began counting on his fingers. '*Tamburlaine.*

The Jew, of course. And, if memory serves, there was more than a little of you in *Henry VI*, Shakespeare's effort.'

'I couldn't possibly comment,' Marlowe smiled.

'*Faustus*, now,' Parry closed to him, 'I've heard *that* is something special. If you dared God out of his Heaven with *Tamburlaine*, what have you done with *Faustus*? I've yet to see it.'

'No one has seen it,' Marlowe told him, 'except for a select few.'

'Then there's hope?' The vicar's eyes shone.

'Not while Master Tilney is Master of the Revels and there is a "y" in the day.'

'Shame,' the vicar frowned, 'a great shame. May I say what an honour it is to have you at St Ethedreda's?'

'Gracious, Dr Parry,' Marlowe bowed. 'Thank you.' He took in the heavy brass crucifix on the vestry wall, in marked contrast to the whitewashed simplicity of the nave. 'You have a beautiful church.'

'Thank *you*,' Parry smiled. 'It has stood here, holding the poor parishioners of Hatfield in its hand, since the thirteenth century.'

'When the Pope ruled.'

The smile froze on the vicar's face. 'Indeed,' he said. 'But I'll wager you didn't come to talk about ecclesiastical architecture – or ancient history.' He offered Marlowe a seat.

'Eunice Brown,' the playwright said.

'Ah yes, poor Eunice. Tragic. Tragic.'

'You know she was murdered, Dr Parry?'

'Surely not!' The vicar looked askance.

'You visited the body?'

'I was called in, yes. Administered the last rites.'

'In Latin?'

'No.' Parry grew frosty. 'In the Queen's broad English. Why do you ask?'

Marlowe chuckled. 'St Etheldreda,' he said, leaning back and cradling one knee, 'your patron saint. She was a princess of East Anglia who wanted to be a nun. Unfortunately, her father had other ideas and she was forced into marriage. When her husband died three years later she fled to a convent in Ely.

Her father was the persistent type, however, and he insisted she marry again – Ecgfrith this time, Prince of Northumbria.'

'I really don't see—'

'She ran away again. Etheldreda was clearly as determined as her dear papa. This time she put on a hair shirt next to her skin and spent the rest of her life praying every night, all night.'

'Fascinating, Master Marlowe.' Parry was smiling again. 'And largely accurate. But I assure you, I didn't choose the name of the church. Neither do I espouse the miracles with which she is associated.'

'Don't you?' Marlowe asked. 'Then why . . . this?' He lunged for the little altar to his left and hauled off the cloth.

'Sacrilege!' Parry screamed, but Marlowe hadn't started yet. He drove his right boot into the wooden panel between the carved ogee arches and a box fell out. Before Parry could leave his seat, screaming as he was, Marlowe had wrenched open the lid and held up the desiccated hand lying there.

'Tell me,' he said levelly, looking Parry straight in the eye, 'am I shaking the hand of a saint?'

'I . . .' Parry's shoulders slumped. Denials now seemed pointless, but he tried anyway. 'I didn't know that was there,' he said. 'Churches all over the country must be full of them, foul relics of superstitious Papist claptrap.'

'I'm sure you're right,' Marlowe told him, 'and well done to be able to recite the mantra by the way – "Foul relics. Papist claptrap" – excellent Puritan rhetoric, isn't it? And I'd be prepared to believe you, were it not for the polished appearance of this reliquary,' he kicked it with his foot, 'and the ease with which the lid opened. This has been handled regularly, recently and – I am prepared to wager – by you.'

It was all over for Parry. He could feel the flames licking around his feet already. And him, the parish priest of Hatfield. 'What . . . what are you going to do?' he asked. 'And please . . . put that back.' He was talking about the saint's relic. Marlowe tossed the hand into the box and sat down again.

'Tell me about Eunice,' he said.

Parry sighed. 'Eunice was one of my parishioners,' he said. 'My *real* parishioners, that is.' His voice had dropped to a whisper. 'The old religion, Marlowe. The *real* religion. I administered the last rites in Latin, as Eunice would have wished.'

Marlowe nodded. 'Does Burghley know?' he asked. 'Cecil?'

'God, no!' Parry was horrified. 'A stauncher pair of Puritans I've yet to meet. And before you ask, my cousin, the Queen's chaplain, knows nothing of this either. Perish the thought.'

Marlowe looked at the man. For much of his adult life, at least since he had met Francis Walsingham, the Queen's estimable former Spymaster, he had been hunting Papists – and finding them, too, very often in the most unlikely places. It came easily to him. But today, he was hunting a murderer. 'Is that why you killed her, Dr Parry?' he asked. 'Eunice? Everybody I've spoken to called her a good woman, devout, Christian to her fingertips. Were you afraid she'd finger you, inadvertently, at her end? That she'd send someone to find her Catholic Father as she faced her Doom? That nice, accommodating Father Parry, who had always been there for her, at secret Masses without number?'

'Of course not,' Parry said, shaking his head. There were tears in his eyes. 'Oh, I won't pretend I've never considered her doing that. She wouldn't have meant any harm, of course, but when a soul's time comes, who knows what truths spill from the mouth?'

'Who indeed?' Marlowe nodded. Then he stood, his mind made up, his questions answered. 'Oh, by the way,' he rummaged in his purse, 'have you seen this before?' He held up the little gem that Lettys had given him, left on a good woman's forehead by an angel.

Parry looked at it closely. He took it and held it up to the dying light of the vestry window. 'A gemstone,' he said. 'No value, I wouldn't think, but as you can imagine, I am no expert. What is it?'

Marlowe took it back. 'It's a relic, Dr Parry,' he said, 'but not the type you believe in.' And he turned to go.

'Marlowe,' Parry was on his feet too. 'Are you going to tell anyone?'

Marlowe looked at him. 'About the hand of a dead woman some ancient, misguided priest of the old religion secreted away years or even centuries ago? No, Doctor, I don't think so. Oh . . .' he opened the door, 'I'd have offered you tickets to my next work, *The Massacre at Paris*, but there's no theatre to put it on in at the moment. And besides,' he winked at the man, 'it's about a clique of rather nasty Catholics – and I don't think you'd like that at all.'

Marlowe rested that night at Hatfield, under the eaves near Burghley's library, soaking up the culture even through the oak panelling. He went over his little chat with the vicar of Hatfield in his mind. The man, he knew, had been a Cambridge scholar, of St John's, no less, which Robert Greene had attended. He had once run a parish in the Vintry, not a stone's throw from Dowgate, where Robert Greene had died. And here he was again, a secret Papist, in at the death of Eunice Brown. But it didn't fit. Nothing fitted. But he made a mental note not to overlook the vicar of Hatfield and he slept with his dagger under his pillow.

ELEVEN

A madman stood at the cross outside St Paul's that Thursday, reminding anyone who cared to listen that the Pestilence had come because of the world's wickedness, that London was the new Gomorrah and that the blackness of death was all that lay ahead. Some confused souls stood around, wide-eyed, listening. Others, dyed-in-the-wool Puritans, nodded solemnly and intoned, 'Too true, brother'. Two members of the Watch, who had been listening to this predictable drivel for years, moved him on with prods from their halberds and threats of the Bridewell.

Marlowe had heard it all before too, but he was not at Harvey's house in Peternoster Row that morning for lunacy, Tom Sledd's unresolved fate notwithstanding. He was there to continue a conversation he had started in Cambridge days earlier. He was there to talk to Gabriel Harvey. The man's hapless secretary was still carrying books, but as soon as he saw Marlowe, he remembered his handiness with a dagger and dropped the lot.

'Is he in?' Marlowe asked the man, who stood frozen to the spot. The playwright decided to give him another option. 'Is he out?'

'What in the name of God . . .?' Gabriel Harvey appeared at the top of the stairs, still in his nightgown. 'Marlowe! Do you know what time it is?'

'Eight o'clock by Paul's time,' Marlowe said, cheerily. 'Time for all good Christians to be up and about their business.' He was already climbing the stairs. 'And what exactly *is* your business these days, Dr Harvey?'

'Marlowe, I—'

'No,' the playwright held up his hand, 'Don't tell me. Sticking your nose into other people's business.' He had reached the landing. 'And you are *very* good at it; possibly the finest in the field.'

'I don't care for your attitude,' Harvey snapped.

'And I don't give a flying fart what you care for,' Marlowe said, now that he was face to face with the man. 'I'm not Secundus Convictus now, Doctor. I am the most famous playwright in London. What are you going to do? Give me a bad review?'

Harvey was white with anger. 'One day, you'll dare God out of his Heaven once too often, blasphemer,' he rasped.

Marlowe chuckled. 'Tell me,' he said, 'whose idea was the proctors? Yours or Andrewes's?'

'I don't know what you're talking about.' Harvey tried to play the innocent, but it was less than convincing.

'All right,' Marlowe said, leaning against the wall. 'We'll let that pass for now. Tell me instead why you went to see Robert Greene shortly before he died.'

'I told you.' Harvey had lost none of the pomposity that Marlowe remembered from his university days. 'I was passing.'

'Yes, but you lied, didn't you? Men like you don't pass Dowgate, especially when there's Pestilence in the wind. What was the real reason? Did you bring him a comforting broth of mushrooms?'

Before Harvey could answer, Marlowe shoulder-barged the door into Harvey's bedroom. There was a shriek and a woman was sitting up in bed, pulling her nightdress closed and gasping, open-mouthed. Harvey grabbed Marlowe's sleeve, but the university professor-turned-critic was no match for a projectioner and he found himself kneeling on the floor, his head wrenched back with Marlowe's fingers tangled in his hair.

'Don't hurt him, Master Marlowe,' the woman found the composure to say.

'Hastings,' Harvey gurgled, his neck extended by Marlowe's grip, 'fetch a constable, for God's sake.'

'Hastings,' Marlowe counter-ordered, 'stay exactly where you are.'

The dithering secretary on the ground floor had only hopped onto his right foot. Now he hopped back onto his left. Marlowe was looking at the woman. 'You seem to know my name, Madame,' he said. 'May I know yours? I assume it isn't Mrs Harvey.'

'You assume right,' she said. 'It's Greene. Doll Greene.'

'No better than you should be.'

There was another half-strangled gurgle from Harvey, but Doll Greene could clearly handle herself. 'What do you mean by that?' she snapped, checking that all was well in her frontage. Harvey's liberality didn't run to a four-poster bed, so she had little to cover herself with.

'I must confess I've never really understood the phrase,' Marlowe said, as if they were discussing the weather, 'along with "buttering no parsnips" and "how's your father?".'. It *was* Mrs Isam's assessment of you, however.'

'That hypocritical bitch!' Doll Greene hissed. 'She's a bawd, Master Marlowe, a keeper of brothels.'

'Your late husband seemed quite content with that,' Marlowe said. 'Oh, my condolences, by the way.'

'Condolences?' she sneered. 'If memory serves, Robyn couldn't stand you.'

'Your memory *does* serve,' Marlowe nodded, 'but then, he couldn't stand old Gabriel here and you both seem to have got over that.' He let go of Harvey's hair and the critic-professor flopped forward, trying to ease the pain in his neck. 'At least,' Marlowe went on, 'I know what Gabriel was doing in Dowgate. Picking you up, I'll wager.'

'I haven't lived with Robyn for years,' Doll said.

Harvey was on his feet again, still fuming, but trying to keep his distance from Marlowe. 'I went to Greene's lodgings to find out what he'd been writing. There was a rumour it was pretty libellous stuff – about me; about all of us, come to that. But somebody had beaten me to it. All his papers had gone.'

And Marlowe knew exactly where they had ended up, on the table of the Queen's Spymaster in Whitehall. How they had got there remained something of a mystery.

There was a faint wailing sound along the landing. Marlowe looked up to see a tousle-haired blond lad, perhaps ten, yawning and scratching himself.

'Fortunatus!' Doll shrieked. 'Go back to bed. The grown-ups are talking.'

The unaptly named boy yawned again, shrugged and did as he was told.

'Gabriel,' Doll Greene snapped at him, 'make yourself scarce. Master Marlowe and I have things to discuss.'

Harvey opened his mouth to say something, but thought better of it and marched down the stairs with as much dignity as he could gather around him, fetching the hapless Hastings a smart one around the side of the head as he passed. To Marlowe's horror, Doll Greene was leaning forward and patting the bed beside her. As invitations went, it left a lot to be desired. He stayed where he was, with his back pressed firmly against the doorframe.

'Could you close the door?' she purred, loosening her nightgown front and showing an altogether different side of her than the shrieking harridan of a few moments ago.

'I could,' Marlowe conceded, 'but I don't intend to. What is it you want, Mistress Greene?'

She closed the nightgown again. All right, Robert Greene and Gabriel Harvey had fallen for her charms, but she was realist enough to realize it couldn't happen *every* time. 'I'll be blunt,' she said. 'Gabriel was rooting around in Robyn's things for any plays, poems and other trifles he could . . . what's that word you University men use? Purloin. So much less criminal-sounding than steal, don't you think? He found nothing, of course. But he left everything else there. Clothes, personal possessions, money. I can't go and get them. Mrs Isam won't give me the time of day. She likes Gabriel, I think, and that reprobate Simon Forman even more. But you've met her, haven't you, Master Marlowe?'

'I have,' he nodded.

'Well, could you pop back? Pick up whatever the poor old sod left behind, other than his winding sheet? You were always my late husband's enemy. Will you be his friend now?'

'I doubt there'll be much left,' Marlowe said. 'Especially money.'

He looked at her, not the most appealing of women; and one with a truly dreadful taste in men. Even so, he heard himself say, 'I'll do what I can.'

Ingram Frizer puffed thoughtfully on his clay pipe. There was some dispute about who had brought tobacco from the New

World but, whoever it was, Ingram Frizer was very grateful. For those moments in life when nothing is going right, tobacco was the only answer. Oh, and ale of course. And perhaps a hot woman or two.

'So, where's he gone?' He passed the pipe to Nicholas Skeres who squinted sideways at him.

'Who?'

'Henslowe. Last time I saw him, he was at the front of the queue, nose to nose with Kit Marlowe outside the Palace of Whitehall.'

'He was.' Skeres remembered. He didn't actually share Frizer's love of tobacco. It was rather a noxious weed, if he was being honest. But being honest wasn't really what Nicholas Skeres did, so he puffed away, just to be sociable, trying to forget that his eyes were watering and his throat felt as if it had been brutally skinned.

'I heard,' Will Kemp took the pipe from Skeres, 'he'd discovered a long-lost auntie out on the Essex marshes somewhere. Time for family time, so to speak.'

'Who?' Hal Dignam was last in the line; by the time the pipe reached him, it had gone out.

The four of them sat side by side on the top of the wall that marked the edge of Master Sackerson's pit. The grizzled, ancient animal looked up at them with his piggy eyes and used his long, pink tongue to lick his nose.

'Wish I could do that,' Kemp said, trying the same technique. 'Might add to the repertoire.'

Frizer *could* do that, but seldom felt the need. 'I don't think you boys are taking this very seriously,' he said, a frown creasing his forehead. 'We were all there the other night, sticking our necks out and our heads over the parapet for the sake of theatre. And for all his fine words, old Henslowe just melted away. They'll be watching all of us now, you mark my words.'

'It was bloody dark,' Kemp remonstrated with his fellow-actor, 'and seen one torch-carrying troublemaker, seen 'em all. We'll be all right. Oh, Henslowe's a marked man, that's for sure. Nice of you to dob him in, by the way, Hal, shouting out his name like that.'

'Who?' Dignam asked.

'What about old Kit, though, eh?' Skeres said. He'd been worrying about it for days. 'Do you think he was in on it, you know, with the Whitehall nobs?'

Frizer thought for a moment. 'Well, he's a University wit, ain't he?' He was reasoning aloud. 'Got more in common with them than us, I suppose.'

'Yes, but his dad's a bootmaker back in Canterbury,' Kemp said. 'You couldn't get more one of us if you tried.'

'Tried what, Will?' Hal Dignam was trying to relight the pipe. ''Ere, do you think bears drink smoke?'

Will Kemp was nearest, so he did the honours, slapping Dignam around the head in time-honoured clown tradition. And it was just the sheerest of luck that he didn't fall into the Bear Pit.

Kit Marlowe was pleasantly surprised how much time the closing of the theatres had given him. He could go where he wanted, when he wanted, without the twin demons of Sledd and Henslowe, one on each shoulder, scolding him for not attending rehearsals or not delivering a rewrite of Act III. He knew he would soon come to miss it but, for now, it was making his life rather easy. For instance, instead of dashing off to the Rose this forenoon having roused Harvey and his unlovely paramour from bed, he had time to visit John Dee, for some well-needed advice and a chance to talk through the teeming ideas which thronged his head.

Jane Dee opened the door to him with a face like thunder, swiftly overlaid with sun when she saw who it was. Looking left and right, she grabbed him by the wrist and pulled him inside.

'Expecting someone?' Marlowe asked, amused.

Jane Dee's eyes rolled up in exasperation. 'Since that idiot Simon Forman has been prancing around London in his gowns and hats, scattering frogs hither and yon, we have had nothing but trouble. Friends, even old friends, come and expect the poor doctor to cure every manner of ill, even the Pestilence, as if he would allow that in the house with the children here! But they don't want to give him time to consult with his books and give them the right remedy, if indeed there is one. No. They want him to light a taper, caper around and, with a burst of stardust, have them cured.' She closed in to Marlowe so their noses almost touched. 'They bought a *dead* woman yesterday.'

Marlowe's eyes widened politely. He had known John Dee have a very serious go at raising the dead before now, but thought it impolite to interrupt.

'Stone dead, she was. You didn't have to be much of a Magus to tell that. I had to leave the doors and windows open the rest of the day. Then, when he can't do miracles, they shout and rave. The *language* sometimes!' She finally took a deep breath and grabbed Marlowe by the shoulders and gave him loud kisses on each cheek. 'But it isn't one of them, it's *you* and if anyone can bring a smile to the doctor's face, Kit, you are that person. In you go. He's in the back room, you know the way.' And she was gone, with broom before to sweep the dust behind the door. Jane Dee probably did sit down sometimes, even sleep now and again. It was just that no one ever saw her do it.

Marlowe tapped on the door but there was no reply.

Jane, whose ears could detect every small movement that might annoy her husband, called through from the kitchen. 'Just go in, Kit. He's hiding.'

Marlowe put his head around the door and saw that the room was empty. It had nothing like the magic of Dee's old house in Mortlake, with the basilisk hanging from the ceiling on a perch and mirrors catching and holding reflections from years ago or the future, depending on who looked into them. But the faint smell of sulphur was there, overlaid now though it was by Jane's liberal applications of beeswax on the ancient furniture, made of dark bog oak as old as time and as tough as iron. The books were the same too, leaning drunkenly on a few precarious shelves or piled up on the floor. The fire burned brightly in the wide hearth and a kettle sang on the trivet, alongside a seething cauldron that always looked ready to boil over and yet somehow never did. But of John Dee, there was no sign.

Marlowe was confused. It wasn't like Jane to not know

almost to the inch where her husband might be found. He looked round behind the door but, apart from a hook holding an old and disreputable cloak, there was nothing there. Marlowe pursed his lips and blew a puzzled breath down his nose. He must go and ask Jane.

'No need to bother Jane,' a voice said in his left ear and he gave a jump. 'My word, Kit,' Dr Dee said, stepping out from behind the door, 'you're nervous today. Come and sit by the fire.'

Marlowe was too old a hand to allow his friend to see how much he had been startled. The cloak, he now saw, was not a cloak at all, just Dee, face hidden, standing in the place a cloak might be expected to hang. A turn of the sleeve, a tug on a hem, he could see how it was done. A useful trick; he must try it sometime.

Dee laughed to see the thoughts going over Marlowe's face. 'It helps if you know the person you are hiding from,' he said, answering the question before it was even formed. 'Some people, and I know you will know the kind I mean, wouldn't have seen me if I was sitting right there in the chair, as long as I kept still. Others, I could fool by simply standing in a shadow or behind the drape. But for you, I needed something a little more, a little glamour, if I can call it that.' He sighed and stretched his arms out to the side, making the elbows crack like a matchlock. 'I'm getting a bit old for clinging to the back of a door, though.'

'You have lost none of your knack,' Marlowe said. 'I would have gone away in another minute.'

'Jane would have had my hide,' Dee told him. 'She worries about me, you know. Needs to know my whereabouts. But I know it is only because she loves me.' A look of wonder came over his face. 'I am luckier than I deserve.'

'We all are,' Marlowe told him. He had known Dee in sadness and in joy and, by and large, he preferred the joy. 'I'm here to pick over your brain in the hope that you can help me.'

Dee rubbed his hands together and led the way to where two chairs faced each other in front of the fire. October was being kind to them in London that year, but winter was knocking at the door and there was a chill in the air. The kettle whistling to itself on the hearth reminded Dee of his hostly duties. 'A cup of my herbal mixture, Kit?'

Marlowe was uncertain. He had drunk Dee's herbal mixture before.

'Don't be afraid, I have completely reconsidered the ingredients and I think you will find it very palatable.'

Marlowe looked askance. 'Does it still have asafoetida in it?' he asked, dubiously.

'Not a grain. Jane hates it as well, though I confess I don't see why. I have replaced the asafoetida with mint, the rue with rosemary, the bitter fescue with clover and with a few other changes I think you will enjoy it. Keeping with the countryside flavour, it is topped up with mead.' He stood and wrapped a cloth around his hand to pick up the kettle. 'Do try it. You'll like it.'

'Well, I will try just a small cup,' Marlowe agreed. It certainly sounded nicer than the original recipe.

'While I prepare it, tell me your conundrum.'

'It is several conundra, really, but I will start with the first and main one. As you know, I have been investigating the death of Robert Greene . . .'

'Have you found the miscreant yet?'

Marlowe was glad to hear that Dee at least felt that there was a miscreant. It wasn't a view to which many subscribed. 'As yet, no. I know who it is not, but that is not much help when the list is so long. But in visiting Cambridge, I happened to meet a boy, bereaved of his brother in what seemed to be a simple swimming accident.'

'But you think not.'

'I do think not, but I just don't seem to be able to put my finger on why. The boy I met, though grieving, seemed to be very lucid and he too had been set upon when his brother was drowned. He remembers being pulled from the water and then pushed down again, repeatedly.'

'That doesn't – at first hearing – sound much like the death of Robert Greene,' Dee observed, crushing some mint at the bottom of two glazed cups.

'No, perhaps not. But then, just this Sunday morning, to be

accurate, one Eunice Brown, one-time nanny to the Cecil family . . .'

'Not Noo-Noo?' Dee looked up from his chopping board. 'You knew her?'

Dee chuckled. 'Well, not *knew* as such. But when Robert was just a little one – a littler one, perhaps I should say – running in his hanging sleeves in the corridors of power, Noo-Noo was never far behind. Mind you, she must have been getting on . . . I assume, from the context, that she is dead?'

'Yes. Extremely.'

'That's a shame. She seemed a nice woman.'

'So I believe.' Marlowe should have known that Dee would know something unexpected. 'She was found dead in her bed at Hatfield, murdered.'

'Murdered?' Dee's eyes were wide. 'I wasn't expecting you to say that.'

'Really?'

Dee bowed his head modestly. 'Well, yes, of course I was. But not because I am unusually prescient, just that murder is almost all we ever talk about.'

Marlowe chuckled. 'Yes, I do see that. The thing about the death of this poor old soul, this *good* woman, was the violence. Her face was bruised with the marks of many fingers and her throat had been gripped hard at least half a dozen times.'

'You know as well as I do, Kit,' Dee said, turning from the fire with two steaming cups, 'that murdering someone by smothering or strangulation is not a simple matter of holding a person's nose or throat for a moment or two. It can take about four minutes, as a rough rule of thumb.'

'Odd you should say that, Doctor,' Marlowe said, 'I detected thumb marks on the poor woman's neck. Is there a way, do you know, of telling one thumb from another?'

Dee laughed, 'Don't be ridiculous, Kit. Miracles, as you know, take a little longer.'

Marlowe took the cup and sniffed it. To his surprise, it smelled quite pleasant. 'I do understand that, Doctor,' he said, 'but I had never seen so many different bruises to achieve one thing before.'

'Perhaps the murderer was weak and had to keep changing

their grip. As I remember Noo-Noo, she wasn't strong. Had
she put on weight? Become a big woman to subdue?'

Marlowe shook his head and took a deep sip of the herbs.
He pointed to the cup. 'This is very nice,' he said, his stage-
craft only just managing to take the surprise from his voice.
'She was tiny. Probably more so than when you saw her last,
chasing after Master Robyn. And to me, although it was two
days later, the bruises looked to be from a man's hand. A
larger woman, perhaps, but I would say a man.' He stopped
for a moment. Betty, the night attendant, was a comfortably
built woman. But would she have the stomach for murder?
He thought not.

Dee could always follow Marlowe's racing thoughts, perhaps
better than any man alive and he did so now. 'So, you think
that the two murders are linked, because the lad who survived
the drowning remembered coming up for the third time and
because poor Mistress Brown was smothered by someone
without the spirit for it.'

Marlowe was disappointed. 'Do you think that's all it was?
It seemed to me . . .'

Dee looked solemn. 'I have never drowned, speaking person-
ally, and also I have never been smothered to death. But I
have spoken to many who were. And the stories are the same.
The drowned ones always say their lives flash before them. I
admit I have always considered that a cliché, the kind of joke
the dead do dearly love to play with us. But I do believe that
as the body fights for air, certain pictures impress themselves
on the brain, not once, but many times. A stutter of the brain,
if you will. So this lad, remembering, sees himself coming up
for air more than once, when in fact, he just did it as he
surfaced the one and only time.'

'He seemed so certain.'

'Yes,' Dee smiled. 'They are. And as for poor Noo-Noo,
she fought, despite her age and infirmity. Perhaps the person
had no stomach for it but, having started, had no recourse but
to go on, because he or she would be recognized and surely
accused had the woman lived.'

'Perhaps . . .' Marlowe had seen the body. He had spoken
to Richard Williams. Dee had done neither. 'One thing, though,

Doctor,' he said. 'Richard, the drowned boy's brother, remembered a person holding him out of the water. He couldn't describe them, he was almost dead at that point. But he did remember him saying something, over and over.'

'And that was?' Despite his easy answers, Dee was intrigued.

'He said that the voice said – he was sure it was a man – he said: "Have you seen him yet?"'

'Did he know what that could mean?' Dee rummaged for a piece of paper and stub of pencil in the recesses of his gown.

'He couldn't think. I have wondered since whether perhaps it referred to his brother, dead by this time and in the hands of the current. But I don't see why it should.'

'Memory is a tricky thing,' Dee pointed out. 'It could be something he had heard hours, if not days, before. Or when he was coming to – I assume they pulled him out of the water insensible?'

'Yes, I believe they did.'

'In that case, it is explained, surely.' Dee drained his cup with a smack of the lips. 'He heard his rescuers asking if anyone had seen the twin.' He put his cup down smartly on the hearth and the subject seemed to be closed.

Marlowe was still not convinced. He had been so near to making a link. 'It's a shame that we can't ask Eunice Brown what she heard,' he said, only half seriously.

Dee's eyes lit up. 'But we *can*!' he said, jumping up. Then his face fell. 'We don't have anything to guide our quest, though, do we? Nothing she had worn or owned. Even touched.'

Marlowe smiled. 'Yes, we do,' he said. He put his hand inside his doublet and pulled out a square of silk, a kerchief his mother had sent him as a gift, years ago, which he had always treasured. He unwrapped it and there, sparkling in the firelight, was the angel's tear.

Dee looked at it dubiously. 'What is it? It doesn't look like anything Eunice Brown would own.'

'She didn't. The First Finder found it on her forehead. She thinks it was left by an angel, to show that Eunice Brown had gone to Heaven.'

Dee took it up carefully between finger and thumb. 'That would be nice, wouldn't it? Even for you, Kit, it would be nice to think we would go to Heaven, escorted there on soft wings. But no, in this case, our First Finder is wrong. This is nothing more or less than a glass bead. Even so, if it was on the dead woman's skin for a while . . .'

'Some hours, I should say. She was cold when they found her.'

'Then, despite the fact that it has been in other hands, then . . .' Dee looked up, eyes sparkling. 'Shall we try?'

Marlowe doubted that the dead, particularly this dead, who was hopefully in the arms of her Redeemer, as she had always wished, could help, but anything was worth a try. 'What can I do to help?'

'Well, you can curb your scepticism, Kit, if you would.'

Marlowe looked wounded.

'Don't look at me like that. I know you believe in nothing you can't see and touch. But the other world is never far away and, with luck, I can bring it here today.'

'Do we need to wait for midnight or anything like that?' Marlowe had seen Dee about his business before and a strange and wonderful business it was. But never by daylight.

'No, no. I have found it works at any time of day, if the spirits are willing. If you could just check to see where Jane is, I will get some things gathered together.'

'Jane doesn't approve, then?'

Dee sighed. 'Sadly, no. But I will prevail, I know. Just put your head around the kitchen door. If she is cooking, we will have at least an hour.'

Marlowe made his way into the flagged kitchen, where Jane Dee held undoubted sway. She had a cook, who spent most of her time sulking in the corner while her mistress turned out pastries as light as air and sweetmeats for which men would sell their soul. Today she was embroiled, almost literally, in the making of a great pie, to feed the entire household. She looked up, brushing a damp frond of hair from her forehead with the back of a sweaty hand.

'Do you need something, Kit?' she asked, her natural sweet nature only just managing to mask the testiness beneath.

'I just wondered if you would like to join us,' he said, pleasantly. 'But you look a little—'

'Busy. Yes.' Her look said it all. Men!

'I'll go and tell the doctor, shall I?'

'Mmm.' She was concentrating on her pie.

Marlowe closed the door of Dee's sanctum behind him firmly. 'She's making a pie,' he reported.

'That will keep her busy,' Dee said, happily. 'It's almost a religion with her, the Thursday pie.' He swept a hand over the table in the middle of the room. 'I have simplified my methods from what you may be used to. I don't use cockerel's blood any more, as you can see. I have found a dried mushroom which has almost exactly the same composition. I still use the sulphur, of course.' He gave a little chuckle at the thought that any conjuring could take place without it.

Marlowe clicked his tongue. The very thought!

'I shall have to burn a feather in a moment, but Jane won't smell that in the kitchen. Then I do need to recite an incantation, so I would be grateful if you could hold that book for me. And lastly, put the little bead on that mirror in the centre . . . yes, just there.' Dee arranged his table to his liking and then pinched his eyeglasses onto his nose.

In other hands, the summoning would be a farce. But as Dee intoned the words in an arcane tongue – along with the smell of the burning feather and the sulphur, and the glint of the tiny bead, which seemed to draw all the light from the room and concentrate it there, on the mirror – the shade of Eunice Brown was almost palpable in the room. She wasn't visible, but Marlowe could smell the scent of lavender and old lady rising above that of the burning. There was a sigh which set the candles guttering.

'Eunice?' Dee asked. 'Eunice Brown? Is that you?'

Marlowe knew it was vital to ask the question outright, otherwise a demon could come uninvited. There was no sound, but the air seemed to give its assent. There was a brief gust of warmth, infused again with lavender.

'She's here,' Marlowe whispered and Dee nodded, almost imperceptibly. He knew that the spirits of the devout could be easily scared off.

'Eunice,' Dee said gently, 'we are here to help you. We want to find out who murdered you.'

The air shimmered and the smell of lavender faded. An enormous crash filled their ears but nothing they could see had fallen over. Even so, they could have sworn that the floor vibrated with the shock of it. The two men froze, waiting for Jane to explode through the door, but no one came. Dee raised his face to the ceiling and whispered, 'Eunice. Eunice. If you are there, tap once.'

There wasn't a sound; even the slight sizzling from the burning feather was silent now. Marlowe breathed in and could smell no lavender. The spirit echo that had possibly been Eunice Brown had gone.

After a few moments, Dee dropped his shoulders and sighed. 'She isn't here, Kit. But she was, I think?' He looked eager.

'She was,' Marlowe agreed, against his better judgement. He found proof of the afterlife difficult to come to terms with these days; if there was an afterlife, might there not also be a God? He smiled to himself – he must be getting old, seeing both sides of an argument. Being certain was perhaps a young man's game.

'I'm sorry, Kit,' Dee said, tidying up his paraphernalia. 'I had hoped for more.'

'Lettys would be happy,' Marlowe told him.

'Lettuce?' Dee had never considered the feelings of vegetables. It was bad enough that little Madinia was beginning to ask why the lambs bleated so piteously when they were passing Smithfield; if vegetables had to be considered too, it would be the end of him.

'Lettys. The First Finder. She was anxious that Eunice had gone to Heaven.'

'I don't think we proved that,' Dee said, honestly.

'It would be enough for Lettys,' Marlowe assured him. He looked down at the scorched table and put Eunice Brown from his mind. There was nothing else he could do for her or Roger Williams or even Robert Greene, for now. But there was one other thing he needed to ask before he went.

'What else did you want to ask?' Dee said, flopping back down in his chair.

'How do you do that?' Marlowe asked him.

'What?' Dee looked beatific.

'Know what I am going to say?'

'Practice,' Dee said, simply. 'That and listening and remembering. Some day, I will find I have remembered too much and that will be the death of me. But until then, I never forget what has been said – it's a blessing and a curse.' His eyes clouded over and Marlowe knew he was remembering his Helene.

Marlowe tried him at his own game. 'Can you speak to Cecil and get him to lift the closing of the theatres?' Boldness was the way.

'I can speak to Cecil,' Dee said. 'I can also ask him to lift the closure. But it won't get the theatres reopened, I fear. Cecil speaks to me because the Queen would wish it. We have had our ups and downs, Gloriana and I, but she is too afraid of what she fears I might do to throw me to the wolves. And so, I am tolerated, no more.'

'But surely, he would listen to you. Your science . . .?'

'Is second to none, of course it is. But for now, no advice counts unless it drips from the oily tongue of Simon Forman.'

'Forman?' Marlowe laughed. 'But they must know him for a charlatan, surely?'

'A charlatan. A rogue. But, sadly, for the moment, a fashionable charlatan and rogue. Go and see him, but make sure you take a heavy purse. They say he doesn't speak to his wife unless she pays him. Were I her, I wouldn't pay, but there's no accounting for taste. Do you know where to find him?'

Marlowe thought for a moment. 'Westminster, isn't it?'

'That's right. Just get to the west wall of the abbey and then follow your nose – the smell of dead newt is almost unmistakeable.'

Marlowe remembered it – it seemed an age since they had resurrected Robert Greene, however briefly; it would be an experience to meet the magus in his own house. It was a pity that he would have to stay polite – playing with charlatans was something he relished, but with a job to do as important as reopening the theatres, he would need his most honeyed words. He would just need to take care that they didn't choke him. But first, he had to tell Noo-Noo's boys some sad news.

TWELVE

The Palace of Whitehall looked less forbidding in the sunshine and there was no army of armed men crouching behind its parapet. Marlowe walked in, having shown his papers to the guard and found his way to the inner sanctum that was Robert Cecil's lair. The little man was perched like a monkey on his windowsill, his back to the panelling, his pipe in his mouth.

'Morning, Marlowe.' He looked up through a wreath of smoke. 'What news?'

Marlowe sat in what was fast becoming his usual chair. It didn't look as though a glass of wine was in the offing, so he began. 'You and your father were right,' he said. 'Eunice Brown *was* murdered.'

Cecil nodded, his large eyes hooded against the smoke. 'And?'

'It's my guess her murderer was a visitor, somebody who was in and out of Hatfield, but with a reason to be there.'

Cecil frowned. That made little sense to him. 'Why would a passing stranger run the risk of getting into the house, finding Noo-Noo's chamber and murdering her? There must be easier targets.'

'I believe I spoke to all your father's servants,' Marlowe told him. 'From Cruikshank to the stable lads. You and I, Sir Robert, are used to interrogating people. We watch for the flutter of the eyelid, the twitch of the mouth. If any of them was lying, I missed it. Nobody had a bad word to say about Goody Eunice.'

There was a clatter in the passageway outside and the sound of raised voices. Cecil hopped down from his perch, extinguishing the pipe, opening the window and fanning away the smoke.

'Father!' he just had time to say before the most powerful man in the country swept in.

Burghley was shouting at someone in the passageway.
'And you can tell the Earl of Essex . . . Never mind, I'll do it
myself.' He turned his attention to the room, frowned and
sniffed. 'Do you drink smoke, Marlowe?' he asked.

The projectioner was on his feet out of respect and he
bowed. 'Anyone who doesn't love tobacco is a fool, my Lord
. . . or so I've heard it said.'

'Have you?' Burghley sneered. 'I should look to your
company, Marlowe.'

'Marlowe has some news, Father,' Cecil said, sitting down
behind his desk. 'About Noo-Noo.'

'Ah,' Burghley poured a goblet of Rhenish and, against
all probabilities, gave one to Marlowe. He didn't do the
honours in respect of his son; presumably wine, like tobacco,
was bad for him. 'I have just come from the good woman's
funeral. Quite beautiful. Parry excelled himself.'

More than you know, thought Marlowe.

'Say on.' Burghley sat on the corner of Cecil's desk and all
but eclipsed the little man behind it.

'Marlowe thinks . . .' Cecil began, but Burghley held up
his hand for silence.

'I know he does,' the old man said. 'That, I assume, is why
you employ him.' He looked at the projectioner. 'Marlowe?'

'I believe that Eunice was killed by someone visiting your
estate, my Lord,' he said. 'I understand they are legion.'

The Queen's Councillor nodded. 'They are indeed. I like
clever men around me, Marlowe, I see nothing wrong with that.
Philosophy, ethics, geography, things of that nature.'

'Politics?' Marlowe threw in. 'Religion?'

'Ah, well, we have to tread warily there of course, in these
dangerous times.'

Marlowe couldn't help wondering whether the times would
be a little less dangerous without these two. 'It's the manner
of Eunice's death that I can't fathom.'

Burghley looked at the playwright with hauteur not unmixed
with contempt. 'Fathoming is what my son pays you to do,'
he said. 'What, in particular, vexes you?'

'There was a great deal of force used on Mistress Brown,'

Marlowe said. 'Much more than was necessary in the case of a frail old lady.'

'Lots of bruising,' Cecil recalled.

'Applied not once, but over a period of time – longer, I suspect, than it would take to actually kill her.'

'Someone who enjoys pain for its own sake?' Burghley was wondering aloud, 'a Topcliffe, you might say.'

The keeper of the Queen's instruments of torture was renowned throughout Europe. He would have made short work of Eunice Brown.

'Yet someone struck by remorse,' Marlowe reasoned.

'I don't understand,' Burghley frowned.

'Eunice's chamber is not cut off from the rest of the house,' Marlowe said. 'Other servants' quarters are nearby. Our murderer had to act quietly and, for his own safety, quickly. And yet, this murder was done slowly, piecemeal almost, as if the man lost his nerve in the process and had to begin again. And I've seen this somewhere before.'

'You have?' Cecil sat up. 'Where?'

'Cambridge, not three weeks ago. That was a drowning accident, or so it seemed. The dead man's brother was also attacked and tells a tale of a tentative killer, who kept letting him go. There are parts of the story which seem to match that of the Hatfield killing, others of which we can never be sure.'

'Never is a big word, Master Marlowe,' Burghley said.

'The murderer in Cambridge spoke. We can't know whether the Hatfield one did the same. But even so, there are resonances. Did Eunice have any connections with Cambridge?'

The Cecils looked at each other, shaking their heads.

'Or Poppleton? The Cambridge scholar came from there.'

'Where in God's green earth is Popp . . . what did you call it?'

'Poppleton. It's near York.'

'No, Marlowe,' Burghley said. 'Noo-Noo was born in Hertfordshire and came to work for us as a girl. Her mother was my wet nurse so, as you can tell, we have known her family as far back as is possible. They all lie in the churchyard at Etheldreda's. You spoke to Dr Parry, I assume?'

Marlowe smiled at the memory of it. 'I did,' he said. 'A good man, I think.'

'The best,' Burghley assured him. 'Could he help?'

'Not at all. I suppose, my Lord, a list of visitors to Hatfield in the last week would be out of the question.'

'Utterly.' Burghley spread his arms. 'Oh, I know I should take more care with people coming to the house. Robert is always twittering about it, aren't you, Robert?'

The Queen's Imp nodded. Both men knew that Robert could twitter until Hell froze over and it would do no good.

'You'd have to question every member of the Privy Council,' Burghley went on. 'Not a few ambassadors from every country from France to Muscovy. And every one of them has more hangers-on than I've books in my library. I suspect you'd grow old before you got through all of them, Marlowe, not to mention the stink you'd cause on the international relations front. We've got enough enemies in Europe as it is, without adding more.'

'Then, for the moment, gentlemen,' Marlowe said, getting up, 'I can do no more. Oh, one favour, my Lord, if I may?'

Burghley looked at the man. He had to admit, he felt a little let down. Francis Walsingham had always spoken highly of Marlowe; his own son did too, albeit through gritted teeth. But Marlowe seemed to have made no progress at all and linking the death of his dear Noo-Noo with some threadbare university scholar was a pointless exercise. 'Name it.' For all that, Burghley was, deep down, a kind man.

'The theatres, my Lord. Rumour has it that the Pestilence is subsiding. Many of my associates rely on their stage income to live. Couldn't the ban be lifted? The theatres be reopened?'

'Dr Forman says "No",' Burghley said. 'And he *is* the foremost authority on the damned disease that we have. Sorry, Marlowe, but there it is.'

'But, Dr Dee—'

Burghley gave a bark of laughter. 'All very well in his day, but he is nowhere near Simon Forman.'

Marlowe would agree with that. He could tell that he had driven that particular pig as far along the passage as it would go and knew when to stop. 'Very well, my Lord.' He bowed to them both and smiled when he caught sight of Cecil's pipe stem sticking out of his Venetians. 'I will wish you both good day.'

In the doorway he turned. 'By the way,' he said, 'whatever happened to Nicholas Faunt?'

'Faunt?' Burghley repeated. 'Why do you ask?'

'As you know, my Lord, I worked with the man several times back in the day. I thought I saw him recently, though it may have been a trick of the light.'

'Nicholas Faunt was Sir Francis Walsingham's creature,' Cecil said, tartly. 'Yesterday's man. He will never darken these doors again.'

Marlowe smiled, bowed again and left. He had just reached the staircase when he heard the clatter of pattens behind him. Lord Burghley, his cup discarded, was scurrying to catch him.

'My Lord?' Marlowe turned to face him.

Burghley was shifty, glancing back over his shoulder. 'Look, Marlowe, I don't want this noised abroad, if you get my drift?' He was nodding in the direction of his son's chamber. 'But Faunt is still in my employ. Robert doesn't like him, so I'm keeping it quiet. But men like Faunt don't grow on trees. He has his uses.'

'I'm sure he does, my Lord,' Marlowe said.

'Where did you see him? Not Hatfield, surely?'

'In Bedlam,' Marlowe said, 'the asylum for the insane.'

For a moment, Burghley turned pale, blinking in the half-light of the stair. 'Yes,' he said, slowly. 'That would make sense.'

And Kit Marlowe was glad of that because, at that moment, nothing else did.

He took to the streets that skirted Whitehall and made for Charing Cross. The ancient monument looked greyer than ever now that the weak October sun had gone and the clouds had taken its place. There was the usual crowd of rough sleepers clustered at its base, the flotsam of a country ruled by the Cecils. One of them, in dark grey, but less ragged than the others, was staring intently at Marlowe. He got up and strolled towards him, tentatively at first, then increasing his stride.

'Master Marlowe!' he greeted him.

Marlowe stood still. There, in the less than flattering gown of a King's scholar, stood Richard Williams, whose brother had died in the Cam not four weeks earlier. 'Master Williams.' Marlowe shook the lad's hand. 'What brings you to the Cross?'

'I have not been well, Master Marlowe.' The boy looked thin and pale. 'After Roger . . . I could not settle to my studies. The Master has given me sabbatical leave; he was very understanding. So I have come to London to stay with my aunt in Clerkenwell.'

'You took the North Road?' Marlowe asked. 'On foot?'

'I did, but I accepted a lift from a tinker's cart and ended up in Hatfield.'

'Hatfield?' Marlowe's eyes narrowed. 'That was out of your way.'

'It was.' Williams felt a little foolish. 'I fell asleep in the cart and, before I knew it, I was lying in a ditch by the parish church.'

'St Etheldreda's.' Marlowe nodded.

'Do you know it?' Williams asked.

'Intimately,' Marlowe said. 'Tell me, Richard. When was this? When were you in Hatfield?'

'Er . . . last week, I think. To tell you true, since Roger . . . I have lost all sense of time.'

Marlowe looked at the boy. Grief and repeated immersion in water had taken its toll. But was there more to it? The boy, himself a murder victim but for the Grace of God, had been in Hatfield, when God or the Devil took Eunice Brown. 'Come with me,' Marlowe said. 'You look as if you could do with a square meal. And then, we'll get you off to Clerkenwell. Your aunt; she's a kind woman, I hope.'

'The kindest,' Williams answered. He squared his shoulders in his ugly gown and took the first step of the rest of his life.

Marlowe was not sorry to have a reason to visit Simon Forman, in his lair. Ever since meeting him accidentally, he had wanted to find out more. It was hard to read his face behind the mask and, surely, there was more to the man than simply conjuring, glamour and some small amphibians? His house was not hard to find. A small gaggle of importunate sufferers from various diseases, some all too apparent, others more covert, stood outside the door. A young man in a dark blue robe stood on the threshold, with a satchel at his hip. As each person moved to the head of the line, the lad put a hand on their head and presented them with a sachet from the bag; from a distance, it reminded Marlowe of nothing so much as the Mass; the benediction and the body of their Lord. He hung back until the last of the sachets had been distributed.

The lad raised his voice so all in the line could hear. 'The magus must be allowed time now to prepare some more tinctures,' he said. 'Please disperse so as to give him the peace he needs; when he knows that his beloved countrymen are suffering at his door, it interferes with his link to the all-healing powers that only he can harness.' The small crowd shifted for a moment, but there was clearly not going to be any more healing that day, so they wandered away, in ones and twos, limping, coughing, in one case carried on a makeshift stretcher.

When they had all gone, Marlowe approached the door and stopped the apprentice as he turned to close it.

'I'm sorry.' The voice was kindly, with a hint of country burr in it. 'The magus must be allowed—'

'Yes. I heard.'

'So . . .' the boy pushed the door to, but Marlowe's foot was in it and it wouldn't close.

'I must see Master Forman.'

'The magus—'

'Can you say nothing else?' Marlowe could see intelligence in the eyes, but there seemed to be no one at home. 'I am not sick, as you can possibly tell. In fact, friends who know these things, Dr John Dee for example, tell me I am in the rudest of health and will live to be ninety. I want to see Master Forman on another matter altogether.'

The apprentice looked doubtful. He felt a bit of a fool repeating his message again, but didn't know what else to say.

Marlowe put him out of his misery. 'Look . . . what is your name?'

'Gerard, sir.'

'Gerard what? Or is it what Gerard?'

The boy raised his eyes and again appeared to recite. 'Until we find our calling, forenames only are all we require. Our name for using about our business will come to us when the time is right.'

Marlowe nodded thoughtfully. 'Hence "Forman", I assume.'

'The magus received his name in a vision, yes. And he is indeed foremost among men.'

There was something in Gerard's manner that made Marlowe look again. What he had taken for possible hypnotic trance, or some herbal tincture controlling him, he saw now was doubt. Something about the magus was troubling the boy and he had time enough to discover what. The garish robe was a little too big and was fraying around the sleeve. The haircut was designed to look monkish but the lad, as lads everywhere will, had brushed it forward over his ears and dampened it down with water; it couldn't control its tendency to curl and it looked rather innocent and pleasing. Marlowe knew how to handle his curls and used them to great effect to extract information from duchess and doxy alike, but he remembered how he had felt about them when he was not yet twenty.

'Well,' he said, confidentially, 'my name is Marlowe, but I have been called many things from Marley to Machiavel. I wonder what I should have called myself had I not kept my father's name.'

Gerard stepped back. '*Christopher* Marlowe?' he said. 'Christopher *Marlowe*? The poet.'

Marlowe shrugged. 'Amongst other things.'

'I wondered if it could be you,' Gerard said. 'But so many people copy your hair, your clothes . . .'

Marlowe found that fact slightly disturbing. He had never noticed although, now he came to think of it, Shaxsper had been doing strange things with his thinning locks of late.

'Your plays . . .' Gerard found he was stage-struck. 'So wise. The poetry . . .'

'Yes. Thank you. Er . . . Gerard, is it?'

'Yes.'

'Gerard, I would like to meet your master, but first, can we walk a little? Do you have to be back inside? Report on the size of the crowd, that kind of thing.' It was the kind of thing that Henslowe did all the time, people running hither and thither, telling him how many groundlings, how many gallants, and so how much his coffers would benefit. And, in their own ways, Forman and Henslowe were but two cheeks of one arse.

Gerard took an anxious look behind him into the dark interior of the house. 'I can spare a little time,' he said. A walk with Kit Marlowe – who wouldn't spare a little time for that?

'There is an alehouse just down the lane – you are *allowed* ale, I assume?'

The apprentice bridled. 'I am allowed anything. We all are. We are not slaves, you know, Master Marlowe, we are apprentices. Full apprentices.'

Marlowe nodded his apology. 'Then come this way,' he said. 'The ale is fresh and the serving wenches clean. Who could ask for more?'

The shakes came upon him a little before noon. The sky over Bedlam was an opaque grey, spitting with rain. For weeks now, Tom Sledd had struggled to live in this place. The grey gruel kept him alive and fleas and lice were his constant companions. He could hear the bell of All Hallows on the Wall tolling, for a midday funeral was his guess. There were never any christenings or weddings, nothing for a fast, happy peal of bells, just the solemn tocsin.

Tom Sledd wasn't really of a miserable disposition, but his weeks in this circle of Hell had all but broken him. All he could remember of the outside world was Robert Greene in his coffin, the worms lining up to eat him, the odd crow circling overhead. And Greene's coffin became, in his mind, Sledd's coffin. He was in it, yet walking behind it, all at the same time. Six men were carrying their solemn load – Kit Marlowe, Will Shaxsper, Philip Henslowe, Richard Burbage, Ned Alleyn and Will Kemp. But *they* weren't solemn. Kemp was whirling his damned pig's bladder over his head. Alleyn and Burbage were trying to outshout each other with the mighty pentameter of Kit Marlowe. The playwrights were reading out competing prologues of plays, their voices rising in crescendo. Henslowe was counting his money, flinging gold coins into the coffin to lie with Sledd. The wreck who was once stage manager at the Rose huddled his knees under his chin and sobbed.

It was a while before he felt the fingers fiddling at his belt, the one he had been toying with using to hang himself with if this madness went on for much longer. A large man was leaning against him, trying to get at the purse which still dangled, empty, from his belt. Sledd frowned, wiping the tears from his eyes and trying to focus. He recognized the man as one who seemed to spend most of his time humping the younger women against the far wall. He had been listening to his grunts and their cries for weeks now.

'Get away!' Sledd shoved him but he was too heavy to move.

'Got any cake?' the man asked, though clearly his real target was altogether rounder and made of silver.

'Cake?' Sledd repeated. 'No, I haven't. Just the slops we all get, same as you. Keep your hands off me.'

'As you wish,' the man grumbled. He half turned, then turned back. '*Pax vobiscum*, my son,' he said, and burst out laughing before rolling away.

'Got him,' a dark voice said in his other ear. Sledd spun round to see the poet looking at him, a smile on his face. 'I knew it could only be a matter of time. And I knew it would be you who solved the riddle for me.'

'Bugger off,' Sledd said. He was exhausted. He knew the poet would not try to rob him and he hadn't the strength to shout at this man.

'When I want provant,' the poet declaimed softly, still smiling, 'with Humphrey I sup, and when benighted, I repose in Paul's with waking souls, yet never am affrighted.'

'All right,' Sledd sighed, 'you're a bloody beggar, cadging meals at Duke Humphrey's tomb and doing Paul's walk. I know.'

'You don't know your arse from your elbow, Tom Sledd.'

Sledd blinked. 'What?' he said. The poet's voice had changed, his eyes no longer rolled from time to time in his head. His gaze was level. And strangely familiar.

'I could pull off the beard and cut my hair and put on my own Venetians and Colleyweston. Even show you Lord Burghley's seal of office. And you still wouldn't have a clue, would you?'

Realization dawned at last. 'You're . . .' Sledd shouted, but the poet's hand was across his mouth in a second.

'Nicholas Faunt, late of Sir Francis Walsingham's secret service, yes. Today, I work for Burghley, but it largely amounts to the same thing.' He slowly let his hand drop and huddled closer to Sledd, not for warmth or comfort but so that his conversation could not be heard. 'I can't believe you didn't recognize me. As soon as I saw you, I said to myself, "Bugger. It's Tom Sledd and he'll see through this stage makeup faster than Roland Sleford chains innocent people up." But no, not you. How many adventures have we had together, one way or another, involving Kit Marlowe?'

'Kit Marlowe!' Sledd blurted out, then hissed, 'the shit! He left me here to rot.'

'He had no choice,' Faunt mumbled. 'He'd come to get you out, then he saw me. *He* recognized me at once.'

'Well . . .' Sledd shrugged, feeling stupid as well as exhausted and witless.

'He realized I was here for a reason and couldn't compromise my position.'

'What reason?' Sledd whispered. He was starting to feel a lot better now that a man of Nicholas Faunt's standing was sitting beside him.

'Your light-fingered friend over there,' Faunt nodded in the man's direction. 'The fornicator.'

'What about him?'

'He's a Jesuit. Name of Ballantine. He's been on the run for weeks now and we got intelligence that he was hiding here. My problem was how to identify him, how to prove he was only mad nor' by nor'west. He could have been anybody.'

'Except me!' Sledd pointed out, trying to keep his voice low and his brain from exploding. 'You knew it couldn't be me.'

'Of course, but I couldn't risk exposing myself even to get you out. I still can't.'

'What?' Sledd grabbed the man by his rags. 'What do you mean?'

'One little slipped "*Pax vobiscum*" isn't enough for the Secretary of State. And let's face it, he hasn't been behaving much like a Jesuit priest, has he? But now I know who he is, I can work on him. Just a day or so, Tom, and we'll both walk out of here; I promise.'

Sledd hesitated. He wanted to hit Nicholas Faunt, over and over again. He wanted to strangle him with his own bare hands; but that way, he knew, he'd never leave Bedlam.

'A day or two,' he hissed. 'No more.'

But the poet who was really a projectioner had already spotted Jack on his late morning rounds, traipsing in their direction. 'I know more than Apollo,' he told the gaoler. 'For oft, when he lies sleeping, I see the stars at bloody wars in the wounded welkin weeping.'

Jack aimed a kick at Faunt's genitals. 'Of course you do, you mad bastard,' he growled.

Inside the alehouse, it was soon apparent that, allowed or not, Gerard and ale were not bosom companions. He took a sip of the thin froth and blinked. 'Strong,' he said.

Marlowe had just been thinking that he might have to change to Rhenish rather than drink gutter water, but he persevered, so the lad felt at home in his company. He nodded his agreement. 'I know we have only just met, Gerard,' he said, putting down his goblet, 'but you strike me as a rather unhappy young apprentice.'

Gerard shook his head vehemently. 'I am very happy,' he said. 'The magus treats us well. The food is good. I will have a profession one day.' It was the final sentence that held the harmony of doubt.

'What profession?' Marlowe took another sip, watching him over the rim of his goblet.

'Healer,' Gerard said, defiantly.

'Healer. I see. And what will you heal? And how will you do it? You can't wear a plague doctor's mask for ever. The Pestilence will not stalk our streets for all of your life, you know. And what will you do then?'

'There are other ills,' Gerard said, a touch defiantly. 'There are always women needing help, the magus says.'

Marlowe heard the doubt again and pounced on it. 'Women? *Just* women?'

Gerard put down his drink so Marlowe could not see how his hand trembled. 'Master Marlowe,' he said. 'Can I tell you something?'

'Anything.' Marlowe could extract the final secret from a clam.

'I have begun to wonder . . . these last days . . . well, I have begun to wonder if the magus might be a sham.'

Marlowe was not much of an actor, but he could feign amazement and did so now. 'A *sham?* The great Dr Forman? But the Queen . . .'

'I *know!*' Gerard lowered his voice and looked round to see if people were staring. 'But I have . . . he has shared with me . . . things I don't really want to tell you, Master Marlowe, if I may keep that secret. It is the way he . . . it's the women, you see.'

Marlowe saw. He knew charlatans much worse than Forman, who used methods far more venal. But they made no bones about it. Ned Alleyn, for example, used his fame and other undeniable talents to ensnare any women who came into his orbit. But he and they knew what would happen and, when it all was over, there were no ill-feelings and in a good week he could double his theatre earnings and more. But Forman preyed on the scared and lonely, and that Marlowe could not abide.

'Don't worry, Gerard.' He had seen the clandestine tear drop into the boy's ale. 'You don't need to do what you don't want to. I feel that you have healing in you. I could see when you were handing out the herbs that you really cared for those poor people. Stick to that, and you won't go far wrong.'

'I'll never be rich, though,' the lad wailed.

'Money isn't everything,' Marlowe told him. 'Being happy is worth more and is often harder to achieve. Just forget what he said to you. Put it from your mind and keep on with your work. I assume you learned your herbal lore from . . . who? Your mother?'

'My grandame. She is a . . .' Gerard had heard what the
village called her, when they came one by one in the night to
her back door, but he wasn't going to use the 'w' word in
front of a virtual stranger, famous though he might be.

Marlowe raised a hand. 'I understand. Follow your grandame
and you won't be rich, but you will be happy. I guarantee it.
But is there something else? You look happier already, but you
still have something on your mind.'

Gerard felt a chill up his spine. This man could read his
mind as well as any seer. For a terrifying minute, he wondered
whether he came from Forman, or from Hell itself. But he
was stepped in so far, it would be tedious now to go back,
so he carried on. 'We have a maidservant at the house. She
hasn't many brains, love her heart, but she means well. After
the magus had given me his talk, he sent me to . . .' His eyes
welled up again.

'Practise?' Marlowe checked.

The apprentice nodded. 'Don't get me wrong, Master
Marlowe. I am no innocent. We tend to make our own entertainment in the country. But I couldn't do what the magus
told me to do. Not to little Tabitha, anyway. So, we just talked.
I told her not to tell anyone that we had just talked but
she was happy to do that. She's just a child and . . . well, we
talked. And she told me that when the magus had told
us he was out in the countryside, bringing healing to the
people, he was at home, stinking in his bed, was what
she said. Apart from Saturday night, when he went out in all
his full finery and didn't get back until late Sunday. He *lied*
to us, Master Marlowe!'

Marlowe smiled and drained his goblet. 'We all lie, all the
time, Gerard,' he said. 'Have you never lied to Master Forman?'

The apprentice blushed.

'You need to work on that,' Marlowe said, waving a hand
in front of the lad's face, which burned all the brighter. 'I'll
take it to mean that you have.'

'We all did,' he explained. 'We were all out in the world,
as the magus puts it, for a week. None of us did very well. I
just camped out for a week. It was relaxing; I met a few nice
people. I gave one boy a tincture for a toenail that was giving

him pain. But I didn't heal the dozens I claimed. Matthias just went home to mother. They live in a big house somewhere near London. Timothy did earn some money, but he lost it when his horse had a foal.'

Marlowe was sure there was a story there, but didn't have time to hear it.

'So yes, we lie. But we're apprentices, Master Marlowe. We're *meant* to lie.'

'That's an unusual view,' Marlowe pointed out, 'but not unique, I'm sure. We should be getting you back, however. Otherwise, you will be practising your lying skills once more.'

'When you see the magus, Master Marlowe, you won't tell him, will you? What we've been talking about?'

Marlowe clapped a hand over his mouth. 'I am as silent as the grave,' he promised. 'Your master will learn nothing from me.'

'Thank you. Let me take you to the magus, then.'

And the two walked up the lane, through the door, and towards the sanctum of Doctor Simon Forman, Magus to Her Majesty.

Forman was otherwise engaged. Mistress Forman was leaning on her fists on his desk and staring him down. He had actually based his famous basilisk stare on his wife, though he would go through Hell and high water before he admitted it.

'But, Jeanie,' he crooned, trying to calm her down.

'Don't "but Jeanie" me,' she said. 'I will not have you sending your boys to practise your vile arts on my Tabitha. She is a good girl, from the country; she doesn't want truck with all that. Besides, I can't get a minute's work out of her today. She keeps bursting into hysterics.'

Forman looked outraged. 'Who was the fellow?' he roared. 'Whoever it is will be sent from this house forthwith.'

'Don't give me your flannel,' she said. 'I didn't come down with the last shower of frogs. It was Gerard. He is a dear boy and did nothing, as it happens. Tab might be a bit slow, but she knew what you had told him to do.'

'Because she listens at doors!' Forman had learned years ago that the best defence is attack.

'So what if she does? I would know nothing of what you do if she never spent a few minutes at a keyhole now and again. But I'm telling you, Simon Forman . . .'

'Simon Erasmus Hippocrates Forman,' he corrected her.

'What?' This stopped her dead. 'When did you get those names, may I ask?'

'They came to me in a dream,' he said, complacently.

She threw up her hands in resignation. 'I give up,' she said. 'Don't do it again.'

'Don't do what?' he tried a winning smile.

'*Anything!*' And with that, she turned on her heel and threw open the door.

Gerard was standing there, with a complete stranger. He looked no better than he should be, clearly some lowlife crony of her lowlife husband. She hauled off and fetched Gerard a handy one upside the head.

Gerard clasped his ear and howled. 'Ow! What was that for?'

But the woman had gone.

Forman stood up behind his desk and tried not to look like a man recently torn into metaphorical shreds by his wife. He gestured for Marlowe to come in and sit, then turned his attention to Gerard.

'I'm sorry, my boy,' he said, and Marlowe had never heard a voice as devoid of sorrow. 'My wife is a little overwrought. Go and get one of the others to put a cold compress on that ear. I would suggest comfrey and knitbone.'

Gerard went off muttering, his head still singing. Mistress Forman had a strong right arm, sure enough, but she hadn't broken anything in his head. It was his heart that was broken – his idol had feet of worse than clay and he had proved it with that stupid remedy. Gerard went straight to his bench, to find himself some self-heal and some camomile.

'So, Master Marlowe,' he said, trying to make it sound like a prognostication from on high, 'it *is* Master Marlowe, isn't it?'

'As you well know, Master Forman.' Marlowe bowed. 'Doctor.'

There was possibly a joke there, but Marlowe wasn't in the mood.

Forman waited for the correction, then gave up. 'What is it you want, Master Marlowe? My time is precious.'

'Hmm. As you say. My request is a simple one, Master Forman. I want you to go to Lord Burghley and recommend that the theatres are reopened.'

Forman goggled. 'A simple request, you say?'

'Indeed. I have reason enough to believe that Burghley regrets the closure. It has caused one riot already and more will follow. You just need to say that when you said the theatres should be closed, you misspoke.'

Forman leaned forward, his eyes icy. It was a look which had quelled many a lesser man. 'I *never* misspeak.'

'Again, as you say. But I will not take no for an answer, Master Forman. If you do not do as I say, I will use my not-inconsiderable influence in high places to ensure that the many husbands you have cuckolded find out precisely why their wives will only consent to Master Forman doctoring at their bedside.'

Forman might have been made of stone.

'Does that sound like something a husband would want to hear?' Marlowe went on. 'I can think of several who would run you through first and ask questions later. Sir George Stafford, for example, has been known to knock a groom unconscious because he touched his wife's knee as she was mounting her horse. So you can see how they might misunderstand what you touch when mounting their wives.'

Forman slammed his fist down on the table top. 'I will go to Lord Burghley,' he said, through gritted teeth. 'But if the entire populace of London dies of the Pestilence, be it on your head.'

Marlowe shrugged and got up. 'As I am one of the populace of London, Master Forman, I doubt I would be in a position to care,' he said. 'But I will bear it in mind.'

Forman stood and went to a hook behind the door. He swung his gorgeous cape around his shoulders and barged past Marlowe. 'No time like the present,' he muttered, and slammed his way through the laboratory and out into the street.

'What's the matter with him?' Matthias asked, with no interest in the answer.

'I think your master has seen a door opening which will give him the result he wants with no loss of face,' Marlowe said, coming through from the sanctum. 'In other words, the theatres open, London alive again and foolish women flocking to his door. It should please you, too. You won't be sent out to earn your bread again for a while.'

Matthias was sorry – his letters, translated with some aplomb by Timothy, had made him long for his French governess even more. Timothy, hard at work among his retorts, looked up briefly. 'Master Marlowe,' he said. 'Timothy.' He bowed from the neck. 'I am pleased to make your acquaintance. Your plays have brought us much pleasure.'

'Thank you, Timothy. And your friend?'

'Matthias. You are quite right, we were beginning to notice short rations. Thank you for making our master see sense.'

'That's not easy,' muttered Gerard through the poultice on his head.

'It has been a pleasure to meet you all,' Marlowe said with an all-encompassing bow and swept from the room, more elegantly than Forman could ever manage and with a good deal less noise. The apprentices heard an excited twittering in the hall as he made his goodbyes to Mistress Forman. Christopher Marlowe was very good at exiting stage right, left or centre.

THIRTEEN

'I remember you,' the constable of the Watch said, looking at Marlowe. 'Still looking for that old enemy?'

'I've found a lot more since,' Marlowe smiled. 'How goes the Pestilence?'

'On the wane, they say,' the other constable said, 'but if you see a cross on the door, I'd keep wide of it.'

'I will,' Marlowe said and strode on between the leaning tenements along Kyroun Lane. There was still no cross on Mrs Isam's door and he banged on it with his fist.

A girl answered, perhaps sixteen, in the clothes of a maid. Her gaze, however, had nothing of the scullery about it. 'Yes?' she pouted.

'Is your mistress in?' Marlowe asked.

'If it's a mistress you're looking for . . .' the girl sidled closer to him, sliding her hand down his doublet.

'Leave the gentleman alone!' a harsh voice snapped. It was followed by a smack around the head and Mrs Isam, responsible for both, stood there fuming. 'Master Marlowe,' she scowled at him, ignoring the protestations of the girl, who sauntered away, holding her ringing ear.

'Mistress Isam,' he nodded. 'May I come in?'

'What do you want? None of my girls, that's obvious.' For the briefest of moments, the bawd wondered whether Marlowe's tastes might run to the older woman, such as herself, perhaps. But there was a look on Marlowe's face that told her not to entertain the idea.

'I have come for Dominus Greene's things,' he said.

'What things?' Mrs Isam asked.

'His effects. You know – clothes, books, pipe . . .' the poet-playwright was already running out of ideas.

'There's no money,' Mrs Isam cut to the chase. 'You can come in and look if you like.'

Marlowe ducked into the dark of the passageway and

followed as the landlady-turned-brothel-keeper led him up a twisting stairway. Almost every riser creaked under their weight. If the late Robert Greene was afraid of his murderer, he would have heard him in plenty of time on *this* staircase.

Robert Greene's room was a tiny hovel under the eaves. Through the cobwebbed window, Marlowe could make out the spars of the ships at the Queen's Wharves from Dowgate to Ebbgate and Oystergate beyond that. Southwark, he knew, stood across the river, with the Rose, locked and barred now, and the bear pits that had once drawn the crowds too. All of it lay hidden by mist, as though time, in a single inked line from Burghley, had wiped out their existence. The bed was small and cramped. It was a bed for sleeping, not loving; a bed in which to die. Marlowe opened the single cupboard door and a couple of shirts hung there.

'Is this it?' he asked Mrs Isam without turning to look at her.

'What did you expect?' she asked. 'I haven't been able to let this room, what with the Pestilence. So I had to make a living somehow.'

'You sold his clothes?'

'Of course. Not that they fetched much. His cloak was pretty threadbare and he'd long ago pawned that stupid bloody earring he used to wear. Anything else, that slut Fanny Jackman must have taken.'

'She was fond of Dominus Greene,' Marlowe turned to her, checking that the cupboard really was empty.

'Fond, my arse!' Eliza Isam toyed with spitting on the floor, but it was her floor and she *might* be able to let the room again, one day. Also, it never did to let the girls see her show her coarser side; she had to keep a distance.

'Tell me, Mrs Isam,' Marlowe said, 'apart from Gabriel Harvey, who spent time with Dominus Greene? When we spoke before, I wasn't quite sure of the situation here. Now, I am.'

'Situation?' she frowned. 'What situation?'

'You keep a bawdy house, Madame,' he told her. 'The girl I just met is one of your doxies. So was Fanny Jackman.'

'How dare you!' Mrs Isam snarled, climbing onto her

dignity and clinging to it for dear life. 'They're serving wenches, that's all.'

'And I'm the Archbishop of Canterbury. I'm also running out of patience. Somebody killed Robert Greene, Mrs Isam, in *your* house. Shall I find a magistrate to start some enquiries? Keeping a knocking-shop is one thing, but allowing the murder of a gentleman . . .' he closed to her, looking down into her twisted face, 'perhaps even *participating* in the murder of a gentleman . . .'

'I never!' she screamed. 'I never did!'

'Then tell me who came here. Who visited Greene in the days before he died?'

Mrs Isam shuddered. This strange, dark man with the singular purpose had not touched her, yet she felt as if he had driven red-hot irons into her flesh.' There was one man,' she said. 'Came twice. Both before and after Dominus Greene died. Name of Johnson.'

'Johnson?' The name meant nothing to Marlowe. 'What did he look like?'

'Er . . . tall. Older than you. Dressed like a roisterer. We don't get many like that in Kyroun Lane.'

'What did he want? One of the girls?'

'No, just Dominus Greene. Said he was an old friend, from way back.'

'He talked to Greene here? In this room?'

'Yes. On the day before he died. He came back the day after.'

'Did he take anything with him? Of Greene's, I mean.'

'Papers.' She was trying to remember. The passing of her lodger had left her, it had to be said, a little unnerved. 'I don't know what they were. Plays and poetry, I suppose.'

'They didn't go with Dr Harvey?'

'No, no. He came later. It's funny. Nobody came at all in those last days and suddenly there was two of them. Well, three, really, if you count Fanny I-can-speak-Latin Jackman, which I don't. Oh, and Timmy, of course.'

'Timmy?'

'My nephew. He comes round to see me from time to time. He's home now, as a matter of fact. Do you want a word?'

Marlowe did. Fanny Jackman had told him that Mrs Isam's nephew often sat with Dominus Greene. Perhaps he could shed some light in the darkness of Dowgate.

Mrs Isam shrieked out the lad's name and there was a clatter of pattens on the risers. A young man stood there on the landing, a young man that Marlowe had seen before.

'Master Marlowe!' the boy stood open-mouthed.

'Timothy,' Marlowe nodded. 'The sorcerer's apprentice.'

'That's right,' Mrs Isam grinned her gappy grin. All in all, Marlowe was happier when she was scowling. 'Although I don't think I care for Dr Forman being described as a sorcerer. He's—'

Marlowe raised a hand. 'Yes,' he said. 'I know what Dr Forman is. Would you leave us, Mrs Isam?'

'Leave?' The woman was nearly speechless.

'It's all right, Aunt El,' Timothy said, patting the woman's shoulder and shooing her through the door. 'Master Marlowe and I are just going to have a little chat.'

'Ah, you University wits, eh? All right, call me if you want me.'

Timothy closed the door behind her. 'She was a good woman once, Master Marlowe,' he said, 'when her husband was alive.'

'And now?' Marlowe eased himself down onto Greene's bed. It wasn't the softest he had ever known.

'The girls.' Forman's apprentice was looking out of the window. 'I've tried to talk her out of it, but she says a woman must make a living. Who are we to judge? God will have the last word.'

'What about Robert Greene's last word?' Marlowe asked.

'What do you mean?' Timothy turned to face him.

'Were you with him when he died?'

'No, I was at the master's . . . er . . . Dr Forman's house in Philpot Lane. Where we bumped into each other, in fact.'

'But you spent time with Greene?'

'Yes, I did. He was quite the philosopher, you know.'

'Really?'

'We had long discussions into the night, about all sorts of things. The exact shape of the world. The existence of God.'

'And what conclusions did you come to?' Marlowe asked.

Timothy looked at him oddly. 'I'm rather more concerned with *your* conclusions, Master Marlowe,' he said.

'Mine?' It was Marlowe's turn to frown.

'Yes. Men say you have dared God out of his Heaven. Men say that you believe that Moses was just a conjuror. Men say—'

'—that I am Machiavel and that there is no God. Yes, I know, Timothy. Men say a lot of things, through spite and envy and malice, those three wise men who ride with us wherever we go, following what star they will.'

'You are making fun of me, Master Marlowe,' Timothy said, a rather sad look on his face.

'Not for all the world,' Marlowe said. 'Rather, I am making fun of myself. Tell me, did Dominus Greene talk of any enemies?'

'Enemies?'

'I received a letter from him, written in the days before he died. He thought that someone was trying to kill him.'

'Who?'

Marlowe shrugged. 'If I knew that, we wouldn't be having this conversation. Whoever it was, killed him slowly.'

'Slowly?'

'With poison would be my guess.' Marlowe knew that it would be civil to give John Dee credit where it was due, but the least said, the soonest mended. 'There was no inquest.'

'The master . . . Dr Forman . . . said there was no need.'

'Did he now?'

'He is a great man, Master Marlowe,' Timothy said, 'except . . .'

'Except?'

'No, no,' the boy shook his head, 'I've said too much.'

'You've said nothing,' Marlowe contradicted him. 'What were you going to say?'

Timothy hesitated. He wasn't wearing his silly robes today – he never did in Dowgate on the principle that he probably wouldn't escape with his life – so, somehow, he felt removed from Forman, at arm's length at least. 'He preys on women. Relies too heavily in my opinion on glamour. He wants faerie dust and flashing lights. And money, of course. The rest of us want science. Even Gerard, in his country bumpkin way.

Actually, perhaps more than any of us; the man knows his herbs, I'll give him that.'

'Does he?' Marlowe raised an eyebrow. 'And what is the good of your science, Timothy?' he asked.

'To find God, of course. Isn't that what all of us are about?'

Marlowe smiled. 'I didn't have Forman or any of his boys down as Puritans,' he said.

'We're not that,' Timothy assured him. 'We just see things differently.'

'So does John Dee,' Marlowe reminded him.

Timothy's mouth hung open. 'You know Dr Dee?' he asked.

Marlowe nodded. 'I am proud to count him a friend,' he said.

'Oh, Master Marlowe. Could you introduce us? The master is a genius, of course, but Dr Dee . . .'

Marlowe laughed, holding up his hand. 'I don't know,' he said. 'One thing at a time. First, I must find out who killed Robert Greene.'

'I don't see how I can help,' the boy said.

'How often did Dr Forman come to this house?' Marlowe asked.

'Now and then,' Timothy told him.

'With you?'

'Hardly ever,' Timothy said. 'He encourages us apprentices to go our own way. Says he doesn't need to hold our hands. Between you and me,' he leaned in to Marlowe, lowering his voice and becoming confidential, 'I think we cramped his style. Ladies-wise, that is.'

'Did he like Greene?' Marlowe asked. 'Spend time with him?'

'I don't know,' Timothy said. 'He never mentioned it. I know he spent quite a lot of . . . time . . . with Fan Jackman.' He looked thoughtful. 'Gerard and Matthias did, though.'

'What?' Marlowe didn't follow.

'Spent time with Greene. I introduced them. Matthias is an Oxford man, so I think he liked teasing Robert with the Cambridge thing, as he does me. Gerard doesn't know one end of a university from the other, so men like Robert impress him.'

'So they both came here? And so did Dr Forman?'

'Yes,' Timothy said. 'Yes, of course. What are you saying?'
Marlowe sighed. 'I wish I knew,' he said. 'Tell me, your
aunt mentioned a Master Johnson who called on Greene in
the days before his death. Do you know him?'
'No,' Timothy said. 'I have seen him, though.'
'When?'
'Ooh,' Timothy had to dig deep into his memory. 'I suppose
it would be the last time I saw Robert, a couple of days before
he died.
'What did he look like?'
'To be honest, I wasn't paying much attention. I assumed
he was a client, you know, of one of the girls. He was a
gentleman, that much is certain. His clothes, his manner of
speaking. He had an air of authority about him.'
'Authority?'
'Yes, you know; as if he was used to giving orders. And
having them followed.'
Marlowe clutched at an impossible straw. 'He wasn't unusu-
ally short?' he asked. 'A dwarf, almost?'
'No.' Timothy shook his head, this time without having to
think unduly. 'Six foot, if he was an inch. Why the interest,
Master Marlowe?'
Marlowe looked deep into the boy's eyes. 'The interest,
Timothy,' he said, 'is that you might just have seen Robert
Greene's murderer.'

As Marlowe made his way back to Hog Lane late that evening,
he was in two minds as to whether he had achieved a lot
that day or nothing at all. He had certainly spoken to a lot of
people, asked them a lot of questions and, in some cases,
requested a boon. But whether any of it would lead anywhere
was anyone's guess. He walked more and more slowly as he
got nearer to his own front door, somehow reluctant to go
in and be by himself, alone with his thoughts. A new play,
rudimentary jottings only, lay on the table in his bedchamber
and in normal times he would feel that itching in his head and
in his hand to get more words down on paper. Sometimes,
he could see them, swirling around his head like moths to a
flame, clamouring to be the next one written, to be forever

part of one of his mighty lines. But tonight, it was faces he could see; Robert Greene, grey and still petulant, even in death; Richard Williams, bereft and suddenly only half of a whole; Eunice Brown, bruised, battered and baulked of a peaceful meeting with her Maker. They seemed to have no link between them and, try as he might, he could not make them fit. And yet . . .

'Kit?' The word was whispered but it hit Marlowe's ear like a gunshot, so deep was he in his own thoughts. He had spun round, dagger in hand, almost before he realized it.

'Who's there?' he hissed. 'Show yourself.'

'Whoa there, Kit.' Shaxsper stepped out into the fitful moonlight. 'It's only me. Will. Will Shaxsper.'

'Are you some kind of idiot?' Marlowe stormed at him. 'Don't you know by now not to creep up on me? I could have killed you.'

Shaxsper was a phlegmatic man but even his heart was beating faster. 'You were very quick on your feet, there, Kit. But I was sure you had seen me – you seemed to be looking straight at me as you came down the lane.'

'I was thinking.' Marlowe sheathed his dagger and Shaxsper did fleetingly wonder why he had kept it in his hand so long. 'I'm sorry, Will. I have a lot on my mind. Did you want me for anything in particular, or were you lounging in my doorway by sheer coincidence?'

Shaxsper laughed. He was clearly forgiven. 'I wanted to see you, Kit. Without the theatres we're all a bit shiftless and I am trying to decide whether to go home and be a glover like my father. Move back in with . . .'

'Anne.'

'I do *know* my wife's name, Marlowe.' Shaxsper was on his dignity. 'I was just pausing for thought.'

Marlowe undid the latch and pushed open his door, gesturing Shaxsper to follow. 'Ah, I see. A little dramatic break, there. Very effective. Keep it in.' He groped for a tinderbox and lit a taper with the ease of long practice. 'Come through into the kitchen. It will be warmer in there and there might be a posset warming on the hob.'

'Your women keep you well, Kit.'

'I'm not too sure whose benefit it is for,' he said with a smile. 'They don't have too hard a life. I am hardly here, when all is said and done.'

The kitchen was indeed warm and comforting, lit softly by the embers of the fire. The smell of cinnamon and nutmeg lightly perfumed the air and the posset pot and ladle were where he knew they would be, in the far corner of the hearth, keeping warm.

'I'll just get an extra cup for you. Sit down.' Marlowe gestured to a chair in the chimney corner. 'Watch out for the cat, she likes to sleep there when it starts to get colder out.'

Shaxsper swept a hand over the shadowed seat but it was unoccupied and he sat down. 'I would never have guessed this of you, Kit. A house. Staff. A cat.'

Marlowe filled the two cups and handed one over. 'A man must live somewhere. And it isn't my cat. As for staff, sometimes I wonder if I work for them, not the other way around. But it is good to have somewhere to sit in the warm and have a drink at the end of the day without having to keep my dagger at my back, it's true.'

Shaxsper sipped his drink. His landlady tended to the watery when she made posset, which was almost never. This was perfect and he gave it all his attention. His eyelids began to close and he was starting to wonder if Marlowe had such a thing as a second-best bed when his host suddenly spoke.

'So, Will. As you were saying. Should you move back in with . . .'

'Ha ha. Very amusing. But . . . should I, do you think?'

'I have never met the woman,' Marlowe hedged.

'That doesn't have anything to do with it,' Shaxsper said, testily. 'She's perfectly pleasant, as far as I recall. It's just that I know if I go back, I won't leave again. My dream of fame, of becoming a playwright . . . that all goes to Hell and I become a glover or end up working on her family's farm. I'm not sure I can do that, Kit.'

'Then don't.' Marlowe had never worried about what his family would think, but he knew with children, Shaxsper's outlook had to be different. 'Look, I perhaps shouldn't tell you this, but I believe the theatres might be reopening soon.'

Shaxsper held on to his cup with difficulty as he jack-knifed upright in his chair. 'What have you *done*?' he asked, his eyes sparkling. 'Have you really got Burghley to recant?'

'Not directly,' Marlowe said. 'And this isn't for public consumption, but hopefully, yes, soon. Probably not immediately – Burghley won't want to lose face – but soon. So, does that answer your quandary?'

'Oh, yes!' Shaxsper leaned his head back in his chair and closed his eyes in bliss. He wouldn't have to be a glover, to have pricked, sore fingers and unsatisfied customers. He wouldn't have to move back in with—

'I know this will surprise you, Will,' Marlowe said, breaking into the would-be playwright's thoughts, 'but I would like some advice from you.'

Shaxsper looked at him wide-eyed. 'From me?'

'Yes, I knew it would surprise you,' Marlowe said. 'I've surprised myself. But with Tom in Bedlam, Nicholas Faunt . . . who knows where . . . and Michael Johns and Dr Dee tucked up in their beds too far away to reach, I am left with you, or so it seems. If you'd rather not, I do understand.'

Shaxsper leaned forward eagerly. 'No, Kit, no, I am truly honoured. I will try to give my very best advice.'

Marlowe smiled grimly. 'Don't overdo it, Will. I just need you to be as intelligent as you know how. Can you manage that?'

Shaxsper wasn't enough of an actor to be able to look intelligent very successfully, but he gave it his very best try, his great brow furrowed, a crooked finger to his chin.

Marlowe sighed. This might well turn out to be a gigantic mistake, but it was too late to renege now. 'You know I was looking into the circumstance of Greene's death, of course.'

'I helped dig him up,' Shaxsper said proudly.

'Indeed. Well, when I went to Cambridge in search of Harvey, I met a lad there whose twin brother had drowned in the Cam. It had been put down as a tragic accident but he – and I – suspect murder. Whoever had killed his brother had also tried to kill him. It isn't often you get to chat with a murder victim, and his story was an odd one. As he remembers it, and Dr Dee says it was his imagination at the point of death, he was dunked under the water repeatedly and a man kept asking him a question.'

Shaxsper had not the same experience of bloody murder as Marlowe, but he thought about it all the time. A play wasn't a play, in his opinion, without at least a couple of horrible deaths, the more the merrier, so he was always concocting new ways to dispatch a person. 'What was the question?'

'"Have you seen him?"'

'Well, that's clear. The murderer had obviously mistaken these boys for someone else, someone who knew the whereabouts of . . . I don't know . . . a loved one, perhaps. Someone who had stolen something.'

That sounded remarkably intelligent and Marlowe almost looked around to see who had spoken; surely the words had not come out of Shaxsper's mouth? 'The problem there, though, is that they were twins. Absolutely identical, according to the surviving brother. It would be stretching credulity to think that this hypothetical person, who knew where another hypothetical person was, was also an identical twin looking very like . . .'

Shaxsper flapped a hand. 'Yes, yes. I do see. But it would explain it, all the same.'

'Then there was another death, in Hatfield. At Burghley's house, as a matter of fact. This time, it was an old lady, who had been savagely smothered, her face and neck a mass of fingermarks, scratches and bruises.'

Shaxsper looked blank.

'I know at first glance it doesn't seem to have anything in common with Greene and the drowned boy and yet . . . it niggles at me.'

'Did anyone see anything? Hear anything?'

Marlowe blew out a frustrated breath. 'Not a thing. The maid along the landing is deaf, although she won't admit it. The house is full of all kinds of people, coming and going. The guests are above reproach and their servants have to be assumed to be so, otherwise we would all be with Tom in Bedlam. It will turn out to be something and nothing, I suppose, but . . . even so . . .'

Shaxsper was tiring of looking intelligent and the heat of

the fire was making him a little drowsy, but he tried his best to stay awake.

'Do you think that the boy heard his attacker speak? That it wasn't his imagination?'

'I hear someone call my name, sometimes,' Shaxsper said.

Marlowe looked encouraging. He wasn't quite sure where this was going.

'At night, you know, between waking and sleeping. Just "Will" like that. Once, when I heard that Hamnet was ill, I heard him call "Papa". But I have never heard a question like that. Not in my head. It seems a bit . . .' Shaxsper sought for the right word – the problem he often had with choosing the correct one frequently drove him to make one up. 'A bit . . . complexible.'

'Complexible? Is that even a word?' Marlowe was beginning to see through Shaxsper's rambling but needed another push to get there.

'Complicated, then. Over-precise. So I think that he *did* hear it, yes.'

'But what did it mean?'

'That I don't know. Perhaps I'm tired. I suppose I should be getting back home.' Shaxsper looked wistfully at Marlowe.

The real playwright let him stew for a moment then reached forward and slapped his knee. 'Don't worry, Will, you can stay tonight. Will the second-best bed do you?'

Over the years working for the Queen's secret service, Kit Marlowe had learned a thing or two about waiting on street corners. London was crawling with coney-catchers, shady characters like Frizer and Skeres who could spot an ingénu a mile away and fleece him of his valuables, livelihood and inheritance before he could so much as sneeze. Dressed down as he was, he tried that ploy today. He had already bearded Forman in his lair, badgering Gerard on his way in and he didn't want to risk it again. He had bumped into Timothy without having to break his stride, but that still left Matthias.

The lad emerged a little after noon, striding down Philpot Lane in the direction of the abbey. Knights of the shire in their formal black robes were crowding into St Stephen's Hall. There was much jostling and shouting as men prepared to debate one of Her Majesty's bills of provision. Marlowe had targeted three of them already, posing as a humble petitioner. In every case, he'd been given a flea in his ear, but it had all killed time that morning and had served its purpose.

'Keep walking,' he muttered in Matthias's ear, getting into step behind him.

The big lad turned with a swirl of his flashy cape. 'Master Marlowe,' he said, but didn't have time for more before he was scuttling down some steps into the basement of an alehouse and bounced into a hard, wooden seat.

'What'll you have?' Marlowe asked him.

'Oh, that's very good of you. Rhenish, if they have any.'

'Pickles to go with that?' The playwright-projectioner clicked his fingers and a serving girl appeared. He was remembering Gabriel Harvey's explanation of what had killed Robert Greene.

Matthias looked up at the girl and grinned. 'No, no,' he said. 'I am about the doctor's business today and my breath must be fresh.' He winked at the girl who smiled coyly, curtseyed and went in search of the wine.

'Tell me about Dr Forman,' Marlowe leaned forward.

'What do you want to know?' Matthias asked.

So much for the loyalty of apprentices. Marlowe kept it simple. 'Everything.'

'Well . . .' It hadn't occurred to Marlowe that *this* sorcerer's apprentice could gossip for England, but the man asking the questions had struck pure gold. 'Not to put too fine a point on it, Master Marlowe, he is a fraud.'

'Oh?'

'His sole purpose in life is to find fame and fortune – in either order. To that end, he has his way with ladies of rank. Or money; he doesn't care which.'

'And men?'

Matthias looked shocked. 'I hadn't heard *that!*' he said, almost indignant.

'No, I mean, how does he manage the men? I assume not all of his clients are female.'

'Oh, I see. Well, he uses his science, of course. I once heard him discourse with two leading scholars from the Inns of Court for nearly three hours. All very plausible, but I'm not sure how much of it was true.'

The girl arrived with the cups and lingered for long enough for Matthias to squeeze her hand. 'You have some tension there, my dear,' he purred. 'Comes of carrying too many heavy jugs, I'll wager.' He beamed at her breasts, threatening as they were to burst out of her bodice. 'If I had more time today . . .'

'You haven't,' Marlowe said, shooing the girl away. 'You're an Oxford man, aren't you?'

'Trinity,' Matthias said, 'although I have not attained my Masters degree yet.'

'Nor will you, away from the college,' Marlowe pointed out. Both men knew that residence at the university was essential for the higher qualification.

'Ah, but I am learning at the knee of the great Dr Forman,' Matthias pointed out.

'His knee may be great,' Marlowe said, 'but you just told me he is a fraud.'

'In his daily rounds, yes,' Matthias sipped his wine, 'a man has to make a living.'

'Can he cure the Pestilence?' Marlowe asked.

Matthias shrugged. 'He says he can. But deep down, in the stillness of the laboratory, we all of us work for one thing.'

'Which is?'

Matthias became confidential. He glanced from left to right. 'To find God,' he said.

Marlowe's eyes narrowed. 'Then you have all missed your calling, Master Matthias,' he said. 'You should have joined the Church.'

'No, no,' the boy shook his head. 'I'm not talking about religiosity, faith, any of that claptrap. I'm talking about science. About the notion of Heaven. Is it real? Are there gates of pearl? Does St Peter keep them, with the keys in his hand? When you and I see a man laid into his grave, Master Marlowe, is that it? Is that all? We believe there's more.'

'We?' Marlowe repeated. 'Do you mean the majority of the world?'

'No,' Matthias said. 'They just repeat by rote. The three of us and the magus *know* there is more. As do you.'

'Me?' Marlowe raised an eyebrow.

'One of the little trifles I've read in my time is a copy of a play of yours that I believe will never be staged again – *Dr Faustus*.'

'Where did you get that?' Marlowe asked.

'Never mind. Faustus sells his soul to the Devil to see things that most mortals can only dream of. Have you seen the Devil, Master Marlowe? Are you really a reincarnation of Machiavel?'

Marlowe looked at the boy. With his golden curls and the smooth curve of his cheek, he had mistaken him for a cherubic oaf, a chaser of girls and a charlatan, posturing, like his master, in a lurid gown for effect. But this jackanapes had neatly turned the tables and it was Marlowe who was stretched out like some hapless thing pinned to a laboratory table.

'Reincarnation of Machiavel?' Marlowe smiled. 'No. Have I seen the Devil? Who's to say? He wears so many guises, Master Matthias. That drunk over there?' He nodded to the far end of the room where a loudmouth was complaining about the taste – and the cost – of the beer. 'The girl who served us, the one you plan to practise the doctor's special massage on? Philip Henslowe, erstwhile owner of the Rose? Lord Burghley? You?'

'Me?' The tables had turned again. 'No, no. I'm looking for God. If I find the Devil on the way, so be it.'

'How do you do it?' Marlowe asked.

'Aha,' Matthias tapped the side of his nose. 'Trade secrets, I'm afraid, Master Marlowe,' he said. 'I can tell you how the others do it. My own methods must remain my own.' Again he became confidential. 'We all risk damnation as it is.'

'I'll settle for that,' Marlowe said.

'Take Gerard. Not a duplicitous bone in his body, or a brain in his head. He will not hurt animals so he uses plants, herbal medicines, that kind of thing.'

'He's a wise man, then?'

'Of sorts. White witchcraft, if you will.' Matthias mouthed the words. An alehouse a mere stone's throw from St Stephen's

Hall and the Abbey of Westminster was not somewhere men bandied such words about. 'He has potions, elixirs, all suggested to him by the doctor. Except that he knows far more about them than the doctor does. By mixing certain elements in his phials, he hopes to make it possible for us to see Heaven.'

Marlowe looked dubious. 'Any luck so far?'

'That depends on who he tries it on. It did nothing for me or the doctor. Timothy – who knows? I'll get to him in a minute. Mistress Forman will have no truck with it, but one or two of our clients seem . . . I'll have to use the word "enchanted".'

'In what way?'

'Well, take Robert Greene. Weeks before he died, Gerard gave him a potion – mandragora, foxglove, bits and bobs.'

'And?'

'Well, if you ask me, Greene was a little touched before Gerard started, but he became even odder later, sitting in a shroud, as if he was already dead.'

'Preparing to meet his Maker,' Marlowe nodded.

'That was Timothy's belief, certainly, when we talked about it.'

'And what is Timothy's method?'

'Well, he's far more adventurous. Rats, cats, dogs, the odd crow. He's working on river trout at the moment.'

'Go on.'

'Well, he kills them – says fresh meat is essential – skins them and pegs them out on his table. He works on the heart, the lungs, the liver.'

'And?'

Matthias shrugged. 'Damned if I know,' he said. 'Don't even know what he's looking for. He's been focussing on the animals' brains recently. There *are* people in this great country of ours who say that the brain is behind it all, that it – not the body – is where the soul is.'

'So you don't think that Timothy is making very good progress?'

'No, I don't, but he's a dark one, is our Timothy. When and

if he finds anything, he's not likely to share it with anybody else.'

'Which brings us back to the doctor,' Marlowe said, leaning back. He wanted to replenish their wine but didn't want the air-headed girl distracting Matthias again, so he went thirsty.

'Hmm.' Matthias leaned back too, steepling his fingers. 'The doctor is a picker-up of other people's ideas,' he said. 'He'll help himself to anything he can from me, Gerard, Timothy, the man in the street.'

'I know a playwright like that,' Marlowe said.

'I doubt you'll get anything particularly original from the doctor. You'll have to ask him.'

'That's a little like handling quicksilver,' Marlowe smiled.

'Quicksilver!' Matthias almost shouted. 'Now, there's a thought!'

'What?'

'Oh, nothing.' The apprentice realized he might have said too much.

'Do you know Cambridge, Master Matthias?' Marlowe asked. 'Specifically the stretch of the river called Paradise?'

'Wouldn't be seen dead near the place,' Matthias laughed. 'Oh, begging your pardon, of course, Dominus Marlowe.'

'Pardon granted,' Marlowe smiled. 'What about Hatfield?'

'Er . . . that's in Sussex, isn't it?'

'No,' Marlowe said, flatly. 'Tell me, when the three of you went on your travels recently, where did you go?'

'Can you keep a secret?' Matthias looked a little concerned.

'Has the Pope put a price on the Queen's head?'

'Very well. I went home. To Chertsey, I don't know if you have ever been there. My people have the old Abbey House there. Lots of good cooking, comfortable beds, motherly smotherings, that sort of thing. We all told the doctor we'd been out administering to the sick. All a load of hogwash, of course. Gerard camped out somewhere along the river. God knows where Timothy went. Some place called Barn Elms, he said.'

'Barn Elms?' Marlowe repeated.

'Do you know it?'

'I know of it,' Marlowe said. 'Pity it's nowhere near Hatfield.'

Matthias clicked his fingers and the blonde girl came running. The apprentice was shaking his head. 'All this obsession with Hatfield, Master Marlowe,' he said, squeezing the girl through her plackets, 'you really should try to get out more.'

FOURTEEN

He drummed his fingers on the sideboard and stared out of the latticed windows. The morning sun was gilding the turrets of Whitehall and the birches flashed silver under their fast-vanishing canopy of leaves. The Queen's Secretary of State had waited long enough. Either Dr Forman had driven back the Pestilence or Dr Dee had had a mercurial hand in it. Or God Himself had decided that enough was enough. Whatever the reason, the Pestilence was petering out and he had it from the mouth of the magus himself. The plague pit was only half full this time and there were markedly fewer men wandering the streets in herb-filled beaks.

Burghley could do what he was about to do without loss of face. He called loud and clear and a liveried flunkey arrived, secretary to the Secretary. 'Get a message to the Master of the Revels, Dickson,' he said. 'Tell him to open the theatres. We'll just have to ride out the wrath of the Puritans. And tell Tilney to put something new on for Her Majesty – the old trout's been bending my ear for weeks.'

'Sir.' The secretary bowed.

'Oh, Dickson – you'll dress that up a bit, of course.'

Edmund Tilney skipped around his chambers on the shadier side of Whitehall. He was clutching Burghley's letter, complete with wax and ribbon, and humming to himself. He even danced a very quick volta with Mistress Tilney and he hadn't danced with her for years. In his head, the orchestra played and a thousand cannon roared their approval, fireworks filling a golden sky.

'Henderson,' he bellowed at an underling, 'write me an edict. Make it in the form of a playbill and run off a hundred copies. No, make that two hundred. Stick them on any available space your people can find. Well, don't just stand there, man!'

'Er . . . the Puritans, Sir Edmund?' Henderson could read the minds of Londoners like an open book.

'Bugger the Puritans, man!' Tilney chortled. 'The theatres are open!'

A horseman was galloping along Maiden Lane, lashing his mount with his rein-ends and ramming home his spurs. Had the Dons invaded? Was the Queen dead? Neither seemed likely, because the messenger was Edmund Tilney. The Master of the Revels dismounted as if he was half his fifty-seven years and threw his reins to Nicholas Skeres, who happened to be sitting by the Rose's gate. With a theatrical flourish, Tilney produced a hammer from his saddlebag and, waving a sheet of parchment, smashed the padlock that held the doors shut.

'Do you work here?' he asked Skeres.

'Used to,' the man muttered, but Ingram Frizer was altogether nimbler and louder.

'No, he don't, sir. But I do.' He bowed low. 'Ingram Frizer, walking gentleman.' It never hurt to get your name lodged in the minds of great men. Unless, of course, those great men were magistrates.

'Well, carry on walking, sir,' Tilney laughed. 'The theatres are open!'

Edmund Tilney had never been hoisted shoulder high before, but he was now, first by Skeres and Frizer, then by actors and stagehands without number who seemed to sprout from the Rose's stonework. They carried him through the vestibule and into the courtyard before placing him carefully on a dais centre stage.

'If it's good enough for the King of France, Sir Edmund,' Frizer said, patting his shoulder, 'it's good enough for you.'

Tilney wasn't quite sure how to take that, but was more comfortable with the effusive thanks he got from Ned Alleyn and Richard Burbage, falling over each other in their hurry to reach him. A rapidly balding actor from Warwickshire was there too, slapping backs and laughing with joy, the tears running down his face.

'Marvellous news, eh, Mistress Henslowe?' he called out to one of the mob standing where the groundlings usually gathered.

It was one of those strange moments when a lull descends, like the eye of a storm, like the silence between the hiss of a fuse and the roar of a cannon. In that silence, all eyes turned to the woman in question.

'Marvellous, indeed,' the woman shrilled, looking about her hysterically. 'My husband, wherever he is, will be delighted.'

Cheers rose again from the crowd and the party began. Fighting his way out at last from the delirious theatricals, Edmund Tilney passed Mistress Henslowe.

'You really don't have to go to these lengths, Henslowe,' he muttered, 'unless of course, there is something you haven't told me?' and he swept on.

The October night was not cold, but even so, Marlowe was happy to be astride the wall of Master Sackerson's Bear Pit, with the musky warmth of the creature making just that tiny bit of difference to the overall temperature. It was too dark to see the details of the bear's moth-eaten coat, but there was enough light still in the sky to reflect in his piggy eyes, so Marlowe knew he was looking up at him. His huffing breath was his way of saying he loved you, or so Tom Sledd always said, so Marlowe decided to take it on trust.

'Don't worry, Master S.,' Marlowe said, throwing down a wizened apple he had brought with him specially. 'Tom will be back soon. I know he's missed you.'

The bear gave a soft little grunt and Marlowe could tell why he and Tom were so close. He really *did* understand every word said to him.

'He knows you do,' the playwright told the bear. 'He's in good hands. Nicholas Faunt . . . you remember him?'

The huff was a little harsher. Faunt had not always got on with the bear; he didn't really understand his point of view, so Tom said.

'Well, he's looking after Tom, so he'll come to no harm. You'll see him soon, don't fret.'

An enormous cheer broke from the Rose, almost visible in the faint glow of limelight spilling through the open roof.

'Someone's having a good time,' Marlowe said, indulgently. 'Theatres open again, everybody happy.' Except. Except Fan

Jackman, Richard Williams, Burghley and Cecil – and who knew how many others, deprived of their loved ones before their time. Marlowe looked down at the bear. 'Have you ever seen Heaven, Master Sackerson?' he asked.

The bear rolled over with a sigh, arms splayed, apple mush on his chin. Heaven was easy for him. Food. A bit of well-chosen company. Years ago, he would have said a female bear, just for a few minutes, now and then, but now, not so much. Marlowe wondered, not for the first time, how it would feel to tickle that vast stomach, to feel the strength still beneath the mothy fur. But he suspected that would be a very fast way of seeing Heaven, or wherever the tickler might be headed. He swung his leg over onto the pavement side of the wall and jumped down.

'Goodbye for now, Master Sackerson,' he whispered. 'Stay safe. And pray for me – I am going to see a man about a God.'

By the time Marlowe reached the house in the shadow of the abbey, the night was pitch dark. The usual detritus of London were still out and about and from time to time a cry of fear or pleasure – often hard to distinguish – pierced the night. But there was no glimmer of light from any of the windows facing the street, nor a sound.

Marlowe was wearing dark clothes with no decoration. Buttons had been dimmed with soot. His dagger hilt was loosely hung with a scrap of black velvet so that no glow of palm-polished silver would betray his position. He didn't know what he might have to do this night – he wasn't even sure if he would find Forman at home, given his well-advertised proclivities. But he had to try. With every day of freedom he gave the man, another soul might find itself set free before its time. And if Kit Marlowe wasn't sure of the existence of souls, he was sure that every man or woman alive had the right to their allotted span.

He eased himself under the deep lintel of the door. The lock was a basic one and soon broached. As he had suspected, there were no bolts drawn across. No man who likes to wander at night has bolts on his doors; all too easy to be locked out.

The hinges were well oiled too – with an inward chuckle, Marlowe wondered whether Forman would appreciate the joke that his nocturnal wanderings had made it so easy for Nemesis to come calling. Marlowe would have wagered a good purse that the stairs wouldn't creak and he would have won. Getting silently from a door to the landing above had never been so easy.

After that, it was a little more difficult. There were five doors off the landing and no other stairs. Like many buildings squeezed into the streets around Westminster, this house had just two floors. Downstairs, there were two large rooms, mainly for show and, in Forman's house, the laboratory and then the sanctum sprawling out at the back. A window at the head of the stairs looked out onto the courtyard, and the windows of the long, low building were dark and blank. One door stood open and in the gloom it was possible to see two little beds, blankets rolled back, and some children's toys. It didn't surprise Marlowe that Forman, for all his brave words about being able to cure the Pestilence, had sent his children away to the safety of the countryside. Many farmers' wives had reason to bless the black death that stalked the city streets – as long as their little guests didn't bring it with them, the money that they did bring could make all the difference between a lean winter and a comfortable one.

He crept along the landing, rolling from heel to toe, slowly, carefully. Just because Forman oiled his hinges and braced his stairs, there was no need to be careless. Marlowe had faced many a man over the years, armed to the teeth and determined that one of them would die. So far, they had all backed the wrong man as survivor, but Forman was cunning, if not, Marlowe guessed, much of a swordsman. Where Marlowe was quick on his feet and ruthless, Forman knew this house like the back of his hand and he wasn't above installing trapdoors to catch the unwary. And he had three apprentices to call upon. Rumour had it that Mistress Forman had a formidable right hook too. So care must be uppermost in his mind.

At the first door, there was a glimmer of light showing around the hinges and through a knothole just below Marlowe's eyeline. It threw a narrow beam across the landing, picking out a detail on a small painting hung on the panelling; a curled finger seemed to beckon in the darkness. Taking care not to get too close in case someone on the other side of the door saw his eye fill the space, Marlowe looked in. The cook and the kitchen maid were tucked up in narrow beds, one on either side of a small chest where a stub of candle burned, the little maid completely fast asleep, as only exhausted people can be. The cook was reading a Bible, running her finger slowly along each line and moving her mouth silently as she did so. Sometimes, when a word was difficult, she had several tries at it and Marlowe found himself holding his breath as she struggled. After a moment or two, she reached the end of the appointed passage for the day and, with infinite care and slowness, she put a bookmark into her place, wrapped the Bible in a cloth and stowed it beneath her pillow. Then she retied the strings of her nightcap, snuggled down into the bed, into the nest her body had made after many nights of sleep and blew out the candle.

In the sudden darkness, Marlowe crept along to the next door. No handy knotholes here and he pressed his ear to the boards. A crescendo and diminuendo of snoring came through the wood, sometimes stopping altogether and then coming back again, like wind through the chimneys on a blustery day. The snores bespoke contentment but, more especially, young males deep in dreams they would rather not share. Occasionally, a bass chuckle broke the rhythm and then the snoring would be off again. It reminded Marlowe of being out in a fishing boat in his youth. The labouring climb to the top of a wave, the silent anticipation at its crest and then the exhilaration of the slide down the other side. This must be the apprentices' room and Marlowe crept past.

At the end of the landing, a door was slightly ajar. The position of this bedchamber suggested that it was bigger than the rest and Marlowe tried to decide whether this would be that of Forman himself or his wife. He had not got to know him well, but he didn't feel that the magus would give his wife the largest room. But on the other hand, he might do that as a sop to keep her quiet. It couldn't be easy to be married to a man who made fornication into a successful business. He had only seen the lady briefly, when she clouted Gerard round the head with a crack that echoed through the house, and he didn't think that she was someone who would let Forman get away with his dubious doings without a serious quantity of quid pro quo.

He pushed gently on the door and slipped inside. He knew instinctively that he was not alone in there. The smell of the rest of the house – of unknown chemicals, herbs, blood and dead vole – was less tangible in here, being overlaid with lavender and roses. The furniture was heavy and dark – the faint starlight coming through the undraped window showed massy blocks of darkness against one wall, a four-poster bed framed by presses. The white counterpane almost glowed by comparison and the bed clearly had an occupant, but from the doorway it was impossible to see who. Marlowe held his breath and crept closer. The figure on the bed writhed suddenly and muttered something he couldn't quite catch. But the voice was a woman's and so either this was Mistress Forman's room or, if she shared it with her husband, he was elsewhere. Marlowe frowned. This might mean making a new plan. But that wouldn't matter; a job worth doing is worth doing well.

He carefully retraced his steps to the door, not turning his back on the bed. Marlowe never turned his back on anyone, on principle. If a blade was coming for him, he would rather see its flight than suddenly feel it between his shoulder blades. He pulled the door to behind him and resumed his slow heel to toe along the landing, back towards the head of the stairs. As he passed the fourth door he listened briefly, just to complete the job. As his ear touched the knotty pine, he heard a noise which made even his man-of-the-world view of life take a pause. It was a low moan, not repeated, then the creak of a bed, the strings protesting as two bodies pressed down and writhed upon them. Surely, Forman didn't bring his conquests *here*? Not to the room next to his wife? No wonder the woman was a little short-tempered. Marlowe had had no second thoughts in bringing Forman to book but, even had he, they would have disappeared with that sound. His hand crept to the small of his back and he flipped the velvet from his dagger hilt. He wanted nothing to impede him when he made his final rush. If the lady was going to be embarrassed, so be it. Perhaps it would be a salutary lesson.

He lifted the latch slowly and was not surprised to find that it slid like silk. As he pushed the door open a little, he saw that a candle was burning on a press under the window. The black night took the flame and reflected it back into the room and so there was ample light to see by. Marlowe stood silently inside the door, eyes downcast for a moment while they got used to the light. At the edge of his vision, he could see that the figures on the bed seemed to have no shame. One was hunched over the other, back bowed and shaking furiously, fast, desperate. He raised his head from time to time and Marlowe could see the monstrous beak of a plague doctor outlined in gold against the light. The sparkle from the adorned robe threw prisms around the room, trembling on the walls and ceiling, reflected again and again from the black window panes. How like Forman to wear his robe when fornicating with some woman in desperate enough straits to be taken in by his lies. This had surely gone far enough. Marlowe reached for his dagger and was unsheathing it slowly, silently, when there came a sound that chilled his blood.

From the bed came a rattle, a rattle he had heard before, of a man breathing his last. The hunched figure leaned over the prone one and lifted the mask. He bent down and seemed to blow into the invisible face of his lover, who bucked and arced in the bed with a crowing shout as the air went back into desperate lungs. And then low, evil, a voice with ice in it – with dark menace that was worse than any dead man's rattle – spoke.

'Have you seen him? Have you seen him yet?'

Marlowe's breath, held for what seemed like eternity, left him in a rush and the figure on the bed spun round, the beak back in place, eyes burning behind the mask.

'You!' he spat and jumped to the floor, gown billowing around him like a cloud. He landed awkwardly, but recovered and went for Marlowe like a madman. The force of his leap sent Marlowe's dagger skittering into a corner, but even as he landed, Marlowe knew that this was not Simon Forman. Forman was a big man, tending to paunchy but still very fit and strong. The demon wrestling Marlowe to the floor now was small, wiry and desperate. Teeth sank into Marlowe's arm and hung on like a wild animal's. Fingers reached up to gouge at his eyes and one hand managed to grab a handful of hair, pulling hard and making the tears spring to Marlowe's eyes. Keeping his head back, he brought his knee up but missed his target, catching his opponent on the thigh. Even so, it was a hard blow and the grip on his hair was released and the teeth in his arm opened in an oath.

Marlowe rolled, in the limited space between the bed and the wall, and pinned the would-be murderer under him, pressing his arm across his throat. The great beak stabbed the air and almost caught him in the eye, but he pushed it back with one shoulder and felt it crack, cascading herbs everywhere. He pressed and pressed and remembered John Dee telling him how long it could take to stifle someone – he felt he had been here for hours already, but he knew deep down it was less than a minute.

At the far reaches of his hearing, he sensed that whoever it was on the bed was stirring, coughing, retching. Between each cough was a desperate whooping sound as air tried to force its way into lungs crushed and bruised, down a throat burning with the fires of Hell. But he could tell that they were beginning to get stronger. Could he hold down this writhing demon until they could climb out of the bed and come to his help?

The clawing hands beneath him were beginning to get weaker now but he dared not let go. It could all be a trap – he had been fooled this way before now and didn't intend it to happen again. But before he had to decide whether to stay there until one more man met his Maker before his time, he heard a heavy thud as the occupant on the bed fell to the floor and, swinging wildly, punched the struggling form beneath him in the side of the head so he lay still.

Marlowe rolled sideways, nursing his bitten arm. He looked to where Simon Forman sat with his back to the press, the candlelight making a halo around his head. And between them, out cold, was a slight figure with a broken mask across the face, dressed in one of Forman's outsize robes and breathing still, but with difficulty.

Forman looked up at Marlowe, a question in his eyes and Marlowe nodded. Slowly, easing the strings from around the ears, the magus slipped off the ruined mask to reveal the face of his apprentice, Timothy, pale in the candlelight, looking like a sleeping child.

'Did you know about him?' he said, quietly, to Forman.

Forman pointed to his throat and shrugged. It would be a long time before his silver tongue could do its work around London. Then he shook his head.

The door flew open and Mistress Forman stood there, her nightcap low on her forehead and her nightdress as impregnable as the Tower. 'Is it too much,' she said, 'to ask for a little quiet . . .?' Her voice fell away as she peered down at Timothy. Marlowe could read every thought that went through her head and he thought it best to intervene before she gave them a clout that would send them to Kingdom come.

'Mistress Forman,' he said, hurriedly, struggling to his feet. 'It's not what you think. Timothy was trying to kill your husband.'

She looked unsurprised. She had had the exact idea in mind for years. A thought struck her. 'What are you doing in my house?'

'Saving your husband's life, I suppose,' Marlowe said, dusting himself off and pulling his doublet back into shape. He saw a glint of metal in the corner, by the bed. 'Could you just reach that dagger for me, Doctor Forman?' He pointed and the magus leaned across and passed it to him. 'Thank you.' He turned back to the lady of the house, still looming white and terrible in the doorway. 'I apologize, I should not have come in without an invitation, but I am sure you can see that I had no choice. I knew there was a murderer here,' though he forbore to tell her he had got the wrong man, 'and I had to move fast.'

The woman stretched out a toe and poked Timothy with it. 'Is he dead?'

'No,' Marlowe reassured her. 'He's asleep. And I suggest we let him lie, for a while. Because when he wakes, his life will not really be worth living.'

She looked at her husband with little emotion, and then to

the unconscious boy. 'I'm sorry he tried to hurt you, Simon,' she said, 'and more sorry that he killed other people. But you put the idea into his head, whatever idea it was, and that was wrong.' She turned to Marlowe. 'Make sure you remember that, that it wasn't just that poor boy who did these terrible things. Sometimes, you don't need to wield a knife to kill someone.' She turned to go and then spoke over her shoulder. 'I am going to tell the others what has happened and send them on their way. They have homes to go to that are better than mine, though I tried, God help me. You,' she pointed at Forman, 'can go as well, as soon as it is light. I am sure there are many homes that will welcome you. And who knows, perhaps one day, this one might as well. Goodnight.' And with that, she shut the door.

The men sat silently for a moment, Forman because he had no choice, Marlowe because he was reassessing Mistress Forman; she was really quite a woman. Finally, he spoke.

'Do you feel well enough to help me get to the bottom of this, Doctor?' he said. 'Don't try to speak, just nod.'

The doctor nodded, carefully, holding his throat and swallowing with difficulty.

'Do you have a herb or something which will bring him round?'

Forman's eyes swivelled then he mimed throwing a jug of water over his apprentice.

'No, no, something which will bring him round in a fit state to answer questions.'

The doctor nodded and got to his feet, pausing on all fours to catch his breath. He pointed to his mouth and, when he knew Marlowe was watching, moved his lips in an exaggerated word – laboratory.

Marlowe pulled Timothy's arms up and hauled him over his shoulder. The boy grunted but didn't struggle and, with Forman carrying the candle ahead, they made their way down the stairs, Marlowe's shadow looking like a giant hunchback shrinking and growing in the flickering light. As they passed the apprentices' door, they could hear Mistress Forman's voice, telling the boys what had happened. The candlelight was streaming through the knothole again, so the cook at least had heard the commotion. But soon they were in the laboratory, the silence only broken by the skitter of Timothy's trapped rats and the hiss of a snake's belly as it circled them in their cage.

Forman made straight for a bottle on the far bench. He poured a cupful of it and drank it greedily, each gulp bringing a whimper. Then, he turned to where Marlowe had slung Timothy into a chair and motioned for him to tip back his head. With no preamble, he poured the liquid into the open mouth and stood back implacably watching while the boy gasped and frothed and tried desperately to get up. Marlowe held him fast and Forman gave him another shot. Soon, the apprentice was sitting looking about him, wild eyed.

'What is that stuff?' Marlowe was impressed.

Forman tapped the side of his nose. 'That's my secret,' he rasped.

'You'll make a fortune if you ever sell it,' Marlowe said and Forman smiled a wintry smile. That was certainly his plan, for a rainy day, which might already be here. 'Do you have some rope?' He was holding Timothy down, but it was getting difficult as the boy regained his strength.

Forman nodded and foraged under a bench, coming up with a coil of hemp, with strands of other materials woven through.

Timothy spat. 'Oh,' he said, 'don't tell me we're using the magic rope.'

How he could inject such venom into such simple words, Marlowe could not see. 'Magic rope?'

Timothy looked at him. 'It's just rope with a few dried flowers in it, but you would be amazed at how many people will pay a guinea a yard for it. It's good for whatever ails you, or so I believe. Or used to believe, perhaps I should say.'

Tied into his chair, the apprentice looked anything but a murderer. His bruises were starting to come out and he had the beginnings of a wonderful black eye. But through the swelling, his pupils were like fire, blazing out of a face contorted with hatred, malice and madness.

Forman leaned forward and swallowed painfully before grating out, 'Why did you do it, Timothy? What were you hoping to achieve?'

The boy laughed in his face. 'I was trying to beat you, to beat you all to finding God. You see,' and his face grew intense, 'I had heard stories, when I was a little boy. My mother, when she was giving birth to me, had died, or so they said. But the nurse brought her back; she threw water over her, bucket after bucket, and finally, she took a great breath and was alive again. That's what they told me. And later, when I was older, she told me that she had been on a staircase, lined with angels, and at the top of the stairs was a light and in the light was . . . God. She could never tell me what he looked like, because she heard me crying and came back to me.' He smiled like a child at each of his accusers. 'So she never saw God's face. But I knew that it could be done, to send someone up that staircase, but higher than she went, until they saw God's face. And then, bring them back, to tell us all about it.'

'But . . .?' Marlowe had seen many things done in the name of God, but this was new. 'How would it help us, to hear what God looks like? Surely, if you believe, you can decide for yourself what He looks like.'

'You *can*,' Timothy said, looking doubtful. 'But isn't it better to *know*?'

'Not if people die,' Marlowe said.

'People always die,' the apprentice said. 'You can't make an omelette without breaking eggs.'

'You killed people,' Marlowe said, bluntly. 'With your bare hands.'

'That wasn't very pleasant, I agree,' the boy said. 'But the herbs were too difficult to get right. I put some extra ingredients into Gerard's potion for Robert Greene and then, when he was almost gone, I would give him the antidote – which is just good old-fashioned mushrooms, by the way. But he never saw God, or so he said. I wouldn't put it past him to not tell me. He was a curmudgeon till the moment he died. And nobody cared, anyway.'

Marlowe couldn't help himself. He slapped the boy so his head snapped back. 'Who are you to judge that?' he snarled. 'Even I cared, and I wasn't even his friend. Who knows what he might have written, given time? Everyone should have the chance to live their span.'

As far as the ropes would let him, Timothy shrugged. 'Anyway, I decided not to use herbs,' he said, dismissing Robert Greene's little life in seven words. 'But I remembered my mother and her being doused with water, so I thought I would try that. The twins were an extra thing I thought I might try. I thought if I killed one, he might wait at the top of the staircase, to show God to his brother. But that didn't work, either. In fact, I did feel a little sorry about them. Well, the one that stayed alive. He looked so miserable, all wet and alone on the bank. But the river was hard work.'

Marlowe felt he would be happier somehow if this poor, mad creature had no scruples. To find he had one or two somehow made it worse. 'And Eunice Brown? How did you choose her?'

Forman cleared his throat. 'You said you were in Barn Elms,' he whispered.

Timothy looked him up and down as if he were a specimen on his slab. 'We all lied to you,' he said. 'At first, we were terrified, because you told us you could see what we did through your scrying glass. But as time went by, we knew it was all just your usual lies – yes, lies, so don't look so horrified – and, in the end, only Gerard believed it, and now not even him. I admit you caught me out, or almost. I thought the story of the horse – which was true, by the way – would be enough, but oh, no, you wanted more. So I told the truth in all but two things. I missed out killing that old woman.' He looked at Marlowe. 'What did you say her name was?'

'Eunice Brown.' Marlowe could scarcely speak for anger.

'Well, her, and also I said Barn Elms, not Hatfield. Master Marlowe can tell you why.'

Marlowe took a deep breath and composed himself. 'Barn Elms, Dr Forman, was the home of Sir Francis Walsingham, one-time Spymaster to the Queen. Hatfield is the family home of Sir Robert Cecil, who has that role now.'

'So, that was clever, wasn't it?' Timothy said. 'A clue.' He nodded at Marlowe, as one clever man to another. 'The old besom struggled. I wasn't ready for that.' Then he caught Forman's eye. 'Any more of that drink? I rather liked it.'

'No,' Forman grated. 'No more for you.'

'That's a shame. Where was I? Oh, yes. Well, tonight was make or break. I knew if I succeeded, the magus here would take all the credit. If I failed, I would have a dead man on my hands. So I knew, when I began, that if he told me what the face of God looked like, it would be knowledge that I and I alone would have. Because, you see,' he said, with a rueful smile at his master, 'either way, I would have to kill you. But you were as stupid as the rest. I have not been able to understand, Master Marlowe, why no one can tell me this simple fact. All I want, and it isn't much, is for them to climb that damned staircase, look into the face of God and come back and tell me about it. Is that too much to ask?' He looked at his captors. 'Is it?'

Marlowe motioned to Forman to follow him into the sanctum. Once there, he turned to him. 'He is quite mad, Doctor, you will agree with me?'

'Totally mad,' Forman nodded. 'I . . .' he bent his head and massaged his brow with his fingers, 'I don't know how I didn't see it.'

'I don't think anyone could have seen it until tonight,' Marlowe said. 'As far as he was concerned, what he did was experimenting, just as he has been doing with his animals, as Gerard did with his herbs. The lives he took were nothing in the search for the face of God. I must ask you, though – why did you set them on such a task? You must have known that had one of them, against all the odds, succeeded, or at least come up with a plausible answer, you would have all been at the very least in the Tower. The Puritans would not have allowed you to live.'

Forman flopped down in his chair and buried his head in his arms. Then, with a convulsive cough and a supreme effort, he spoke in almost his normal voice. 'I didn't think. I knew they could never find God, could never have a view of Heaven. When I took them on, I was proud to be able to mould young minds. I could send them out, in my image, through the land, making money. Healing people, of course, but mainly, making money.' He coughed again and eased his throat, flapping his hand to ask for a moment.

'But you didn't know how bright they would be, did you?'

Marlowe went on. 'You didn't know that you had taken three young minds into your home which would not be easy to mould. At first, of course. Give them a robe with glass beads on, gold-coloured lace, fringes and furbelows. Ironically, it was that that led me to one of you in the first place. Whoever killed Eunice Brown left a bead on her forehead in the struggle. But there were four robes and four sorcerers. But you were the one to give them some explosions, some scrying glass nonsense. And of course, your pièce de résistance, your special massage.'

'Perhaps, in retrospect, the special massage was a mistake . . .'

'Certainly in the case of Gerard it was. The scales fell from his eyes well and truly then. But eventually, of course, they all outstripped you. They could actually heal people, not just fool them. Gerard knows more about hedge magic now than you will if you live to be a thousand.'

Forman ducked his head.

'Which I daresay you have claimed will happen.' Marlowe sighed. 'And so, the worms turned. And, in turning, in Timothy's case, became totally unhinged. I have brought you through here so I can make a suggestion. By rights, we should hand him over to the magistrates, who will make sure that before many more weeks have elapsed, he will be dead. Or, we can do a kinder thing.'

Forman's eyes opened. 'What? Kill him ourselves? I'm not sure I—'

'No, not kill him ourselves.' Marlowe had killed men in his time, in hot blood and cold, but putting the poor mad thing in the next room out of his misery, as one would a horse or dog, was just not going to happen on his watch. 'I was thinking more of . . . Bedlam.'

Gerard and Matthias stood, irresolute, on the street outside Simon Forman's house. It had been an eventful few days, to be sure, but this night had finally topped the lot. First of all, it was shock enough to wake and find Mistress Forman leaning over their bed, nightcap ribbons flying, her nightdress buttons undone. The tale she told would have been difficult enough to follow even in broad daylight, but by the light of a flickering candle when she had dragged them from sleep was unbelievable. As they understood it, Timothy had gone mad and had killed the magus, who had been brought to life by a demon in black clothes who had been hiding under the bed.

'It sounds a bit unlikely,' Matthias said, as he hefted his bag over his shoulder.

'I should say so,' Gerard agreed. 'I don't think demons hide under beds, do they?'

Matthias was doubtful. 'I don't know. I know my grandame always said there was one in the press in my room who would eat me if I wouldn't go to sleep.'

Gerard thought for a moment. 'I think that was a story, Matthias,' he said, gently. He had, after all, seen his own grandmother do some rather incredible things which he had been told never to mention. A demon in a press might just be Matthias's family talent.

'Either way,' Matthias said, 'I'm for home. Soft beds. Good food. I might get my Masters degree after all.'

'Home for me, too.' Gerard didn't remember the beds as being any too comfortable, but at least he had one to himself. And his grandmother wasn't getting any younger; perhaps she would like an apprentice. 'Which way are you heading?' he asked.

'West. You?'

'East. Perhaps we'll meet again one day.' Gerard stuck out a hand and Matthias shook it in his fearsome grip.

'Perhaps I'll see you in my scrying glass,' the young giant said, and loped off up the road towards the river.

'Not if I see you first,' muttered Gerard, and turned his face to the rising sun.

'Shut the bloody Hell up!' Jack's guttural voice echoed and re-echoed through Bedlam's halls, bouncing off the dark passageways and running through the latrines. At first, his calls for quiet had been met with the usual echoing crescendo of the inmates and the rattling of chains. But now they could all see that Jack meant business. He had cracked his whip over their heads, so had Nat, their eyes blazing, their knuckles white around their weapons.

Roland Sleford waited until his gaolers had achieved their effect. Then he stepped up onto a table in the central hall. There was only one wolf-whistle and Nat put an abrupt end to that.

'Listen to me,' the master of Bedlam said, 'you worthless scum. If you thought you were mad, you've seen nothing yet. We are about to have a guest – and believe me, he'll be here for the duration. He'll also be in chains, for your safety and his.'

'Nice of him to think of our safety,' Tom Sledd murmured to Nicholas Faunt.

'Stow it!' Jack, who had the ears of a bat, stood alongside him.

'Gentlemen,' Sleford said, 'if you would be so kind.'

Jack and Nat shunted the crowd back as they all edged forward to see who this guest was. There were cries of delight when Simon Forman swept into the circle of daylight, his gown sparkling and his face imperial. Anyone who dressed like that *had* to be an Abram man at the very least. Then came a little weaselly one, shorter than Forman and with heavy chains around his ankles and wrists. Behind him came a dazzling roisterer who had been careful to leave his dagger at the door.

'Ki . . .' Tom Sledd was on tiptoe, but a sharp finger in the ribs from Faunt silenced him immediately.

The crowd looked at each other. Either of the prisoner's escort should have been their new guest, but not the little one in the middle. Not, that is, until he spoke.

'Good morning, gentles,' Timothy said, beaming at them in their rags. 'I have great and wonderful news. One of you will see God soon. It might not be today, but I promise you it will come. You, sister,' he lunged at an old crone, who was already hauling up her shift. Then she saw the light in his eyes and dropped it again, stepping back to hide behind a kindly lunatic. 'Will it be you?'

'Never!' she screeched.

'What about you, my good man?' Timothy had battened on somebody else and the man ran away, whimpering. 'Don't be afraid of His light. With my help, you'll see him clearly; I know you will.'

The numbed silence had gone now, now that the inmates realized that the newcomer was as mad as they were. Simon Forman took Sleford aside. 'That man was sane once,' he said. 'At least as sane as you or me.' He reached under his shining gown, dropping a toad to the flagstones as he did so. It quickly became the old crone's next meal, as a welcome change from cockroaches. 'Here's his keep for the next month. I'll be back every fourth Wednesday with more. Tell me, must he stay in chains?'

'For his safety and theirs,' Sleford nodded. 'What is he to you?'

'He's my . . . *was* my apprentice.'

'Well, he's indentured here for ever,' Sleford said. 'If he annoys the others too much, they'll kill him; whatever me and my lads try to do about it.'

'You know best, Master Keeper,' Forman said. He turned to find Kit Marlowe, but the projectioner had already disappeared into the dark passageway by which they had come in. Forman took one last look at his apprentice, surrounded now as he was by ragged lunatics who prodded and poked him, stroked his shoulders and licked his hair. In some ways, Forman knew, the apprentice had come home. And perhaps he had found God, too.

'Time, I think,' Faunt said, when Forman had gone. He stood up from his crouching position, screwing his poem into a ball and throwing it into the straw. He stopped after a few paces and turned back. 'Are you coming, Tom?'

The stage manager leapt up and stumbled forward, unsure what was happening.

'Master Sleford,' Faunt called across the open space. 'A word?'

The keeper pushed his way past the crowd around Timothy and faced the asylum's poet. 'Master Faunt,' he nodded. Sledd stood there, open-mouthed. It was as though a play was unfolding before his eyes and he couldn't believe it.

'My colleagues and I must be on our way. May I?'

'Be my guest,' Sleford bowed, though Nicholas Faunt had been that for more weeks than he'd strictly enjoyed already. Lord Burghley's man suddenly sprang to one side, hauling a large man off a naked woman and pushing him against the wall.

'I'll give you a moment to compose yourself, Father Ballantine,' he said, glancing downward.

'What are you talking about?' the man bellowed, subsiding rapidly as he did so.

'Well, once upon a time,' Faunt smiled, 'there was this man called Martin Luther and . . . well, it's a long and complicated story that you, I suspect, know better than I do. I'd like you to tell it, in fact, along with any other Papist secrets you have. You'll have a small audience, probably only one. His name is Richard Topcliffe. And the venue? Oh, it's perfect. It's called the Tower and nobody can hear you scream there.'

Ballantine made a wild grab but Faunt was faster. He caught the priest's arm and pulled it sharply against the joint with a dull crack. The Jesuit jack-knifed in pain, the fight out of him and he slumped against Faunt's shoulder. The three of them marched past Forman along Sleford's passageway to find Kit Marlowe waiting there.

'You've settled up for this one?' Faunt asked him, nodding at Sledd.

'All done,' Marlowe nodded.

'Send your bill to Burghley,' Faunt said, pushing the sobbing Ballantine ahead of him. 'You might get the refund before Hell freezes over.'

Marlowe chuckled. 'We both know, Nicholas,' he said, 'that that's never going to happen.' He smiled at the stage manager. 'Guess what, Tom?' he said. 'The theatres are open.'

'Are they?' Sledd scowled, 'Are they, really?'

Faunt cuffed him around the head. 'This man has just paid Sleford a king's ransom for your freedom, ingrate. The least you can do is be civil.'

'Oh.' Realization dawned. 'Kit,' Sledd nodded, 'I'm sorry . . . I didn't know.' He clasped Marlowe's hand in both of his.

'Don't worry about it, Tom,' Marlowe said. 'Now, get home to that family of yours. The least Johanna's going to say is "What time d'you call this?"'

'I will, Kit,' Sledd laughed. 'I will. But first, I've got

somewhere else to go. Thank you, too, Master Faunt, for . . . well, everything.'

'You're welcome,' Faunt said. 'I can't stay, Kit. Places to be, you know. But . . . sometime soon, we'll get together. Catch up.'

'Don't doubt it, Master Johnson,' Marlowe said and watched him go.

'Well, come on, you people!' Philip Henslowe was himself again. He would always watch his back, lock his door, carry not one dagger but two, and he'd keep his ears well and truly open for any rumour that might fly from Whitehall, but the Rose was back in business again. The playbills announcing *The Massacre at Paris* were fluttering in the October breeze and God, probably, was in his Heaven. 'We've got a play to put on.'

Will Shaxsper was back in his Prince of Condé costume again, extending his left leg, unlike Alleyn, who was extending his right and he was just congratulating himself on a role well-rehearsed when he saw Tom Sledd running across the O which he had done so much to build.

'Nice of you to call,' Henslowe roared as he saw the same sight.

Sledd ignored him. That was because he was making for the Prince of Condé. As he reached the Warwickshire man, he swung back his arm and shattered Shaxsper's nose.

'I think it works,' Henslowe applauded, 'keep it in.' Then he suddenly frowned, looking down at the script. 'Tom,' he said, 'what scene are we in?'

The rest was legend. Shaxsper's awful performance as Condé, delivered in the flat vowels of Warwickshire, was explained away (by him) as Tom Sledd's fault. As for Tom, he had added to the legend by going straight round to the Curtain after the Rose and giving Hal Dignam a black eye. He had also hit Will Kemp with a pig's bladder, but his had contained a brick.

And so it was a very contrite and rather rattled Hal Dignam who tentatively visited the Rose two days later. His face was purple and he was hobbling a little where he had fallen badly after Tom's attack. He crept around each corner he came to, looking out for any still-annoyed stage managers who might be in the offing. Much to his relief, all he saw, standing by the apron, making notes on the rehearsal, was the playwright, Kit Marlowe. He slapped him gingerly on the back, afraid of any sudden movements or sharp noises.

'So, how are things at the Rose, then, Kit?'

Lightning Source UK Ltd.
Milton Keynes UK
UKHW010824110920
369735UK00001B/19